WHEN THE VISCOUNT SEDUCES

ROGUE RULES
BOOK THREE

DARCY BURKE

Zealous Quill Press

For a trio of truly wonderful friends:

Christina Dodd, Rachel Grant, and Jayne Ann Krentz.

You really know how to fire up a scene (pun intended).

WHEN THE VISCOUNT SEDUCES

After a disastrous Almack's debut, bookish and clumsy Gwendolen Price is determined to improve her reputation and make her parents proud. The Viscount Somerton, her brother's friend and one of Society's most eligible bachelors, offers to help her, and she's certain his attention will increase her standing—even though he's exactly the kind of rake she has vowed to avoid.

Lazarus Rowe, the eminently unserious and dashingly handsome Viscount Somerton, has spent a lifetime hiding his shameful secret: he simply cannot read well. With a speech to Parliament looming, he's desperate to remedy this deficiency. The chance to help his friend's hopelessly bluestocking sister seems the perfect trade—his presence as her devoted escort in exchange for her help as his tutor.

As sparks fly between them with every lesson, Gwen refuses to fall for a rogue while Lazarus, begins to reconsider his rakish ways. When a woman from his recent past makes a shocking revelation, Lazarus fears all is lost. Will Gwen retreat to the safety of her books, or do she and this almost-redeemed rake have a chance at a real life happily ever after?

Don't miss the rest of the *Rogue Rules*!

Do you want to hear all the latest about me and my books? Sign up at <u>Reader Club newsletter</u> for members-only bonus content, advance notice of pre-orders, insider scoop, as well as contests and giveaways!

Care to share your love for my books with like-minded readers? Want to hang with me and see pictures of my cats (who doesn't!)? Then don't miss my exclusive Facebook groups!

Darcy's Duchesses for historical readers
Burke's Book Lovers for contemporary readers

Want more historical romance? Do you like your historical romance filled with passion and red hot chemistry? Join me and my author friends in the Facebook group, Historical Harlots, for exclusive giveaways, chat with amazing HistRom authors, and more!

THE ROGUE RULES

Never be alone with a rogue.
Never flirt with a rogue.
Never give a rogue a chance.
Never doubt a rogue's reputation.
Never believe a rogue's pledge of love or devotion.
Never trust a rogue to change.
Never allow a rogue to see your heart.
Ruin the rogue before he can ruin you.

He that loveth a book will never want a faithful friend, a wholesome counsellor, a cheerful companion, an effectual comforter.

-Isaac Barrow, 1630-77

Thank you Toni Lee for your always sharp eye and for seeing Gwen in this quote.

CHAPTER 1

London, April, 1816

*G*wendolen Price's stomach churned from a combination of anxiety and anticipation as she and her mother neared the fabled entrance to Almack's. Gwen had long dreamed of this night, of making a triumphant entrance into this hallowed place where she would be anointed a diamond of the Season.

Her father, arriving later, would nod at her with pride in his dark gaze, and her mother would beam with the same emotion. Gwen would not trip or knock her elbow into anyone, and she would absolutely not bore those she met with a description of the latest novel she'd devoured.

The latter was much easier than the former. Although, both could be extremely difficult, especially given Gwen's nerves. She wanted so badly to impress people and, most importantly, to make her parents proud. Sometimes, she forgot to modulate her speech and her movements, and that was when disaster happened.

She'd executed her presentation to the queen with a shocking grace. Right up until her headdress had listed sideways. In her efforts to right it, she'd bumped into the young lady she'd been standing next to, causing her to fall into the young lady next to her, and so on, for several young ladies. It had caused a stir, all while other young ladies were still being presented. The queen had halted the proceeding until Gwen could get her headdress back on straight, which had required help from her mother *and* someone else's mother.

Then there were the two balls she'd attended thus far this Season. At the first, she'd forgotten not to talk about books. But it hadn't been her fault. She'd been so bored! At the second, she'd danced twice, and both sets had been riddled with her stepping on others' feet or running into them as she moved the wrong way. Then after she'd been holding up the wall for over an hour, a gentleman had finally asked her to promenade, for which she was most grateful. She could walk without incident. Usually. Unless she waved her arms as she talked animatedly or looked at her companion instead of where she was going. Which was precisely what had happened.

She'd been so excited by her discussion—about books, naturally—with her companion that she'd failed to see the Dowager Duchess of Sale, and she'd marched straight into the seventy-some-year-old woman, nearly knocking her down. Thankfully, her companion had moved quickly and saved the dowager from certain doom. Gwen and her mother had gone home after that.

Somehow, despite all that, Gwen had obtained a voucher to Almack's. Her mother had called in every favor, and Gwen's father had used his position in the Treasury to apply pressure to those who could help his daughter gain the patronesses' notice—and in a positive way. Miraculously, Lady Sefton, who was generally seen as the kindest of the ladies who sat in judgment over who was admitted, issued her an invitation. But only for the month of April, not the entire Season. It appeared to be a test, and Gwen vowed she was going to pass it.

"Are you sure you want to do this?" her mother asked. "You haven't even practiced dancing in the past week since Monsieur Leclerc ceased your lessons."

Gwen cringed inwardly in reference to the *third* dancing master who'd decided Gwen was hopeless, that she would never become an accomplished dancer. He'd only lasted a fortnight, the briefest one yet. "I have practiced, Mama. With Badge."

"Your maid does not signify as a dancing partner." Mama shook her head, but a smile teased her mouth. "You do try so very hard, my darling. I am sorry this isn't easier for you."

The coach came to a full stop. "Dancing may not be my forte, but I have other skills. It's really too bad I can't display my watercolors when I attend a ball." She exhaled as the door opened. It was time to go inside.

A footman helped her mother to descend, then provided the same assistance to Gwen. Taking a deep breath, Gwen walked to the entrance with her mother and sent up a silent prayer that nothing horrible would happen. Not tonight.

"Last chance to change your mind," her mother said, glancing over at her. Gwen's mother was incredibly beautiful, with rich sable hair without a single strand of gray, luminous hazel-brown eyes, and satiny olive skin. Though Gwen had the same hair, she was paler in coloring and her eyes were solidly brown. Uninterestingly flat brown without Mama's green and gold flecks. "We can always retreat to Bath," Mama added.

The question of whether Gwen ought to have a London

Season or a Bath Season had been long discussed. Her readiness for London had been in question for several years, and so Gwen had asked for more time to attain additional polish. Finally, her parents had relented last summer and agreed she would debut in London this year. Unfortunately, things had not gone well, but Gwen was determined that would change.

"I'm not ready for that," Gwen said firmly. She knew her mother had her best interests at heart. She didn't want Gwen to feel bad or as though she had failed. But Gwen just wanted her parents to be proud of her, and for that reason, she was going to be a success.

"I love you," Mama said with a soft smile. "No matter what."

"I love you too, Mama. And if tonight is a disaster, I will reconsider. It's not going to be, though. Tonight will be *spectacular*."

It was not spectacular. It was, instead, spectacularly boring.

One hour into her arrival, Gwen had not yet been asked to dance. Some young ladies making their debut had at least one dance arranged for them by the patronesses, but Gwen had not received that benefit. She assumed everyone knew her to be a poor dancing partner.

She turned to her mother, who didn't appear at all troubled by Gwen's lack of partners, but then Mama excelled at looking serene. "I'm going to have a glass of orgeat. Do you want any?"

Her mother's nose wrinkled. "I would advise against it. I thought I mentioned how ghastly sour it tastes here."

"You did, but I'm thirsty, and it seems as though I need to discover the vileness for myself."

Chuckling, Gwen's mother inclined her head toward the supper rooms. "Help yourself, then. And Gwen, do not be concerned that you haven't danced. We arrived very early."

That much was true. The ballroom had been far emptier when they'd first arrived. Over the past hour, many people had flowed in, but the space was still not a crush. Indeed, Gwen's father and brother had not yet arrived, nor had she seen any of her friends.

Gwen made her way along the edge of the ballroom, careful to avoid catching her elbow on anyone. Inside the supper room, the crowd was sparse. It could not even be called a crowd. Most everyone present was either dancing or gathered along the periphery of the ballroom, situated on couches as they conversed.

As she walked to the table holding the orgeat, Gwen's evening gown swirled about her. She glanced down at the peach silk and was glad she at least looked the part of a young Society lady, even if she didn't embody her.

Apparently, her glance down lasted longer than an actual glance, for when she raised her gaze, she nearly strode directly into a gentleman.

"Careful there," the Viscount Somerton said.

Gwen exhaled with relief, glad her near collision was with someone she knew. The viscount, broad shouldered with gloriously blond hair and a dazzling smile, was a good friend of her brother's. She'd spent time with Somerton in Weston, where she and her mother—and her brother this past year—whiled away the month of August with friends near the sea. Somerton and her brother, along with others, spent a great deal of their time at the Grove, an estate owned by the Duke of Henlow. His two children, the Earl of Shefford and Lady Minerva, stayed there in August. Min was a dear friend of Gwen's. Indeed, she was one of the friends who had not yet arrived this evening.

"My apologies, my lord," Gwen said, dipping a brief curtsey. Though her grandfather was a viscount, she was not a member of the peerage herself.

"You needn't use such formality with me," Somerton said with a wave of his gloved hand. "No curtseying permitted." He winked at her, his roguishness on full display.

A year and a half ago, Gwen and her friends had drafted "rogue rules," a guide for steering clear of rakish gentlemen and their scandalous behavior. It had been the result of one of them falling prey to an especially horrid scoundrel. The Earl of Banemore, once a member of that elite group of male friends who gathered at the Grove, had ruined Gwen's friend Pandora Barclay. Pandora had expected a marriage proposal, but when she and Bane had been caught in a compromising position, he'd informed her that he was already betrothed to someone else. Someone he'd married not long after that awful occurrence.

The rogue rules had seemed vital to their own protection, and they generally adhered to them most strictly. For Gwen, she was especially careful with the first two: not to be alone with a rogue and not to flirt with one. Not that she'd had occasion to do either of those. The third was to never give a rogue a chance, which she meant to follow, but about which she was admittedly skeptical. Two of their set, Pandora's sister Persephone and Tamsin, now the Duchess of Wellesbourne and the Lady Droxford, had married supposed rogues. Though, Tamsin's husband was really only a rogue by association, and it didn't seem fair to characterize him as one.

Somerton, however, was most definitely a rogue. He flirted with ease, and charm seemed to drip from his every word and gaze. Gwen wondered if giggling and swooning had originated with women who spent time with knaves such as him. She had no trouble believing it.

"It's hard not to curtsey," Gwen said. "We are at Almack's, and I am trying to make a good impression."

"Well, I'd say you're doing a fine job." He regarded her

intently, his gaze sweeping her from the top of her head-dress to the tip of her slipper peeking from the hem of her gown. "You look lovely. Peach is a very fetching color on you."

"Thank you. That means a great deal coming from you." Gwen had noticed that the viscount possessed a sharp sense for fashion. Of all the gentlemen who gathered in Weston every August, he always seemed the most ready to saunter into a London ballroom.

Tonight, he was impeccably outfitted in a dark green coat, black breeches, a gold embroidered waistcoat, and impossibly glossy Hessians. He laughed at her comment. "Does it? I can't imagine my opinion is all that vital, but I am glad to offer it, and you do look most ravishing." His mouth twisted. "Forget I said that. Poor word choice for a friend's sister. You look very pretty."

Gwen smiled. "Thank you again, and I won't tell Evan what you said. I'm going to get a glass of orgeat. Do you want to join me?"

He made a face. "That noxious brew? I'd rather inhale beetles."

She blinked. "That's a rather…specific alternative."

Leaning close, he spoke in a low tone. "I inhaled a beetle once. I was about eight years old. The insect was on my horse, and as I was riding, it somehow came loose from the animal, caught the wind, and I sucked it directly into my mouth. It was absolutely revolting."

Gwen's mouth opened, but she snapped it closed as she considered the horror of a bug being sucked inside. "That's perhaps the worst anecdote I've ever heard."

"Which is why I'm telling you in confidence." He arched his brows and gave her a mischievous smile.

It occurred to Gwen that he might actually be flirting, but could one really flirt about inhaling a beetle? Or with a friend's cousin? Somerton was cousin to Gwen's dear friend Tamsin.

"I'm bound for the ballroom," Somerton said, straightening. "I won't be staying much longer, but if you'd care to dance the next set, I'd be happy to partner you."

Gwen stared at him. "Truly?" Her eyes narrowed slightly. "Is this a pity dance?"

He cocked his head to the side, and his hesitation answered her question.

"It's all right," she said. "I'm not above accepting that. As you can see, I'm rather desperate."

"You don't look *desperate* to me," he said softly, with kindness in his eyes. "You look like a young lady who deserves to dance."

"Thank you."

"I'll search you out in a bit." He gave her a swift, shallow bow and departed for the ballroom. Appreciating the viscount's kindness, Gwen went to take a cup of orgeat from the table. She took a sip, and good heavens, sour was not a strong enough description. It was bitter. Like the heart of a woman scorned.

Pandora again came to mind, and Gwen instantly refused to compare her drink to one of her friends.

She returned to the ballroom, her mind on Pandora and whether she would ever recover from the scandal enough to reenter Society or find a husband. Though, Gwen was fairly certain she didn't want the latter. So far, she didn't particularly want the former, and Gwen couldn't blame her.

Somehow, Gwen forgot how awful the orgeat tasted and took another drink as she walked into the ballroom. Her eyes squeezed shut as she forced herself to swallow the acrid liquid. In that barest moment, disaster struck. And it wasn't a *near* collision.

She walked straight into a gentleman, spilling her repellant beverage onto his immaculate blue coat and canary-yellow waistcoat. The remainder sloshed toward the floor, splashing his shiny Hessians and the lower part of her skirt.

"Watch where you're going!" the gentleman declared, his gloved hand brushing at the droplets clinging to his front. "You may well have ruined this waistcoat. It's *silk*. And I just picked it up from Savile Row this very afternoon."

Gwen cringed and waved her hands as if she meant to help him tidy himself, but stopped herself from doing so. What that did, however, was splash the remainder of the contents of her orgeat onto the man's waistcoat. Horrified, she stared at the stain darkening the canary silk. "I'm so sorry."

He sputtered. "You're a menace!" Then he stalked off.

Pivoting on her slipper, Gwen took a step after him—what was she going to do?—and promptly slipped. She'd put her new slipper, the soles of which were still quite smooth, directly on the spilled liquid, and there was simply no help for it. She was going to fall.

Her foot slid forward, and her arms windmilled as she fell to her backside. Her skirts rose to her knees, exposing her lower legs. Somehow, she managed to keep hold of the stupid, now quite empty, cup.

While the music kept on, every other sound in the ball-room seem to grind to a halt. Certainly, the conversation stopped. A brief glance around revealed that everyone in Gwen's vicinity was now staring at her. She hurriedly brushed her skirts down her legs, frantically working to cover her exposed calves and ankles. Heat flooded her neck and face. She prayed her mother wasn't watching, but of course she was. Instead, Gwen prayed her father and brother hadn't yet arrived.

A strong hand gripped her arm and put a hand to her

back. "Permit me to help you," the man murmured, his voice familiar.

Gwen turned her head and saw the arresting features of the Viscount Somerton, his green eyes fixed intently—and sympathetically—on her, his jaw firm, his lips impossibly supple. Could a man have supple lips? Regardless, Somerton did.

He helped her swiftly and effortlessly to her feet, then took the empty cup from her. In a fluid movement, he deposited the vessel on a tray of a footman standing against the wall. The viscount's actions were so graceful, so easily maneuvered that Gwen wanted to weep with envy.

"Time for our dance," he said, sweeping her toward the dance floor.

"But it's the middle of a set."

"It's a line. We can simply insert ourselves." He gave her a confident smile, and Gwen had to bite back an absurd laugh.

"It might be simple for you," she muttered as he guided her to the end of the line of ladies.

"Never fear," he whispered. "We are late enough joining that we may not even have a turn before the set ends."

She snapped her gaze to his, a rush of gratitude flowing over her. "You are brilliant," she whispered.

Inexplicably, a shadow passed over his features. "I'm not. Understanding the mechanics and timing of a dance doesn't signify above-average intelligence, but I appreciate you thinking so." He flashed a smile, and she wondered if she'd imagined the momentary darkness.

Unfortunately, their turn came up before the set ended, and Somerton did his best to keep Gwen from losing her balance or bumping into someone. She managed fairly well, though her dancing would never be called elegant. When they reached the end, the music drew to a close.

Breathing heavily from her exertions, Gwen curtseyed as

the other ladies did to their partners, and Somerton bowed. He offered her his arm and escorted her from the dance floor.

"Where shall I escort you?" he asked.

"My mother is over there." Gwen inclined her head toward where she'd left her mother earlier, hoping she would still be there. She'd no desire to wander the ballroom in search of her. The stares and whispered comments around her at the moment were difficult enough to bear.

"Just hold your head high," Somerton said quietly. "And laugh. As though I've just said the wittiest thing."

She did as he said and laughed. At least her laugh wasn't embarrassing.

"Now look at me," he said.

She followed his command and nearly tripped, for he was already looking at her, his eyes glowing with a particular heat she suddenly felt in the very core of herself. He put his hand over hers on his arm. "Steady there," he whispered. "Smile."

Realizing her lips were parted, she pressed them closed and smiled. Her pulse had begun to slow after the dance, but was now picking up speed again.

His hand remained over hers, a warm presence that gave her a comforting sense of security. She felt protected with the viscount walking beside her, and it actually wasn't difficult for her to keep her head up.

They arrived at her mother, whose skin looked a bit pale. She smiled upon seeing them. "Good evening, Lord Somerton."

"Good evening, Mrs. Price. Your daughter and I enjoyed a splendid dance."

"I thank you for your attention to Gwen," Gwen's mother said.

Somerton took his hand from Gwen's, and she reluctantly

removed her grip on his sleeve. Her charming anchor was now gone, and she felt the chill of the ballroom in every part of her.

He bowed to Gwen. "Thank you, Miss Price."

She curtseyed again even though he'd told her not to. "Thank you, my lord."

Then he was gone, and Gwen braced herself for her mother's concern. She would be disappointed, of course, but she would try very hard not to show it.

Summoning a somewhat encouraging smile, Gwen's mother said, "I'm a bit fatigued. Shall we go?" It was so like her not to mention what had happened, at least not here. And if she did bring it up—which she surely would in this case—she would do so with a great deal of care.

"Yes, but have Papa and Evan not arrived yet?"

"Not that I've seen." Her mother started toward the door to the entrance hall.

Gwen was relieved to hear that at least. Once they were finally settled in the coach, she let herself fully relax. Though, there was still a faint tremor of excitement left over from Somerton. The way he'd come to her rescue had been unexpected and absolutely wonderful—she would never forget it.

She also ought not to forget that he was a rogue, the sort of gentlemen she and her friends steered clear of. Still, apparently, a rogue could possess a great measure of kindness.

"Tomorrow, we can discuss whether it makes sense to remove to Bath," Gwen's mother said.

Taking a deep breath, Gwen gathered her courage to ask what she most wanted to know. "Are you disappointed, Mama?"

Gwen's mother patted her hand and gave Gwen a warm smile. "Of course not. What happened tonight was an accident. However, I know you are clever enough to understand that it was still…unfortunate."

That was a nice word. Damaging or disastrous might have been more accurate, however.

"While I expect it makes sense to not return to Almack's, I am hopeful my Season can continue," Gwen said cautiously.

Giving Gwen's hand another pat, her mother then withdrew her hand to her own lap. "We'll discuss it, dear. I know you'll be amenable to whatever your father and I decide."

Because she always was. What choice did Gwen have? If they didn't wish her to continue her Season, she would not. Just as she hadn't had a Season until now—that had been their decision, not hers. She'd just gone along with it, both because she respected their wisdom and because she would never demand something they didn't support.

For these reasons, she would retreat to Bath. And that was exactly what she expected to happen.

CHAPTER 2

*L*azarus Rowe, the Viscount Somerton, had promised his mother two visits to Almack's each Season, the first of which he'd completed this evening. And what an occasion it had been.

While his mother fervently hoped he would search for a wife, Lazarus went only to placate her and generally suffered through his evening there. Tonight, however, he'd helped a friend's sister and he'd been glad to do it. However, his mother was not yet in London to see his good deeds as she was tending to his middle sister who had just welcomed another child a few weeks ago.

Poor Miss Price. He could not stop thinking of her sprawled on the floor of the ballroom, her skirts about her knees so that all and sundry could see her lower legs. She had rather marvelously shaped calves, not that he should note such things about his friend's sister.

Having freed himself from the strictures of Almack's, he made his way to Coventry Street where the Siren's Call, a well-appointed gaming hell owned and run by women, was located. Stepping into the familiar interior with its lush purple-and-gold décor, Lazarus was immediately greeted by one of the women who worked there. Becky was a tall Scottish lass with bright red hair and a brogue as thick as an ancient tree.

"Evening, Somerton," she said. "Sheff's over at your regular table." Becky inclined her head to the back of the main room.

"Thank you, Becky. You look lovely as ever," he added with a grin, taking in her enticing emerald costume. The women of the Siren's Call dressed seductively, but the patrons were not allowed to touch them. Their goal was to lure the men to the hell so they would gamble—a true siren's call.

She curtseyed and gave him a saucy smile. "Thank you, my lord. You are always too kind." She fluttered her lashes, and Somerton chuckled as he went to join his friend, the Earl of Shefford.

"How was Almack's?" Shefford asked, his dark blue eyes lifting to meet Lazarus's. Heir to a dukedom, Shefford held himself with the prestige and privilege owing to his rank, his shoulders pushed back, his square chin slightly jutting.

Lazarus slid into the chair next to Shefford. "Far more entertaining than usual."

Arching a brow, Shefford regarded him with interest. "Don't tell me you've found a bride. I can't lose another friend to the parson's trap."

The trap had already claimed the Duke of Wellesbourne, the Baron Droxford, and the Earl of Banemore, three of their closest friends. Lazarus had no plans to fall as they had.

"Entertaining was perhaps not the best choice of word," Lazarus said with a faint grimace. "Price's sister was there, and there was a rather unfortunate incident."

Shefford grimaced as well. "She's prone to those, I'm afraid. What happened?"

"She spilled orgeat on that dandy Eberforce. He was none too kind about the mishap. I expect he's maligning her at every opportunity."

"Pompous idiot," Shefford muttered before taking a drink of ale. "He'll say anything to gain attention. Price will not be pleased."

"You're referring to Evan?" Lazarus asked. "Or their father?" He was a Lord Commissioner of the Treasury and a highly regarded member of Parliament.

"Both of them, I suppose," Shefford replied. "Poor Miss Price. I imagine she'll be shuffled back to Bath. Or perhaps home to Bristol. Evan told me her Season has not been going well and that her debut at Almack's tonight was critical to her success."

Lazarus hated to think of the charming Miss Price having to flee London in embarrassment. Was there no place in Society for someone who wasn't entirely coordinated? "After she spilled her drink on Eberforce, she slipped into an ungainly mess on the floor. I rushed to help her up, then I took her to dance so she could hold her head up."

Shefford fixed his gaze on Lazarus. "That was bloody heroic of you. Careful, or you'll be seen as a suitor."

Lazarus shrugged. "There are worse things, and anyway, I'm not."

"How did the dance go?" Shefford looked at him with sympathy. "She is not the most…graceful."

"She acquitted herself quite well," Lazarus said. "I would dance with her again, in fact."

"Listening to you talk, I would scarcely believe you to be the scoundrel I know you are." Josephine Harker, the daughter of the owner of the Siren's Call who oversaw the other ladies and who was dressed in a more conservative gown, sauntered closer to their table and deposited a tankard of ale in front of Lazarus.

Lazarus gripped the tankard. "Evening, Jo. Thank you."

"Forgive me for eavesdropping," she said. "I try not to, but it's deuced difficult to avoid it in here, and I do find I like hearing what you lot have to say." She laughed, her wide mouth spreading to reveal remarkably even, white teeth. Jo fixed her gaze on Lazarus. "That was most kind of you to help Miss Price in her moment of need."

"Do you know her?" Lazarus asked. Jo had many friends in Society even if she wasn't actually a member herself.

Jo shook her head. "I only know what her brother has mentioned of her. I have the impression she struggles to meet Society's expectations, which, to me, recommends her most brilliantly."

Shefford laughed. "Because you refuse to meet them, much to your father's chagrin."

While Jo's mother owned the Siren's Call, Jo's father was an artist and man of science who'd been taken up by certain members of Society for his intelligence and wit. As far as Lazarus knew, Jo's parents were estranged, having chosen different paths for themselves.

Jo gave him an impassive stare. "Because Society's rules are ridiculous. And don't pretend you follow them either. If you did, you'd be married with an heir and a spare."

Shefford twitched as a shadow of revulsion passed over his features. "You know me too well, Jo."

A faint smile teased Jo's full lips. "I'm just glad to hear you aren't making fun of Miss Price. That would be too easy to do. Instead, you're championing her." She returned her gaze to Lazarus. "Perhaps she's captured your attention. Or something." She laughed softly before taking herself off to mingle about the room.

"Has that happened?" Shefford asked, a touch of apprehension in his tone.

"No," Lazarus assured him. "I've not developed a tendre for Evan's sister. But I do consider her one of our set—by relation—and I couldn't stand by and watch her flounder."

"You're an excellent friend," Shefford said. "But that has never been in question." He lifted his tankard in a silent toast, and Lazarus did the same.

"Evening, gents." Evan Price took the empty chair beside Lazarus. Lean and muscular, Evan was regarded as a sportsman. He was a superior rider, swordsman, marksman, and pugilist. His skill was almost embarrassing. His dark hair fell across his forehead, and the gold flecks in his brown eyes seemed to glitter in the lamplight. He had an intense look about him.

"Evening, Price," Lazarus said. "Is all well?"

Angling himself toward Lazarus, Evan said, "I understand I've you to thank for saving my sister from complete ruin, though I daresay she's nearly there." He frowned briefly. "I feel quite badly for her."

"It wasn't as bad as all that." At least Lazarus hoped it wasn't, but he feared Evan was right.

"I arrived at Almack's just after she and my mother left," Evan said. "Upon learning they'd departed, I didn't bother staying."

"We must have missed each other in the crush," Lazarus noted. "I departed a while after."

"Unsurprising since I was overcome with people asking about my sister and warning me to stay clear of Eberforce, who was still wandering the ballroom ranting about his ruined waistcoat." Evan scowled.

"Damn, that's as good as any of Droxford's scowls," Shefford said, referring to their friend the baron, who was well known for his sober nature. However, he seemed to have lightened up a great deal since marrying more than six months earlier. It seemed marriage agreed with him most heartily.

Evan grunted. "People should have been warning Eberforce to stay clear of *me*."

Shefford sipped his ale. "Since you did not encounter him, I think you can assume that likely happened. Or that Eberforce is not as foolish as we take him to be. He can't be stupid enough to pick a fight with you."

"Eberforce is all bluster," Lazarus said. He looked to Evan. "I'm just sorry he was the recipient of your sister's drink since he's such a nincompoop. I wish it had been me, for I would have laughed it off."

Evan's gaze remained intense. "You danced with her after. I can't thank you enough. I'm sure that lessened the impact of what happened. People were talking about that almost as much as her mishap. Or perhaps that's just my wishful thinking," he muttered.

Becky brought a tankard of ale for Evan, but didn't linger. Lazarus inclined his head at her as she moved away.

"I was happy to be of assistance," Lazarus said. "Your sister's a good sort. Hopefully, she will recover from this incident."

"It isn't just tonight, though." Evan took a long pull from his ale and set the tankard back on the table. "She's had a rough go of it this Season. I'm fairly certain our mother is already making plans to withdraw to Bath. I suspect our father may even suggest they go home to Bristol and perhaps try again next year." Evan sighed. "Though, I'm not sure what good that will do. Gwen is just abysmal at playing Society's game. She's a terrible dancer, which I'm sure you discovered, Somerton."

"She wasn't that bad." But then it had been the easiest of dances. "Not everyone needs to possess the grace of a swan."

Evan went on. "And she gets nervous if she has to talk to too many people she doesn't already know. She's more comfortable alone in a library. Indeed, she spends far too much time reading books, according to our father. She can read several books in a day. I forget how many." He shook his head in disbelief.

Several books in a day? How had Lazarus not known that about her?

Because while he knew her somewhat, he didn't know her well.

Lazarus couldn't read a book in a week let alone several in a day. Oh, to be able to read with even a modicum of ease! It always took him so much time and effort to get through a single page of correspondence. His secretary believed Lazarus didn't care to read—not that he struggled, however —and thankfully communicated the contents of written messages and other pertinent information verbally.

In a few short weeks, Lazarus was to give a speech in the Lords. He could memorize it—and planned to—but if he needed to refer to the written speech at all, he would be lost. Plus, he needed someone to help him memorize it by reading it aloud and having Lazarus repeat it back. That would be far easier than if he tried to read it and memorize it himself. The entire situation was giving him fits, and he was close to bowing out.

But he didn't want to. His father would have been so proud to hear him speak. He'd been the one person who understood Lazarus's deficiency and had done his best to help him overcome it. That Lazarus read at all was a credit to his father's love and dedication. Lazarus had been just seventeen when his father had died in a riding accident, and the loss was the most painful thing he'd ever endured.

"Did we lose you, Somerton?" Shefford asked. "Or will you come to the Rogue's Den with us?"

The Rogue's Den was an invitation-only brothel, however the proprietress preferred the term "pleasure house." Normally, Lazarus would join them, but at the moment, his mind was rife with ideas.

"I may stop in at the Phoenix Club," Lazarus said. "That is more my interest this evening."

Shefford nodded. "Fair enough."

"Actually, that sounds more appealing to me as well," Evan said to Lazarus. "Mind if I join you?"

"Not at all." Lazarus could then potentially ascertain a little more information about Evan's sister, for Lazarus had a plan involving her. He saw the potential for them to help each other. She could assist him with his reading, and he could bolster her chances for a successful Season. If his attention tonight had helped her, he could continue in that vein.

"Aren't you both boring?" Shefford said with a grunt. "Fine. I'll go to the Phoenix Club too. But let us finish our ale. The Siren's Call has some of the finest."

"That they do," Evan agreed.

Lazarus hid his smile as he took another drink. Tomorrow, he would call on Miss Price and present his proposal. He was a bit surprised that he wasn't nervous to reveal his shameful secret to her, but he just knew she wouldn't find fault with him. On the contrary, he was confident she would be the soul of kindness and understanding.

They could help each other immensely. He hoped she would agree.

~

*T*he following afternoon, Gwen settled herself in the coziest chair—in her opinion—in the drawing room to reread one of her favorite novels. It would be a welcome escape after last night's mishap and this morning's discussions regarding what they would do next.

Two pages in, Gwen's mother entered the drawing room, looking more elegant in her simple blue day dress than many women appeared in their evening finery. "Your father's just left."

Gwen closed her book and set it in her lap. "You've reached a decision, then?" They'd been discussing whether Gwen should remain in London and attempt a recovery from last night's debacle or if she should flee to Bath or even home to Bristol. She tried not to fidget as she awaited her fate.

"Your father and I think it may be best if we repair to Bath. We know a great many people there, and things are just...less stringent." Mama gave her a hopeful smile. "We also discussed whether you might be open to an arranged marriage. That way you can avoid the pressures of Society's expectations. Your father and I would only attempt such an endeavor with your approval and input."

An arranged marriage.

Gwen couldn't say she was surprised to hear those words, but it was disheartening all the same. Because the realization that she couldn't attract a groom on her own made her feel lacking. And she didn't think she *was* lacking. But what did she know?

"You also don't have to marry," her mother said. "Your Aunt Araminta didn't wed."

Aunt Araminta was her father's older sister, and while she seemed quite content as a spinster with a menagerie of animals, Gwen didn't see herself living that life. She wanted a family of her own that was as close and loving as hers had been when she was growing up.

"I'd hoped to wed," Gwen said softly. Even more, she'd hoped to fall in love, but that seemed an elusive dream. She'd never met a gentleman who put her at ease enough to even consider friendship, let alone love.

For some reason, she thought of Somerton and how he'd helped her last night. He *had* put her at ease, but then he'd rescued her when she'd needed it most. Anyway, he was not a potential suitor, let alone bridegroom.

Gwen's mother came toward her, sympathy softening her features. "I know, dear. I hope you'll fall in love too, as I did with your father. It may happen yet—and it may not be during a London Season."

While that was true, Gwen was twenty-two and it hadn't happened yet. Not in Bristol, where she lived and spent most of her time, nor in Weston where she sojourned every August. Perhaps London was too overwhelming, and Bath would be a better place to find what she sought.

It wasn't that she'd had *no* interest. She'd attended assemblies in Bristol and on two different occasions, overzealous gentlemen had tried to steal a kiss in the garden. But those men had not been interested in courtship, and Gwen had known it. They'd been rogues doing as rogues did.

Before Gwen could agree to remove to Bath, their butler, Lake, stepped over the threshold of the drawing room. "Lord Somerton has called. Is Miss Price receiving?" he asked Gwen's mother, then glanced toward Gwen.

"I believe so." Gwen's mother looked at Gwen in question.

Gwen nodded. "Yes. I can receive him here."

Inclining his head, the butler then turned and departed.

Instinctively, Gwen lifted her hand to her hair and hoped she looked presentable. But why wouldn't she? The most strenuous thing she'd done was walk up and down stairs.

"You look lovely," her mother said with a smile. "The viscount danced with you last night and now he's calling. One must wonder at his motives," she added with a wink.

Gwen should have told her mother the truth right then—

that Somerton had only supported his friend's sister at Almack's to be kind. Although, why *was* he calling?

"I'll move to the sitting room and leave the door open," Mama said, nodding toward the doorway at the back of the drawing room.

Lake returned and announced the viscount. As soon as Somerton sauntered into the room, the air seemed to lift and brighten. Perhaps it was his brilliant smile or his effusive charm, which seemed to radiate from him, despite him not yet saying a word.

He bowed to them and addressed Gwen's mother first. "It's a pleasure to see you again, Mrs. Price." Then he transferred his gaze to Gwen. "And you, Miss Price."

"Good afternoon," Gwen said, dipping into a curtsey.

"We're so delighted you've called," Gwen's mother said. "Did you enjoy Almack's last night?"

"As much as one ever does," the viscount quipped.

Gwen's mother laughed softly. "It is a necessary endurance. I'll leave the two of you to visit." She turned and glided to the sitting room, leaving the door open as she'd said she would.

Somerton arched a thick blond brow, then glanced toward the doorway to the sitting room. "Your mother is very trusting."

"Do you plan to seduce me here in the drawing room with my mother next door?"

He put his hand to his chest with a faint grimace. "Is my reputation that poor? Don't answer that."

Gwen grinned. "I did ask the question, which means I'm giving you the benefit of the doubt. Don't make me regret it. I'm already breaking a rogue rule being alone with you, though I can't say we're really *alone*." They spoke in moderate tones, such that it was unlikely her mother would hear them, not that they needed to hide anything.

"I confess my roguish behavior does not stretch to seducing young ladies under their own roofs with their mother in the next room. What rogue rule are you referring to?"

While Gwen and her friends had never said the rules were private—they'd been embroidered by Pandora and given to the two who had married—she wasn't sure she ought to share them with one of the roguiest among the rogues. "Er, just a few guidelines we young ladies follow to ensure we aren't caught unawares."

"There is more than one?" He smiled bemusedly. "What are the other rules?"

There were eight, but Gwen only mentioned a few. "Never flirt with a rogue and never give a rogue a chance."

He fully winced now and put his hand to his forehead as if he might faint. "You wound me. I came here today hoping you would give me a chance."

Gwen's pulse sped. What sort of chance was he referring to? "To do what?" she asked.

"May we sit?" He looked toward a seating area near the windows that overlooked the street below. That would put them as far away from the sitting room—and her mother—as they could be.

"Certainly." She walked to a compact settee covered in a floral pattern set against dark green. She sat and he joined her there, which made them rather cozy. Her heart continued its rapid pace.

"I hope you won't think me too forward," he began, his eyes crinkling as he smiled.

Forward. Gwen's imagination began to leap.

Angling himself toward her, he went on, "I wondered if we might help one another. You seem as though you could benefit from some...support this Season, and I'm in need of someone to help me with a...delicate matter." He flinched, his neck twitching as his head tipped slightly. It was a movement of unease. Whatever the matter, it bothered him.

"I can't imagine what I could help you with," she said with a light laugh. Somerton seemed...perfect.

"It's extremely personal," he said quietly. "Indeed, no one is aware of this...problem. At least not the extent of it."

Concern and sympathy overtook everything else in Gwen's mind as she inched closer to the viscount. "How can I help?"

He seemed to relax, his shoulders settling—but only briefly. As he started to speak again, the tension returned and he did not meet her gaze. "I am not a good reader." He exhaled, and his pulse worked along his throat as if he were upset. He flicked his eyes toward hers, but only briefly. "That was difficult to confess aloud."

Gwen could see that, and she felt an instant and necessary urge to comfort him. And help him, if she could. "It is very brave of you to do so," she murmured. She also had questions. "What does that mean exactly? Can you read?"

"Yes, but it is laborious. I'm appallingly slow. I usually have my secretary read everything and give me a verbal summation. He believes I just don't care to read, as does everyone else." Gentle lines formed across Somerton's brow. "And no one questions that, given my reputation."

Gwen wasn't certain of the entirety of that reputation, just that he was a rogue. Perhaps he had a different reputation among his peers. "Does that go beyond your roguish tendencies?"

He looked out the window but didn't appear to focus on anything. "I'm generally regarded as an unserious member of the House of Lords, more intent on my wardrobe or what horse I'm riding or vehicle I'm driving." His gaze moved back to her, and she could see he was anything *but* unserious. "I should like to be a more active member in the Lords, but it's difficult."

"Because you read slowly," she said. "And you're hiding that fact."

An expression of alarm passed over his features. "Can you imagine what people would say if they knew?"

Gwen knew that people talked about her...deficiencies. Would they do the same to a viscount? Probably. People could be cruel.

"No one needs to know." She gave him an encouraging smile. "But I'm not sure I can really help you."

"Your brother said you can read multiple books in a day. I was hoping you might be able to help. Or at least try." He sounded hopeful, but there was a measured quality to his gaze, as if he were preparing himself for disappointment.

"Of course, I can try. I'd be delighted." And she meant it. "I would have gladly extended whatever help I can offer without your assistance in return."

"That is most kind of you," he said softly. "I'm sure I don't need to say this, but this arrangement must stay between us."

She cocked her head. "How do you plan to help me exactly? By swooping in and saving me from future disasters? By dancing with me?"

He rested his arm on the back of the settee. "By paying you attention and showing the ton that you are a highly desirable young lady."

Gwen was aware of his bare hand so near to her head. He'd obviously left his hat with a footman and apparently his gloves too. From the corner of her eye, she saw that his hands were large, his fingers long and slender. They would surely fly over the keys of a pianoforte. Unlike hers, which never moved as agilely as she wanted them to. At least not with the musical instrument. With a paintbrush, she was able to create art. Or something resembling it.

Clasping her hands in her lap, she said, "As it happens, my mother was just informing me that we are going to Bath for the remainder of the Season."

His eyes rounded and his nostrils flared. "Then how can you agree to help me?"

"I will convince my mother that we should stay, that all is not lost." Gwen glanced toward the sitting room and recalled her mother's curiosity regarding Somerton's call. "My mother likely wonders if you wish to court me since you came calling. And danced with me last night."

"I see." He looked toward the window again, his expression contemplative. "I *could* court you, but I would hate to cause any ill will when we do not wed. Though, my goal is to ensure you are in high demand, that you will have many suitors. You will have your choice of husband."

"I don't share your confidence, particularly since I plan to be discerning. I won't accept just anyone."

His hand moved from the settee to her jaw, where he lightly grazed his fingertips against her. "Nor should you, Miss Price. Do not sell yourself short. You are beautiful, witty, and I have it on great authority that your dancing is quite passable."

Though Gwen was distracted by his touch—in a lovely and somewhat confusing way since this was her brother's friend who had no romantic interest in her whatsoever—she laughed at his description of her. "You flatter me. Or tease me. None of what you said is true."

He gasped in mock distress. "It's all true, and I am offended you would think otherwise."

Now Gwen couldn't help but roll her eyes. "I can't decide if you are a terrible tease or a rogue."

"I can be both, I'm afraid, but I am serious about how I see you. You are beautiful and witty, and my sole experience dancing with you indicated you *are* passable. That you cannot see those things in yourself is perhaps why you continue to falter." He grimaced faintly. "I mean no offense."

"I don't take any." She considered his argument and had to confess it had merit. Her self-doubt and continued mishaps had made her feel inadequate. Perhaps she was too focused on that. "You will bolster my confidence, then?"

He put his hand back on the settee, which was a relief, for his touch had been a terrible—or wonderful—distraction. "I will make you the most confident young lady in London and the most sought-after."

"If I can find half your confidence, I'll have more than enough." She considered him a moment—his dashing looks and his air of authority. "Or is it arrogance?"

"You will have to decide that for yourself," he said with a laugh.

"How do you do it?" she asked sincerely. "Your reading deficiency troubles you, and yet you swan about as if you haven't a care in the world."

He lifted a shoulder. "I've hid that problem my entire life. Only my father was aware." He abruptly stopped, and his gaze traveled to the window once more.

Gwen watched his throat work and suspected he was trying to hide the emotion he was feeling. "You and your father were close?"

Nodding, he swallowed. When he looked back at her, his expression was pleasant, and whatever he'd been feeling was gone. "When shall we begin? We could promenade this afternoon, if you'd like."

"So soon?" Gwen blinked, her mind working.

"Shouldn't we move quickly since your mother is planning to take you to Bath?" He made an excellent point.

"How are we going to conduct your lessons?" she asked. "I don't think I can do it here without my mother finding out."

He stroked his hand along his jaw while drumming the

fingers of his other hand on the back of the settee. Snapping his gaze back to hers, she saw the light of an idea in his green eyes. "What about the Droxfords? You are close to my cousin Tamsin, aren't you?"

"I am." Gwen had become quite friendly with her during their time together in Weston the past two Augusts. Indeed, Gwen had attended her wedding in Cornwall in September.

"This will work well, I think," he said with enthusiasm. "You will call on Tamsin, and I'll visit Droxford at a prearranged time. We'll just need to organize things with them—a private place for us to work."

"That gives us both reason to be there," she said. "But what will be our purpose? You don't want them to know about your problem."

"We'll tell them you're helping me with my speech. This will please Droxford greatly. He's been harassing me to do more in the Lords and will gladly support anything to do with that."

"Tamsin will want to help even without knowing the reason. She has the most generous heart of anyone I know."

Somerton's mouth spread in a wide, heart-stopping grin. Good heavens, he was so handsome Gwen wondered how she would stop herself from staring at him when they met. "I think we have a plan."

"It seems we do. But let us start tomorrow. I need to spend time today thinking about how to approach your reading problem. I will tell my mother you've invited me to promenade tomorrow. That ought to stall our departure from London."

"Excellent."

"You're way over there," Gwen's mother said as she walked into the drawing room. "It was so quiet, I had to see what you were doing." There was no accusation or insinuation in her tone or expression, just a genuine curiosity.

Gwen stood. "Lord Somerton was about to take his leave, Mama."

The viscount rose. "I'll see you tomorrow in the park, then." Another stunning smile curved his lips. He gave her a courtly bow, then offered one to her mother. "A pleasure, Mrs. Price."

"Good afternoon, Lord Somerton."

Mama watched as he left, and the moment he was out of sight, she hurried to Gwen, her eyes glowing with delight. "You must tell me everything."

"There isn't much to tell. He invited me to promenade tomorrow."

"You must have a new hat." Mama pressed her lips together, and Gwen could tell she was already planning Gwen's costume.

"I don't think that's necessary."

"A viscount has called on you, Gwen. This is splendid." Mama grinned. "I suppose we don't need to go to Bath after all."

Gwen hated that she wasn't telling her mother the truth. Mama was going to be disappointed when she learned there wasn't really a courtship, that her association with Somerton was entirely for show.

Perhaps Gwen should tell her a partial truth, that the viscount had offered to help his friend's sister. But before she could, Mama had turned and was walking away. "We'll need to go to Bond Street straightaway. Meet me in the foyer."

There was no use protesting, so Gwen resigned herself to a shopping trip she didn't need. She'd plenty of hats. As if a new bonnet would snare a viscount anyway. Or any other man.

No, Gwen was going to have to do that on her own. Except that wasn't true anymore—she had help. With Somerton's guidance and attention, could she really do as he predicted? Could she have her choice of husbands?

Wishing she could stay home and work out her plan for improving Somerton's reading skill, she trudged from the drawing room. She would find a way to help him, regardless of whether his plan to make her desirable worked. Because the truth was that her task would probably be far easier than his.

CHAPTER 3

*L*azarus strolled into Hyde Park the following afternoon with a buoyant optimism. If anyone could help him finally master reading and feel confident giving a speech, it was Miss Price. Her eagerness to help had both delighted and relieved him. She hadn't been judgmental, nor had she demonstrated pity. He could not have found a better person to provide support where he needed it most.

But today would be about her. Lazarus was most eager to provoke envy in at least a few gentlemen today.

Making his way from the Grosvenor Gate to the Ring, Lazarus exchanged pleasantries with many people. He did not stop to converse. However, he did inform everyone he could that he was on his way to meet a special young lady. That would set tongues wagging.

He spotted Miss Price immediately as he approached the Ring. She stood with her mother, her mouth spreading in a smile the moment she saw him. Honestly, she *was* attractive, certainly pretty enough to garner attention from a number of young bucks. If not for her tendency toward clumsiness and her obvious dancing…issues, she would likely be popular. Her father was a prominent member of the government, and her grandfather was a viscount. That alone ought to propel her into the orbit of an appropriate gentleman.

Lazarus suddenly realized he was practically playing the role of matchmaker. The thought of a rogue such as him attempting to orchestrate a union for nonroguish people provoked him to smirk. He quickly suppressed it.

"Good afternoon," he said, greeting both ladies as he arrived at their side. He noted Miss Price's exceptionally lovely costume—a smart walking dress of dark blue with a matching spencer decorated with gold buttons and a simply marvelous hat. "Your bonnet is particularly cunning, Miss Price. Exceedingly current." Indeed, she would draw envious stares from other ladies, he would wager.

"It's new," Miss Price murmured, her expression one of both pleasure and appreciation. She flicked a glance toward her mother, who beamed with pride.

Lazarus had the sense they enjoyed a close relationship. It reminded him of what he'd shared with his father and how much Lazarus missed him.

"Shall we promenade?" He offered Miss Price his arm.

"Enjoy yourselves." Mrs. Price glanced up at the gray sky. "I do hope the rain holds off."

"We'll hasten back if it does not," Lazarus assured her as Miss Price put her hand on his sleeve. She had small, dainty hands. Very feminine.

What an odd thing for him to note. He was typically more interested in a lady's other physical attributes. But then, he was not regarding Miss Price the way he did most other women. She was his friend's sister and now his friend.

They started along the Ring, and she looked up at him. "Did you speak to Lord Droxford about our proposed arrangement?"

"Not yet, but I plan to. Have you spoken to Tamsin?"

"I will tomorrow," Miss Price replied. "She is coming to visit."

"Splendid. I'll be sure to hunt down Droxford this evening, then. If I can. He doesn't go out much, especially now that he is married." Lazarus inclined his head toward a group of ladies they passed. He noticed how they looked at Miss Price's hat. Masculine in shape, it boasted gorgeous peacock feathers and was trimmed in gold and green. It was somehow ostentatious and tastefully elegant at the same time. When they were past the ladies, he leaned his head slightly toward her. "Your bonnet is causing a stir. It really is remarkable."

"My mother insisted I needed a new hat. We went to Bond Street after you left yesterday, and it was delivered just this morning."

"There will be copies made tomorrow, I can assure you," he said.

"I doubt that will happen. My mother chose something and gave strict instructions for the milliner to make adjustments. She and this particular shopkeeper have an arrangement that she will not duplicate what she fashions for my mother—or me—for others."

"That is surprising. I should think she would want to increase his profits."

"The milliner may make something similar, but not exact. Knowing she made this hat is enough for others to want to buy from her. Or so my mother says." Miss Price wrinkled her nose slightly. "I confess that fashion is not one of my strengths. I am fortunate, and glad, to have my mother's influence. I think every shopkeeper on Bond Street knows her," she added with a laugh. "Though, it's the same with me and booksellers on Paternoster Row."

"You spend a great deal of time in bookshops?" Again,

Lazarus nodded toward a group of ladies, one of whom was giggling and blushing as she eyed him. He was used to such attention. If he had not been in the company of Miss Price, he would have gone to speak with her and probably flirt.

"I do," Miss Price said eagerly. "As much as I'm allowed. I have an allowance for book purchases, and I confess I always spend it all."

"You must have a large library."

"My father let me have a portion of the one at home in Bristol. This is my first time in London, and my books are stacked in a trunk unfortunately. Papa has assured me he will buy a bookcase for my bedchamber."

"Miss Price, I hope you won't think me too forward, but do you speak to all gentlemen in this manner?" He glanced at her and saw her brow furrow.

"I think so." She didn't sound entirely certain. "Am I doing something wrong?"

Lazarus chose his words carefully. He didn't want her to feel badly. "Not wrong, exactly, but discussing plans for your bedchamber is perhaps not the best course of conversation, nor is your passion for books. At least not on a first promenade."

She turned her head toward him, her eyes wide. "I didn't realize I was supposed to be behaving in a specific manner with you. That is, you aren't an actual suitor."

She was right that he wasn't, nor had he set any expectations or requirements for their walk today. He probably ought to have done the latter. "You are correct, but perhaps we should practice how you speak with potential suitors. Unless you really are conversing with me in an entirely different way and already know what not to say."

"Er, no." Pink flagged her cheeks. "I'm sure I've mentioned the plan for a bookcase in my bedchamber and how I spend my entire purse on books." She exhaled. "What gentleman will want a wife who spends his money on books?"

"A smart man will realize you won't do that. You didn't say you've a pile of IOUs scattered about Paternoster Row."

Miss Price laughed. "I do not. Would they even allow a young lady such as me to offer an IOU?"

"I can't imagine they would." He narrowed one eye at her. "I haven't given you any ideas, have I?"

"Not at all. I am not foolish enough to spend money I don't have. My father prides himself on his economy and financial prowess." She lowered her voice. "He has actually amassed a fair amount of wealth for a second son. Honestly, I thought that alone would encourage suitors, but I don't think his prosperity is well known. I believe my father prefers that anyway."

Now it was Lazarus's turn to laugh. "That is not something you ought to share either, particularly if your father doesn't like people knowing."

She sent him an apologetic glance. "You are exceedingly easy to talk to. I feel as if I could reveal anything."

"This is entirely my fault," he said. "We did not set any rules. First, anything you say to me will be kept between us."

Miss Price nodded. "The same for me, especially regarding your half of our arrangement."

"That is comforting to know," he said softly with a faint smile. "Second, let us set specific times when you will behave as you ought with a potential suitor. Perhaps that should be whenever we are together except for our meetings at the Droxfords."

She was slow to respond. "For the rest of our promenade, I will endeavor to do that. Why does that make me suddenly nervous?"

"Don't be."

"That's easy for you to say. You don't have any trouble

charming people or moving with grace and ease." She spoke lightly, but he detected her underlying concern.

"You have many wonderful qualities. I only meant that I don't want you to feel nervous with me. Ever. Can you do that?" He met her gaze, and she nodded. "Excellent. I am here to help. Let us start with appropriate topics of conversation."

She tightened her grip on his arm, sending a jolt of awareness through him. "Please say I can talk about books."

"It depends." He worked to focus on her tutelage, not his body's vexing response to hers. "I would not discuss romantic novels, if those interest you."

"They do indeed, but so do mysteries and biographies. I like any book that tells a good story."

"No poetry or scientific treatises for you?"

"Oh yes, both of those things can also tell a good story. My father's library includes several writings by the scientist Edmond Halley. I adore reading his work. And poetry nearly always tells a story."

Lazarus felt a bit of heat rise in his own face. Today was supposed to be about her, but she'd reminded him how little he knew about literature. "I haven't read any of those things," he said quietly, eager to return to helping her instead of thinking of his inadequacies.

"My apologies," she whispered. "You will love Halley's writing, particularly about the comet. I promise we'll read it. Should I just avoid discussing books?"

Relieved that she'd diverted the conversation back to her, he replied, "I don't think so. Just be measured about it and pay attention to your companion's engagement. If he is interested in pursuing the topic, then by all means, go on. However, if he becomes glassy-eyed or attempts to change the subject, I recommend abandoning the conversation."

"The entire conversation? I can excuse myself?" She sounded almost giddy. "Because I can't see myself in a courtship with someone who isn't interested in books or reading."

That would include him, Lazarus realized, not that they were in danger of falling into an actual courtship. Although, interest wasn't really his problem. He lacked the ability to support that interest. And as such, he'd never pursued it. He couldn't say whether he liked books, and reading was a chore, not an enjoyment.

"There are ways to cordially remove yourself from a conversation. It depends on where you are or what you are doing. Obviously, if you are dancing, you can't just walk away." He laughed, and she joined him.

"What if we are promenading like this?" she asked.

"Well, again, you can't just leave without causing a scene. I suggest you find another topic of conversation to see you through until you're back with your mother."

"I could also walk faster," she said with a mischievous smile.

Lazarus laughed again. "You certainly could."

"Except I'd likely trip and cause an even bigger scene," she said with a sigh. "As much as we may perfect my conversation skills, I'm afraid my clumsiness and poor dancing ability are unfixable."

He hated to hear her denigrate herself, but even more he didn't want her to lose hope that she could change and grow. If she wanted to. "Do you think my reading deficiencies are unfixable?" he asked.

She jerked her gaze to his. "Absolutely not." Her eyes narrowed. Then she laughed. "You are very clever, my lord."

Lazarus wasn't a clumsy person at all, but he nearly tripped. That was the second time she'd commented on his intelligence. And in a favorable way. He couldn't help smiling. "I'm only saying that we can improve or enhance things about ourselves, if we want to."

"I do agree with that sentiment, but while I may learn the technicality of dancing, I'm not convinced I'll master the grace or elegance of it. And perhaps that is acceptable. At least to me."

He felt her tense suddenly and looked toward her. Her attention was fixed just off the path to her right.

Virgil Eberforce stood with a pair of dandies, their garish costumes screaming for attention. As Lazarus and Miss Price neared, Eberforce turned his back to them and spoke loudly enough for them to hear. "That is the unfortunate chit who ruined my waistcoat at Almack's. She should be banned from public spaces, just as she has surely been from private ones. I hear her remaining vouchers to Almack's have been revoked."

Miss Price sucked in a breath and indeed began to walk faster. Lazarus, on the contrary, wanted to stop and have strong words with Eberforce. No, that wasn't quite true. He wanted to pummel the man into the ground.

"Why are you stopping?" she whispered urgently.

"Eberforce deserves a bruising setdown."

"Unless it includes actual bruises, I must insist we be on our way. I don't want to overhear another word."

They hadn't overheard anything. Eberforce had spoken loudly with cruel intent. She was meant to hear every word. Which was why Lazarus wanted to put him in his place. "I'd be happy to plant him a facer," Lazarus offered.

"I spoke in jest," she said, pulling at him so that he began to walk at her faster speed. "You can't hit him. I may be naive about a great many things, but even I know that will not help me. You do recall what happened to Tamsin and Droxford?"

"I do." Droxford had hit a man who'd grabbed Tamsin and attempted to pull her away. The man had been warned not to do it a second time and had failed to behave accordingly. If Lazarus had been there, he would have defended his cousin in the same manner. Of course, he would have been applauded for doing so, and no one would have expected him to marry her.

That Droxford had gone to such extremes for her indicated their relationship was close. Rumors would have arisen, and reputations would likely have been damaged. Hence, they had wed. Fortunately for them both, all had turned out well since they were now madly in love.

"I won't promise not to speak with Eberforce at another time," Lazarus vowed. "Or ensure that your brother does." Yes, that would be far more appropriate, and Evan would be eager to keep Eberforce from verbally attacking his sister. "He's a menace," he added.

"I don't disagree," Miss Price said. "Thank you for your support. It means a great deal to me."

He cast her a sidelong glance and was arrested by the sincerity in her gaze. "You shall have that support—always." The same jolt he'd felt earlier when she'd gripped him more tightly shocked him again. The need to protect Miss Price nearly overwhelmed him.

Her gaze shifted forward. "There is my mother. We hardly practiced how I am to talk with a suitor, but I do feel a bit more educated on that front. When I see you next, I will behave entirely as if you are a potential suitor. When will that be?"

"Are you attending the Oxley ball in two days?"

"Yes. So there, then?"

He nodded. "But I hope to see you before then—regarding our other matter."

"I do too, and I shall *not* be talking to you as if you are a potential suitor." She gave him a winning smile. "I doubt that would serve your interests."

He found he could hardly wait. Because he would at last make some progress with reading—or so he hoped.

〜

*T*he following afternoon, Gwen awaited the arrival of her friends. They gathered at least weekly to keep abreast of what was happening with each other, and it was Gwen's turn to host them.

Tamsin Deverell, Lady Droxford, was the first to arrive, and that was because Gwen had dispatched a note yesterday asking her to come early. This was so Gwen could propose her secret meetings with Somerton.

Now that the moment was upon her, she hoped Tamsin wouldn't refuse. But why would she? Tamsin was, as Gwen had told Somerton, the most generous person she'd ever met.

Garbed in a fetching dark-rose-colored gown trimmed in dark blue, her light brown hair artfully styled, Tamsin appeared every bit the Lady Droxford. She gave Gwen a quick hug before they settled themselves on a pair of chairs next to one another in the main seating area of the drawing room.

"Your new costume is so lovely," Gwen said. "My mother could have chosen that."

"Isaac's Aunt Sophia has been overseeing my wardrobe, which needed complete replacement—at least according to her. I suppose most of my garments aren't appropriate for London."

"Is it terribly overwhelming?" Gwen asked.

Tamsin lifted a shoulder. "Not terribly. Persuading Isaac to accept a modicum of invitations is my biggest challenge," she said with a laugh, her blue-green eyes sparkling. "He doesn't attend everything with me, which is fine. I go with Sophia or with Min and Ellis and their chaperone, Mrs. Dalwhimple." She gave Gwen a sympathetic look. "I understand things haven't been going well for you, and I'm sorry to hear it."

Gwen waved her hand. "We can discuss that when the others arrive." She cocked her head. "I asked you to come early because I need your help. What I'm about to ask is both necessary and secret. I've no doubt you will keep my confidence, but Droxford will need to be in on the secret. Hopefully, Somerton is speaking with him today if he hasn't already."

Tamsin shook her head as if it had cobwebs. "I'm confused. Why is Somerton speaking with Droxford? And what has that to do with your secret?" Tamsin's eyes rounded. "Are you and Somerton going to have an affair?" She giggled, and Gwen could tell she was joking.

"No!" Gwen laughed with her.

"I did hear that he came to your rescue at Almack's. That gossip has spread rather quickly." Her features creased as she added, "I am so sorry we didn't arrive before you left."

"It's all right. I'm sorry you dragged Droxford there for no reason," she said with a chuckle.

Tamsin appeared relieved. "It's good for him to get out once in a while. I'm just glad my cousin helped you."

"He was very kind," Gwen said. "And he suffered my dancing most admirably. He was keen to help me—since he knows Evan."

"Well, he knows you too from Weston," Tamsin pointed out.

"Yes, but not well. He's the sort of rogue we don't allow ourselves to get close to." And yet here Gwen was planning to be very close to him for the next several weeks. But nothing untoward would happen. He was not interested in her as a rogue might be, and she was absolutely *not* drawn to him in that manner.

"That is very true," Tamsin said. "My aunt hopes he will settle down soon, but Grandmama doesn't see that happening. She predicts he won't marry until he's at least thirty, and that's still a couple of years off." Tamsin and Somerton's grandmother resided in a cottage in Weston. They both stayed with her in August.

"It's very sweet that Somerton stays at your grandmother's cottage instead of the Grove," Gwen noted, referring to the estate outside Weston owned by Shefford and Min's father, the Duke of Henlow. "I would expect a rogue to lodge with his friends."

"He is quite fond of Grandmama, as she is of him. Somerton isn't *entirely* a rogue, but then, as his cousin, I am likely biased."

"Or that you are exceedingly optimistic and want to believe the best of him," Gwen said with a light laugh.

"That is also true." Tamsin grinned, then fixed Gwen with an expectant stare. "Now, tell me this secret before I expire from curiosity."

"Somerton has asked for my help in polishing a speech he's to deliver in the Lords."

Tamsin blinked, her surprise evident. "Has he? I'm equally surprised that he is giving a speech, for he hasn't ever seemed that engaged in his position, and that he has enlisted your aid. Forgive my impertinence, but why would he ask you?"

"I may have gone on about reading a great deal," Gwen said offhandedly. "That led us to his speech, and he asked for my help." It seemed a stretch to believe, but Gwen couldn't disclose the truth. Instead, she embellished the need for them to meet and would tell Lazarus what she'd done. "He is also going to help me improve my status on the Marriage Mart. We would like to meet—in private—periodically to accomplish both of those things. In trying to come up with a plan to do this without him calling on me here too often, we thought we could meet at your house. I would call on you, and he would call on Droxford at around the same time. It would all look perfectly innocent."

"Is it innocent?" Tamsin exhaled. "Perhaps I am not as blind to my cousin's roguishness as I thought. Of course it's innocent, else you wouldn't be doing it. How will he help you? With dancing?"

"Er, yes. Mama has not yet been able to secure a new dancing master for me." Unfortunately, Gwen had earned the reputation of being a hopeless student. Her inability to be trained could reflect poorly on the instructor, which gave them pause.

Tamsin gave her an earnest look. "You know I will help you in any way I can. I must speak with Isaac, however, since this involves him too."

"Somerton will be speaking to him, if he hasn't already."

"That will be best," Tamsin said with a flicker of relief in her gaze. "Isaac won't mind, but he won't want to support anything that might harm someone's reputation. He's very *non*roguish in that respect."

"Sometimes I do wonder how Droxford became so close with these other gentlemen, including my brother," Gwen said. "But I suppose that's a long story."

"Somewhat, yes. Isaac formed a particular bond with Shefford while they were at Oxford. I do think Sheff feels protective of him. It's rather sweet."

"Sheff seems like the older brother who wants to watch out for everyone," Gwen said, thinking of how he'd taken her brother, Evan, under his wing last Season. Min had said it was to replace the loss of Banemore, who'd disappeared into the north with his new wife. Whatever the reason, Evan thought highly of his friend, and Shefford seemed to think the same of him.

"Everyone except Min!" Tamsin said with a laugh. "I jest. They do seem fond of one another, even if they tease each other mercilessly."

"Speaking of Min." Gwen glanced toward the doorway.

"Before she arrives, can we set the first meeting for me and Somerton for tomorrow afternoon?"

"I have no quarrel with that, and Isaac is due to be home," Tamsin said. "Unless you hear something different from me later or tomorrow morning, count on it."

"Brilliant!" They'd finished not a moment too soon as the butler announced the arrival of Lady Minerva Halifax and her companion, Miss Ellis Dangerfield.

Elegant and impeccably dressed, Min glided into the drawing room. Her dark hair was swept into a cunning style, and a beautiful garnet cross rested against her pale skin above the bodice of her ivory-and-pale-yellow-striped gown. Ellis was Min's companion and always dressed far more subtly. She wore a light brown, high-necked walking dress with a diminutive floral pattern. Her blonde hair was pulled into a more simple, severe style.

The new arrivals situated themselves on a settee across from Gwen and Tamsin. "We are all here, then," Min said.

Earlier in the Season, they'd met at Persephone's, as she awaited the birth of her child, but she'd delivered a beautiful son a fortnight ago. It would be some time before she joined them once more.

"Indeed we are," Gwen said. "Does anyone want tea?" There was a pot along with some cakes on a table nearby.

"In a bit," Min replied. "We simply must discuss what happened at Almack's the other night." She looked at Gwen with sympathy. "I should have called on you sooner, but things have been hectic at Henlow House. We've a new housekeeper." Min brushed her hands against her lap and fixed a worried stare at Gwen. "The rumor is that you fell into an ungainly heap in the ballroom and that you ruined Eberforce's waistcoat. Then Somerton of all people helped you up and took you to the dance floor in the middle of a set?" She glanced toward Ellis, her companion for nearly fifteen years. "Terrible night for us to arrive late."

"That is a fairly accurate description," Gwen said slowly. "Eberforce was quite rude." She considered telling them about what had happened at the park yesterday, but she was embarrassed.

"He's horrid," Min said vehemently. "And I hear he gave you the cut direct and made insulting comments at Hyde Park yesterday. I'm considering asking Sheff to call him out. Though, I suppose your brother ought to do it."

Or Somerton.

Where had that thought come from?

Gwen knew precisely where—from him. He'd been clear about his desire to do physical harm to Eberforce. Still, that didn't mean he wanted to call him out. Or should. He definitely should not. Again, Gwen thought of Tamsin and how she'd ended up betrothed to Droxford. All because the baron had sought to defend her from an overzealous suitor. It was disturbing and frustrating that protecting a woman should cause a scandal. The scandal should be gentlemen who behaved badly. Rogues. It all came back to rogues.

"He didn't!" Tamsin said with genuine horror. "I don't think I've met Eberforce, nor do I want to."

"He tried to offer for me during my first Season two years ago," Min said. "I danced with him once. He called on me the next day, and I think we spent ten minutes speaking. He was incredibly pompous. That evening, he approached my father outside Brooks's—because he wasn't a member himself—and asked if he could call the following day to negotiate a marriage contract."

"I can't imagine your father thought much of that." Gwen had heard enough anecdotes about the Duke of Henlow to know that he possessed a short temper and did not give time to those he considered beneath him.

"He did not," Ellis murmured with a small smile. "He still tells that story when he's trying to make a point about how people should not attempt to rise above their station."

"It's shocking Eberforce is still unwed," Gwen quipped.

Min grinned. "Completely. Though I am as well," she added. "And so far, my prospects seem bleak this Season as many matrons have written me off as approaching spinsterhood."

"You're only twenty-two," Tamsin said.

"And I just turned twenty-two," Gwen said. "Am I nearly on the shelf?"

"No," Min said firmly. "Nor am I."

"You do, however, have the reputation for being discerning to the point of harming your potential," Ellis pointed out. "Which I wholly disagree with."

"Is that true?" Gwen asked. "Is your reputation suffering?"

"It's not quite as sparkling as it was last Season, I suppose. Because I've turned down so many offers," Min replied with a sigh. "I simply refuse to marry a rogue. My standards are quite high."

Gwen gave her an encouraging nod. "As they should be. I've no wish to wed a rogue either. Though, if that's the only offer I get, I may have to swallow my pride."

"No!" All three of Gwen's friends snapped their heads toward her and answered practically in unison.

Min gave her an earnest stare. "We must protect our pride and our self-respect. You don't want to be caught in an unhappy marriage."

Ellis gave Min a sympathetic look, and not for the first time, Gwen had the sense that Min's parents' marriage was not a happy one. She'd never seen them together, but then she'd only come to London about six weeks earlier.

"I must concur," Tamsin said softly. "I feared I was at first —because Isaac and I were forced to wed by circumstance. I never told you, but after the wedding, he said he wanted the marriage to be in name only."

Gwen gasped. "Why didn't you tell us?"

A faint blush washed over Tamsin's cheeks. "I think I was just shocked. He said it was 'for now,' so I expected it would change—and it did, thankfully. I did speak with Persey about it. Since she was married, I thought she could offer advice as to whether I could manage that."

"And what did she say?" Min asked.

"That I would be disappointed to not have a real marriage. And she was right. I'm sorry I didn't tell any of you."

"There is no need to apologize," Min said warmly. "Persey was the right person to give you counsel. However, I could also have told you that a marriage in name only would be hugely disappointing. But I suppose that depends on what that meant. I actually think I could survive without love if the physical aspects were acceptable."

Tamsin laughed. "You shouldn't know about that."

"When your brother is a known libertine, you learn things you should not." Min's gaze and tone were deeply sardonic.

Gwen found this conversation most interesting. "So, it's better for me to agree to marry a man with whom I can enjoy bed sport even if we don't love one another?"

"You must decide for yourself," Ellis said. "Min is being a tad cynical." She cast her friend an arch look. "However, I still believe in love—for some people. Look at Tamsin. And Persey. They are both happy and in love. And I daresay, they're fortunate enough to enjoy the bed sport too—given the way their husbands look at them."

Min snorted. "Like doe-eyed puppies following their master."

"It's quite nice, actually." Tamsin's gaze held an almost smug glee that made Gwen feel completely happy for her.

"All right, then, I shall be in search of a besotted gentleman whom I can love, or whom I can at least enjoy in the bedroom," Gwen said.

"Just so," Min said with a wide grin. "In all seriousness, you deserve that, Gwen. We all do."

Everyone nodded. The conversation turned to the upcoming social events, which included the Oxley ball as well as the weekly Phoenix Club ball. Though themes were usually reserved for the first Fridays of the month, this week they were having a medieval festival.

By the time Gwen's friends left, she was feeling better about her Season. But more importantly, she was looking forward to her meeting tomorrow with Somerton. Hopefully, he'd spoken with Droxford, and they would, in fact, meet tomorrow.

She was eager to do her part in their arrangement. Hurrying to her sitting room to prepare, she hoped he would be pleased with her plan.

CHAPTER 4

*D*roxford's butler showed Lazarus to the library at the back of the ground floor. Several cases stuffed with books lined the walls, which were covered in a green patterned paper. There was a seating area near the hearth, an alcove for reading, and a table situated near the window that looked out to the back garden.

Lazarus could imagine himself sitting there with Miss Price as she transformed him into a magnificent reader. Then, when she next mentioned poetry or scientific works, he could claim to have read them. How he'd hated that moment with her. He'd never been more ashamed not to be better at reading.

Droxford strode into the library then. "Afternoon, Somerton. Miss Price has not yet arrived, of course."

They'd arranged that Lazarus and Miss Price should time their arrivals at least a quarter hour apart, so they would not be seen coming—or going—at the same time. Not that anyone was going to be marking their arrival or departure.

Giving him a rare smile, Droxford came to stand before him. "I know I said this already, but it bears repeating—I'm thrilled you've decided to increase your participation in the Lords."

Lazarus had told him that Miss Price had agreed to help him hone his speech about soldiers returning from war and how to best support them. Upon learning she had a special interest in the topic, which Lazarus actually had no way of knowing, he said that he'd asked for her assistance, particularly given her way with words. Or so Lazarus had told his friend. He certainly wasn't going to admit to the truth behind their meeting, that he struggled to read.

"It's about time," Droxford added. "I feared you simply didn't possess the passion to do your duty."

Though Lazarus knew Droxford meant well, his words rankled somewhat. Droxford saw his own position, which he'd only inherited after several family members had died, as one of honor and responsibility—a great privilege.

Lazarus, on the other hand, had been raised from birth to know what was expected of him. His father had guided him to one day be the viscount. That it had happened much sooner than either of them had expected was a tragedy.

His father would be so glad to see that Lazarus had finally found the courage to do more, to face his fears. Only, Lazarus had been coerced into agreeing to the speech by Shefford's father, the Duke of Henlow. Not because Henlow had persuaded him, but because Lazarus deeply opposed the duke's position and felt compelled to speak against it.

"I've always had the passion," Lazarus said quietly. "I just haven't felt the need until now."

Droxford nodded. "That is more than fair. Tamsin mentioned you have another reason for meeting Miss Price, that you intend to help her with her Season in some way."

"Did she?" Lazarus wondered why Miss Price had revealed that part of their arrangement, but presumed she had a good reason. "I suppose I neglected to tell you about that aspect. Perhaps because I was certain you'd be more interested in my speech."

"You know me well," Droxford said with a rare flash of a smile. "You have my full support in this, and I'm not saying that because we are family."

More than anything, Lazarus wanted to make his father proud. That at least one of his friends was behind him would have to be an acceptable replacement.

Feminine voices preceded the arrival of Tamsin and Miss Price. They entered the room, and Lazarus noted the immediate softening of Droxford's features as his gaze fell on his wife. Lazarus was so pleased they'd found happiness together. No one deserved that more than Tamsin. Except perhaps Droxford.

"Good afternoon," Lazarus said.

"Good afternoon," Miss Price repeated. She carried a small fabric bag with pink flowers and a dark brown wooden handle. It complemented her rose-colored gown trimmed in a simple ivory lace. She did not wear a hat, and he surmised she must have left it in the entrance hall. "I'm glad we could arrange to meet today." She glanced at their hosts. "Thank you both for agreeing to allow our scheme."

"I am delighted to support the cause," Droxford said. "We'll leave you to it, then." He gave Lazarus a meaningful look, perhaps to communicate that Lazarus had promised him that nothing inappropriate would occur.

Lazarus nodded in silent reply and watched as he and Tamsin left the library. They pulled the door mostly closed, but not entirely. That would not do.

He moved past Miss Price on his way to the door, then shut it firmly but quietly. Turning, he said, "Droxford informed me that you told Tamsin we were also meeting so I could help with your Season."

"Oh yes. I hope you don't mind. When I said that I would

be helping you with your speech, she was surprised and perhaps even a little skeptical? Only because it seems an odd thing for me, of all people, to do. So, I mentioned the other part of our arrangement."

"That seems reasonable. I commend your quick thinking." Glancing toward the bag she carried, he asked, "What's in there?"

"Some materials I brought to assess your abilities."

"There's a table over here where we can work." He walked by her once again, this time to the opposite side of the room, to the rectangular table. There were four wooden chairs, one on each side.

Miss Price set her bag at one end of the table and removed her ivory kid gloves. Setting them next to the bag, she opened it and pulled out two books, some parchment, and a pencil.

"I also brought something," he said. "My speech." He removed the folded parchment from a pocket inside his coat and handed it to her.

"Oh, good. Though I don't think we'll get to that today. We've only an hour." Clasping the speech, she glanced down at it before meeting his gaze. "Is this a copy for me?"

"I hadn't thought to bring one." Now he felt a little foolish.

"I should have asked for it," she said sheepishly, her dark lashes sweeping briefly over her eyes. "If you don't need it back immediately, I can copy it down later and return it to you next time we meet."

"That would be fine."

Smiling, she tucked the parchment into her bag.

"You're not going to read it?" he asked.

Her eyes widened briefly. "I will, but did you want me to do so now?"

"No, that isn't necessary." He realized he had wanted to hear her opinion. But that could wait.

"Your handwriting is very neat," she said.

He moved to stand near the chair at the end of the table opposite her bag. "That isn't mine. I can't write particularly well either—spelling the words out is difficult. I spoke my thoughts to my secretary, and he organized them into a speech." Why did he suddenly feel nervous?

She pushed the books along the table until they rested in front of the chair on one of the long sides. "Is that how you draft your correspondence?"

"Yes. Since my secretary believes I dislike reading, I've told him my thoughts flow better if I can say them aloud, which isn't a lie."

"That's fascinating," Miss Price said, pulling out the chair in front of the books.

Lazarus rushed to hold it for her. "My apologies," he murmured.

She slid onto the chair and looked up at him over her shoulder. "No need."

He took the chair at the end, and she turned her body toward hm. "How did you manage at Oxford? You did go to Oxford, or have I confused you with someone else?"

"I did go to Oxford, but I struggled. I covered for my inadequacies by being an unserious student."

"But you weren't really, were you?"

"At Oxford, yes. There was nothing else for me to be. I didn't go to Eton or any other school. Before Oxford, my father taught me personally." Lazarus hesitated. He never talked about how his father had helped him. But that was because hardly anyone knew of his shortcomings. "I knew everything they were teaching because my father had already taught me. But I wasn't able to adequately demonstrate my knowledge, and I barely graduated."

"Why even bother going at all, then?" she asked, appearing genuinely curious as she leaned slightly toward him.

"It's a rite of passage, or so my father said. He didn't want anyone to question why I didn't attend Oxford or Cambridge or some other school. I'm fairly certain my father made special arrangements for me. I'm only sorry he wasn't able to see me finish." Lazarus allowed a faint smile, but it quickly faded.

Miss Price touched his forearm for a brief moment, her fingers pale against the dark blue wool of his coat. "I'm so sorry. I'm sure he's very proud of you."

"I hope so. That is all I want. Which is why I'm going to all this trouble with this speech. I'll need to memorize it, and that will require your assistance."

"Yes, that is why we're here." She gave him an encouraging smile. "Shall we begin?" Opening one of the books to a particular page, she turned it and placed it in front of Lazarus. "I'd like to get a sense of how you read. Can you read this sonnet to me?"

Lazarus took a deep breath and rested his hands on the table on either side of the book. He fixed his attention on the sonnet and attempted the first word. S-h-a-l-l.

"Shawl," he started, but quickly followed that with "Shall. I. Com…pare. Thee to a summer's day. Thou art more lovely and more temperate. Rough winds do shake the darling buds of May, and summer's lease—"

"Stop." Miss Price gaped at him. "You're an excellent reader. You started slowly, but perhaps you're just nervous?"

He gave her a sheepish smile. "I know this sonnet. As soon as I recognized the first few words, I recited it from memory. This is why I want you to help me memorize the speech."

"How did you memorize the sonnet?"

"My father would read things to me over and over. Eventually, I would memorize something. I then matched up the words I knew in my mind with how they looked. But when that same word is somewhere else, I can't always recognize it immediately." He hated that sensation—he knew the word, but couldn't quite form it in his mind. He got there, but it was slow.

"This is fascinating to know and will help me. Memorizing words and using that skill to recognize words when you see them is an excellent adaptation. Perhaps we can work specifically on honing that ability." She seemed so engaged, so eager to help him, even excited by the prospect.

For the first time since his father had died, Lazarus felt at ease reading with someone else. He could not overstate his sense of relief and even joy. He met her gaze with gratitude. "Thank you."

She grinned. "Let me find a sonnet you don't know." Waggling her brows, she pulled the book back in front of her and flipped through some pages, her eyes moving quickly as she scanned the words.

"Are you reading that fast as you go?" He couldn't keep the awe from his voice.

"Er, yes." Pink dots bloomed in her cheeks as she glanced at him. "But I am very familiar with this book. I love Shakespeare's sonnets." She kept turning pages until she abruptly stopped. Sliding the book toward him, she gave him a mock stern look. "This one, but you must tell me straightaway if you know it."

He laughed softly. "I promise." Sobering, he concentrated on the text. The letters looked foreign for a moment, which was normal. The first few words were easy, thankfully. "From you have I...be-en...been...ab...sent in the..." He hated words like the next one. Multiple letters that when put together were difficult to read. "Sp—"

"Spring," she said softly, her tone warm and encouraging. "That is a challenging word, I think. S, p, and r is a complicated sound. Spr. Can you repeat that?"

"Spr. Spring. Sprightly. Sprig. Spray. Spread. I can say the words." He frowned. "I just can't read them very well."

"You will." She pulled the parchment and pencil to her and wrote the letters S P R. "I'm making notes about what we can work on. Shall we continue?"

He went on reading the sonnet, pausing often. She didn't rush him, nor did she hurry to help him, but she did when he needed it. She was the epitome of patience and gentle support.

"You read wonderfully," she said. "Your voice is a lovely baritone. I do wish I could hear you deliver your speech in the Lords."

"You'll likely be sick of it by then," he said with a half smile. He expected to be, but that would be for the best. He needed to know it inside and out.

She scratched another note on her paper and set the pencil down between them near the edge of the table. "Do you want to write for me, or should we do that another day?"

The pencil rolled off the table, and Lazarus immediately bent to retrieve it.

Miss Price did the same, and they knocked their heads together.

"Ow!" she cried as Lazarus grunted.

They were still slightly bent over, their faces close as their eyes met. "I'm so sorry," she said. "I'm the clumsiest person. But then you know that."

"You are not. That could have happened to anyone."

"Perhaps, but it will always happen to me." Her lips twisted in a charming, lopsided smile. She seemed to accept that she was not as graceful as others, but Lazarus didn't want her to see herself that way.

"I don't consider you clumsy," he said softly. "Only look at how beautifully you read. And how kindly you tutor."

"You flatter me, my lord." She straightened. "If only my bookishness would snare me a husband," she added with a laugh.

"Is that what you want most?" he asked. "A husband?"

She lifted a shoulder. "It will make my parents happy. And proud. Like you, I just want to make them proud."

"I'm sure they are already." If they weren't, they were fools. Their daughter possessed more grace and generosity of spirit than a good many of the young women who were pressed onto the Marriage Mart.

"Will you write for me now?" she asked.

He didn't really want to, but he supposed he must. "Fair warning, I am going to fetch the pencil now." He watched her for a moment, and she nodded at him. Bending once more, he took up the pencil and situated himself. Then he wrote his name and her name—Miss Price. He thanked heaven she didn't have a long, ridiculous name such as Featherstone-haugh. "What else should I write?"

"Can you write the sonnet you have memorized? Just a few lines."

He recited the words in his head and scrawled them on the paper. She'd complimented his handwriting earlier without knowing it wasn't his. Now, she would see the truth and be horrified.

When he was finished, he sat back, his nose wrinkling as he looked at his uneven letters. They were abysmal *and* they'd taken an inordinate amount of time.

"Do you practice writing?" she asked.

"I used to. When my father was alive, and when I was at Oxford. I confess I've become lazy since then." And now he was annoyed with himself. He ought to have kept up with that, if only for his father's sake.

"Do not chastise yourself," she said firmly. "I can see it in your eyes. This is a great deal to manage. I want you to write five lines every day. Can you do that?"

"Yes." He resolved in that moment to do whatever she bade him. "What shall I write?"

"You're to copy the words of your speech."

The task seemed impossible. It wasn't, of course. "Only five lines?"

She nodded. "But, and this is the challenging part, you must read them and then write them. Don't just copy the letters without saying them in your head."

He blew out a breath, wondering how long this would take him. Clenching his jaw, he vowed not to be defeated, particularly when he hadn't even yet tried. He would do this for his father. And for Miss Price. He looked forward to her praise when he showed her his accomplishments.

"I'll do it." He glanced toward the clock. "Our hour is nearly over."

Surprise flashed across her features. "Goodness, that went quickly. When can we meet again?"

"Two days' time?" he suggested.

"Perfect. You'll bring your writing." Her dark eyes rounded. "Oh, wait. I'll need to give you your speech back so you can do your writing. I can give it to you at the Oxley ball this evening."

They stood, and she packed her materials back into her bag. "I look forward to reading your speech," she said.

"I'm eager to hear your thoughts, and I am open to revision."

"Are you?" She sounded surprised. "Well, I can't imagine what I could contribute, but I'll keep that in mind."

"You are very clever, Miss Price. I've no doubt you could contribute a great deal. Never doubt that." He glanced toward the door. "I suppose I must go, since I arrived first. I'll see you this evening."

She nodded, and Lazarus reluctantly left the library, leaving the door open and casting her a final glance before making his way toward the entrance hall.

"I trust you had a fruitful meeting," Droxford said, coming from another room into the entrance hall.

"Quite. We should like to meet again in two days. Same time, if that is convenient."

"I'm sure it will be."

Lazarus fixed Droxford with a grateful stare. "Thank you. Truly. This is very helpful to me." The man could have no idea how much.

"I'm pleased to hear that. I'm here for whatever you may need." Droxford clapped him on the shoulder.

As Lazarus took his hat and gloves from the footman, he realized he'd never felt more optimistic about reading. He wasn't sure he could ever aid Miss Price in as meaningful a way as she was helping him. But he would try. If she wanted a husband, he would ensure she had the best one in London.

❧

"I'm so pleased I chose that emerald velvet for your costume for the Phoenix Club ball tomorrow night." Gwen's mother said from beside her in the coach. They were stopped in an interminable line of vehicles approaching the Oxley ball. "And I've asked the modiste to fashion a circlet for you as well. You will look like a princess of old." That was because the ball's theme was a medieval fair.

"I didn't think we were going to the trouble." Gwen was never as interested in clothing as her mother.

"A viscount has danced with you, called on you, and

promenaded with you in the park," her mother said with a glint of pride in her eyes. "People will be watching you now. You must look your absolute best."

Her mother was giddy at the prospect of Gwen snaring a viscount. Which was, of course, not going to happen.

Torn between not wanting to disappoint her mother and hating that she was lying to her, Gwen couldn't find the words to tell her the truth. But she must—soon. Perhaps after she attracted another suitor or two. Hopefully, that would happen tonight.

Unless people were paying more attention to the way Eberforce spoke of her rather than the manner in which Somerton was nearly courting her. If that happened, Gwen's Season might truly be finished, regardless of what the viscount tried.

She thought back to their meeting that afternoon. Working with him had been more satisfying than she'd expected—and she'd anticipated it would be most exhilarating. It was beyond that, however. Somerton had revealed himself to her in ways he likely hadn't with anyone else, and she honored that very much. She was desperately eager to do all she could for him.

As soon as she'd arrived home, she'd read his speech. It was wonderful, and she could hear his baritone strongly delivering it over the House of Lords. The original copy was folded and tucked into the rather small pocket of her gown so she could return it when she saw him.

As the coach approached the entrance to the Oxleys' home, Gwen looked over at her mother. "Mama, I do hope you aren't counting on a betrothal from the viscount. We have not at all decided if we will suit."

"I understand, my dear. You must be sure, particularly with a man like Somerton." She'd cautioned Gwen about his reputation—that he hadn't yet been serious about marriage and was a terrible flirt—but had still maintained her enthusiasm for his interest in Gwen. "I confess I wonder if he would be the right husband for you, but his attention is certainly most welcome at this particular stage of your Season."

It did seem her mother wouldn't at all mind that Somerton was merely helping her, that his interest wasn't romantic. Relieved, Gwen opened her mouth to tell her mother the truth, but then the door opened, and a footman helped them down from the coach. The evening was chilly but dry. Gooseflesh rose on Gwen's skin as they hurried into the entrance hall.

A short time later, Gwen and her mother entered the ballroom. The fragrances of dozens of kinds of flowers filled the air, and the light of hundreds of candles made everyone sparkle. Couples were just moving onto the dance floor as the orchestra, situated in an alcove overlooking the ballroom, struck up a melody.

Though it wasn't Gwen's first ball, she was still awestruck by the spectacle. Perhaps she always would be. The idea that she might have to execute such an event as a hostess someday was incredibly daunting. Not just because she didn't know where to begin, but because she honestly wondered if she would find it boring.

She hadn't inherited her mother's taste for fashion or her ease with planning dinners and soirees. Her mother hadn't ever hosted a ball, but Gwen felt certain she could. However, she was also just as certain that her father would never agree to the expense.

Tamsin and her husband's aunt, Sophia, Lady Droxford, approached them and exchanged greetings. As the two older women began to talk to one another, Tamsin sidled closer to Gwen.

"What does Somerton have planned for you this evening?" Tamsin asked.

"Nothing in particular," Gwen replied. "I'm to behave with him as if he's a suitor, meaning I shouldn't speak about books or share too much information about myself or my family. I've a tendency to chatter on."

"I love that about you, but I am not a suitor," Tamsin said with a faint sigh. "I am so pleased Somerton is helping you. Honestly, I'd have thought he was too roguish for that." Her features tightened briefly. "That isn't kind of me to say since he is my cousin."

"He *is* a rogue, isn't he?" Gwen asked, thinking of how they'd defined rogues when they'd come up with their rogue rules nearly two years earlier. "He flirts excessively, frequents gaming hells, and has even been known to *entertain* certain widows on a regular basis."

Tamsin's eyes rounded. "I'd forgotten about the widows. But not the Rogue's Den. Don't forget that he is seen there regularly as well."

As proper young ladies, they shouldn't know about widows or establishments such as the Rogue's Den. But Gwen had a brother, and she'd overheard her father lecturing Evan about his visits to the brothel that catered to the loftiest men in London Society.

"Does he really go to gaming hells or just the Siren's Call?"

Brow furrowed, Tamsin hesitated a moment. "Remind me what that is?"

"It's a gaming hell owned by a woman and run by women. Attractive women. However, it is just a gaming hell. At least, that's what Evan told me. He likes it a great deal. He says the employees are charming and pleasant to talk to, and the food and drink are excellent."

"I doubt Isaac has ever been there, at least not to gamble,"

Tamsin said. "He hasn't wagered a day in his life. It sounds like a brilliant business, though."

"If I remain unwed, I could see myself owning a business like that," Gwen mused. "Only it would be a library."

Tamsin giggled. "Of course you would. But you won't remain unwed—not unless you want to."

"The offers are not pouring in," Gwen said wryly. "But with Somerton aiding me, that may change."

"He's taking a risk, though, isn't he?" Tamsin mused. "His interest in you will lead people to conclude he is ready to wed, but in reality, the opposite is true. In my grandmother's last letter, she made a jest about him wasting another Season since he has no plans to wed."

"Do you mean he'll be the recipient of endless attention from young ladies and their mothers looking to secure a husband?" Gwen asked. She was now more grateful to him than ever, for he couldn't enjoy fending off that level of interest. "I do hope it doesn't cause him upset. I would hate to do that."

"He'll be fine," Tamsin assured her. "This is going to work splendidly for you. Here's Miss Gwendolen Price, turning the head of one of the most roguish rakes in London." She grinned.

Gwen could only hope their plan would work. She talked with Tamsin for some time, during which no gentlemen approached.

Finally, Gwen's mother told her it was time to take a stroll around the ballroom. Gwen said good evening to Tamsin and Droxford's aunt and linked arms with her mother.

"How can you not have danced yet?" her mother asked. "I felt certain you'd be asked not long after we arrived."

"It may be that I don't receive invitations to dance, Mama. It is not my forte."

"I am hopeful that I may find a new dancing master yet," Mama said firmly. "I just received a name this afternoon. We must pray that he will take you on."

Gwen didn't see the point. Indeed, she was beginning to wonder why she'd wanted to come to London at all.

What a terribly defeating attitude. If Somerton could work to improve his reading, she could do the same with dancing. How could she encourage him to work hard and keep applying himself if she didn't do the same? She would redouble her efforts, for she owed it to herself to at least try, even if it seemed hopeless.

"Here comes Lord Somerton," Gwen's mother whispered urgently, her arm tightening against Gwen's before she unlinked herself. "Goodness, but he presents himself well. That cravat is knotted to perfection."

Somerton strode straight for them, and indeed his intricately tied cravat was most impressive. As was the cut of his midnight-black coat.

"Good evening, ladies," Somerton said as he bowed gracefully.

If Gwen tried such a maneuver, she'd probably fall over. Mastering the curtsey she'd delivered to the queen a few weeks ago had been extremely difficult. In the end, Mama had instructed her to just not dip as deeply as the other young ladies. Then she'd shared with several people that Gwen had twisted her ankle the day before. It had been a lie, but served to explain Gwen's deficiencies.

"Good evening, Lord Somerton," Gwen's mother began.

"I hoped I might take a promenade with your charming daughter." He smiled toward Gwen.

Gwen's mother beamed. "Lovely. Please enjoy yourselves."

Taking Somerton's arm, Gwen nodded at her mother. When they were away from her, she murmured, "I really need to tell her you aren't actually courting me."

"Is there a problem?" he asked.

"Not really. I don't think she sees your attention as the prelude to a serious courtship." She glanced at him. "Because of your reputation. You haven't indicated you are interested in marriage." Gwen thought that was a better way of saying, *You're a terrible rogue.*

"I see."

"I do hope this scheme won't prove difficult for you," Gwen said. "I fear you may become the focus of a gaggle of young ladies—and their mothers—looking to snag a title."

"I shall survive," he said glibly, a smile teasing his mouth. "I must thank you for our meeting earlier."

"I do hope you found it helpful."

"Time will tell, but I am hopeful for the first time in years. And I am committed to doing whatever you tell me." His gaze met hers with an earnest warmth. "I am yours to command, Miss Price."

Gwen's chest expanded. She would do everything in her power not to let him down. Pulling the folded speech from her pocket, she tucked it into his hand. "I thought your speech was wonderful."

He transferred the speech to his free hand and slipped it into his coat. "I am delighted—and humbled—to hear that."

"Good evening, Lord Somerton." A feminine voice to Gwen's left drew them to pause in their promenade. There were a pair of ladies, young and pretty, their gazes fixed on Somerton. It was as if Gwen wasn't there.

"Good evening," he responded.

"I've dropped my fan," one of them said, her lips pressing into a plump pout.

"Allow me." The viscount bent—without releasing Gwen —and plucked up the fan. He presented it to the pouter, and her lips curled into a flirtatious smile.

She batted her dark lashes at him. "You are most kind, my lord."

"It is my pleasure to help."

"Perhaps we'll see you later?" the other young lady said with a hopeful lilt.

"One can never tell." He grinned, and Gwen could practically see their pulses flutter and their breath seize in their lungs.

"It's happening already," Gwen said.

"What? Those young ladies?" He lifted a shoulder. "That's typical, even before I started helping you."

And why wouldn't it be? Somerton was an exceedingly charming and attractive viscount, even if his reputation was rakish.

"So I'm not interfering in whatever you would normally be doing?" she asked.

"What would that be?"

"Flirting?"

He laughed. "I can flirt with you, can't I?" He waggled his brows at her, his green eyes piercing her with a sharp interest. In that moment, Gwen realized the strength of his flirtation, and she too felt her pulse flutter and her breath catch.

"You can, but what would be the point?" she asked nervously, adding a smile so he wouldn't realize she was seriously asking. Why would he flirt with her when their near courtship was only pretend?

He paused, turning toward her slightly. "The point is in showing everyone within eyesight and earshot that you are a woman worth flirting with. Because you are." He leaned close and whispered, "Don't ever think you shouldn't be flirted with. Now, bat your eyelashes. And smile. Everyone will wonder what I've just said to you."

She did, and when he straightened, she sent a furtive

glance around and saw that there were indeed people watching them. "Perhaps your plan has merit."

"Tomorrow at the Phoenix Club ball, you will have three dances and at least two promenades. And not with me."

"How can you promise that?" She was consistently amazed by his confidence. In this, anyway. He'd been different that afternoon, more vulnerable. She thought she might prefer that version of the roguish viscount.

"Trust me, Miss Price."

She couldn't help but do so—not when he looked at her as if he ruled the social world. And perhaps he did.

"I forgot to speak with you as if you were a potential suitor," she said with a faint grimace.

"We did forget that. Ah, well, next time perhaps—if it's even necessary," he said. "Allow me to return you to your mother."

When they parted a few minutes later, she noted that her pulse was still fluttering, and her breath was perhaps a little short.

CHAPTER 5

$\mathcal{E}$very Friday during the Season, the Phoenix Club, London's premier gentlemen's *and* ladies' club, hosted an assembly. The balls on the first Friday of the month were themed, but tonight's mid-month ball was as well—a medieval festival.

Fridays were the one night of the week where the sexes mingled within the club, save Tuesdays, when the ladies were invited to the men's side of the club. The closest the men ever got to the ladies' side was their half of the ballroom, the width of which spanned both sides on the ground floor.

This was the club's third Season, and it had only gained in popularity. The club's owner, Lord Lucien Westbrook, was one of London's most charming gentlemen. Everyone wanted to be his friend or find their way into his bed. To the latter's chagrin, alas, as Lord Lucien was recently married and utterly devoted to his new wife.

Lazarus arrived at the club and entered through the men's side. Instead of going straight to the ballroom, he went up to the members' den, where he was sure he'd run into at least some of the gentlemen he sought. He was not disappointed.

Shefford sat with a friend of theirs who'd only recently returned to London Society after losing his wife two years ago. Roman Garrick, Marquess of Keele, had long been focused on rebuilding his family's tattered reputation and squandered fortune, but since his wife's death, he'd seemed to double his efforts.

"Evening, Somerton," Shefford said. "Join us for a drink?"

Keele looked up at Lazarus from his chair, his steel-gray eyes sharp as they fixed on him. "The whisky is excellent."

"The Phoenix Club always has the best liquor." Shefford swirled his glass and studied the amber liquid. "I'd ask Lord Lucien how he does it, but I understand Lady Evangeline is responsible." He referred to the manager of the club.

"I must find out where she gets it," Keele murmured before taking another sip. "Shouldn't you two go down to the ball?"

Lazarus noted that Keele was not dressed in medieval garb to match the theme. Shefford had donned a costume, however. He wore a black doublet shot with silver thread.

Predictably, Shefford wrinkled his nose. "I'll get there. Eventually. Or not." He looked up at Lazarus. "Sit with us."

"I cannot. I've things to do." He gestured to his own costume of a dark green gipon edged in gold. "Besides, I would never let this attire go to waste."

"Of course you wouldn't. Only you could make this ancient clothing look fashionable." Shefford frowned. "Rumor is you've been practically courting Evan's sister. What the devil are you about?"

Lazarus sat down at the table with them and spoke in a low tone. "I'm helping her gain admirers. I thought if I paid her attention, others might too. My goal tonight is to ensure she has three dances." And two promenades. He wasn't sure he could manage all that, though he would try.

"That's very kind of you," Keele said.

"You should tell her brother. Last night, he was going on about you promenading with his sister at the Oxley ball and wondering if you are going to offer for her."

Inwardly grimacing, Lazarus wondered if Miss Price had spoken to her mother yet. If not, she probably should. Lazarus didn't wish to cause unrealistic expectations or disharmony.

"Is there any chance you may decide to court her?" Keele asked.

"He's not ready to marry," Shefford said, flicking a glance toward Lazarus as if to make sure.

"I am not," Lazarus confirmed. And yet, he was thinking of Miss Price a great deal. He enjoyed her company, and she'd seen a side of him he'd only fully bared to his father. She hadn't only seen it, she'd embraced that part of him, giving her unconditional support.

Then, last night at the ball, those two young ladies had interrupted their promenade and he'd been irritated. He hadn't wanted to pick up the fan the chit had purposely dropped—he'd watched her do it as he and Miss Price had approached—but he'd politely done so. He'd smiled at them and even flirted in return because that was what he did. Except afterward, he'd felt uneasy about it. Especially when Miss Price had said she wasn't worth flirting with. She was far more worthy than insipid title hunters who dropped their fans to get attention.

Keele's mouth ticked up in a wry smile. "Are you certain, Somerton?"

"So help me, if you decide to wed, I am going to have to write you off," Shefford threatened. "I can't lose another friend to the parson's trap."

"You haven't lost any friends," Somerton said with a fair amount of exasperation. "Except Bane, perhaps, but then who knows what he is about."

"He's expecting a child," Keele said, swirling his whisky. "Any time, in fact. Or perhaps the birth has already come to pass."

"I didn't know that," Shefford said. "How do *you* know?"

"My mother-in-law is cousin to his mother-in-law," Keele replied. "She knows that I have been acquainted with Bane for some time."

"Well, that is excellent news," Somerton said, though he honestly had trouble imaging Bane as a father. He glanced toward the clock. "I need to get down to the ball." He stood. "You sure I can't persuade either of you to join me?"

"Absolutely not," Keele said firmly. "I may be back in Society, but my time attending balls is finished. Good luck to you, my friend."

"I'll be down when I finish my whisky," Shefford responded, though he did not sound enthused. "If only to ensure you don't do anything foolish such as get caught in a compromising position with Evan's sister and be forced to wed."

Lazarus snorted. "That can't possibly happen again, not after Droxford and Bane."

"Just be *careful*," Shefford pleaded.

Nodding, Lazarus waved at them as he turned to go downstairs. Entering the ballroom, he was struck by how grand everything looked. The club had outdone itself tonight with the medieval festival theme. There were flowers and greenery, and a dais with two chairs made to look like thrones. He had no idea what they were for, but they'd never been there before. They must have something to do with the theme.

And a great many of the attendees had embraced the medieval aspect, their costumes hailing from another time. There were more women than men who were dressed appropriately, but that was to be expected.

He scanned the ballroom and located Mrs. Price. She was not difficult to spot as she was taller than most ladies and always one of the most elegantly dressed. Tonight, her attire was flawless, with an exceptional medieval headdress and a golden velvet gown with flowing sleeves. Miss Price was not with her, however. Lazarus wondered if she might be dancing.

Pivoting, he looked toward the dance floor and found her. She *was* dancing. And she was also spectacularly garbed in an emerald gown with a matching circlet atop her head. Her sable hair hung down her back, a stunning style of curls and braids beneath a sheer veil. Isaac realized their costumes matched, which they, of course, had not planned.

He saw that her brow was puckered as she concentrated on the steps. He found himself murmuring what she should do, as if she could hear him. Perhaps they should have practiced dancing at their meeting yesterday. Tomorrow, he would suggest it.

Suddenly, she turned the wrong way and bumped into one of the other people in her set. Lazarus winced. He ought to walk away because watching her was rather torturous—he wanted to rush in and save her. However, he stayed rooted and continued to think the steps in his mind as if he could convey them directly into her brain.

"Somerton."

Turning his head, Lazarus saw Gwen's brother, Evan, heading toward him. He had a near-olive complexion like his mother along with her ink-dark hair. He was also wearing medieval dress, perhaps because his mother had insisted.

"Evening, Price," Lazarus said.

Stopping alongside him, Price followed his gaze. "Are you watching my sister dance?"

"Not your sister in particular, but I do see her."

Price frowned. "Are you courting her?"

Lazarus tried not to betray anything. He kept his focus on the dance floor. "Not at the moment."

"That's a strange answer." Price turned toward him. "I thought we were friends. I should like to know your intentions toward my sister."

Exhaling, Lazarus looked at Price and inclined his head toward the wall. Silently, they walked to the perimeter of the ballroom. "I am merely trying to help your sister by paying her attention. I am not planning to court her."

The gold flecks in Price's eyes seemed to catch fire. "She bloody well thinks you are."

She did? *Shit.* Lazarus glanced toward the dance floor. No, she didn't. She couldn't. They had an arrangement. She could not mistake what they'd agreed to. "Did she say that?"

Price frowned. "No. But my mother keeps talking about your interest."

"Your sister isn't expecting my courtship. She knows I am helping her. My goal is to ensure her Season is not a failure."

Price blinked, appearing nonplussed. "Why are you doing this?"

"Because I wanted to."

"It's just…you risk your own reputation by paying her attention as you have."

"I've been judicious in how much time we spend together," Lazarus explained. "I have no plans to dance with her tonight or even speak to her." Then why had he been ogling her as she danced as if he were a hungry kitten who'd just spotted a bowl of cream?

He'd only been watching her out of concern. He wanted her to be successful.

And how was his observing her going to ensure that?

"I confess I'm surprised you would go to all this trouble to help my sister," Evan said bemusedly. "But I do appreciate your assistance. Provided it really doesn't amount to anything between you. I mean no offense, but I don't think you'd be a good match."

Lazarus wanted to ask why, but he already knew the reasons. His reputation, for one. And her brilliance, while he was generally regarded as unserious and perhaps even doltish. What she really ought to do was frequent literary salons. The perfect gentleman for her would likely be found there. Lazarus pondered a way to introduce her to such people. Could young unmarried ladies on the Marriage Mart even attend such salons?

"Rest assured that I have no marital intent toward your sister," Lazarus said. "Now, if you'll excuse me, I've rounds to make so I may surreptitiously compliment your sister and draw attention to her considerable attributes."

Walking toward the other end of the ballroom, Lazarus tried to shake off the persistent feeling of irritation brought on by Price's comments. Could he really not be a good match for Miss Price? He was a viscount after all. And he possessed charm and wit. He wasn't a *complete* blackguard.

This was an absurd line of thought. Lazarus wasn't ready to marry anyone, let alone Miss Price.

Why, exactly?

His usual excuses, that he hadn't yet been inspired to wed or that he hadn't encountered a woman who made him want to give up his current lifestyle of excess, somehow rang hollow just now. Perhaps he needed to spend the evening at the Rogue's Den in the arms of the beautiful Thomasina. Except even that sounded distasteful at the moment.

Because he needed to focus on helping Miss Price. He spent the next half hour circuiting the ballroom and refreshment area. He struck up conversations about ladies on the Marriage Mart, and complimented Miss Price wherever he was able.

He was about to depart the ballroom and retreat to the

members' den when he encountered two young bucks, one of whom he thought was actively seeking a wife. Lazarus didn't know them well—the taller of the two, a barrister called Markwith, was the gentleman in search of a bride. The other, shorter man's name slipped Lazarus's mind. Both were dressed as medieval knights, without the armor.

"Evening, gentlemen," Lazarus said. "Enjoying the ball?"

"Far more than regular balls," Markwith said. "I've only recently joined the Phoenix Club, and this is my first one. Are they always this extravagantly decorated?"

Lazarus laughed. "Quite. Though I haven't determined the meaning of the dais with the thrones."

"It's for the king and queen, who will be crowned at midnight," the shorter man responded. "You can vote for your choice next to the dais."

There was indeed a small table with a pair of footmen— rather a footman and a footwoman, since the ladies' side only employed women—dressed as medieval pages, over-seeing a large box. A few attendees were writing down their votes.

"Have you voted yet?" Lazarus asked.

The shorter man shook his head. "Haven't decided. On the queen, anyway. I'll be voting for myself of course." He laughed.

Markwith joined in, and Lazarus smiled.

"I'll be voting for Miss Gwendolen Price," Lazarus said. What a boon it would be for her to be chosen! He wished he'd known sooner for he would have made a specific campaign. Well, it wasn't too late. Instead of going upstairs, he'd do his best to ensure she received the most votes. Starting with making his way to the voting table.

"Why Miss Price?" the shorter man asked. "She's pretty enough and her family's highly regarded, but have you seen her dance?" He shook his head. "Clumsy as a drunken soldier. Ruined poor Eberforce's expensive new waistcoat. I was with him when he picked it up on Savile Row."

"That's hardly charitable," Markwith said with a slight frown.

Lazarus was glad the man had spoken so that he could take a moment to form his own response. Else he would have jumped down the shorter man's idiotic throat. "I've danced with Miss Price, and she is a lovely partner. She is exceedingly intelligent and quite witty. You won't find a more engaging companion on the dance floor."

"Intelligent, you say?" Markwith said. "Precisely what most interests me in a bride. I shall seek her out forthwith."

"Don't blame me when she stamps on your foot," the shorter man said. He shot a look at Lazarus. "I am not disparaging her. It is a fact. A friend of mine limped all the next day after dancing with her a couple of weeks ago."

Lazarus wanted to say that wasn't possible, but he knew otherwise. "Comparing her to a drunken soldier is the definition of disparaging." He glowered at the man. "Do better."

Inclining his head toward Markwith, Lazarus stalked away toward the voting table. He soothed his irritation by thinking of how delighted the man would be when he spent time with Miss Price and determined for himself that she was very clever. Perhaps Markwith would be the one to sweep her off her feet and into his arms.

That thought had the opposite effect of soothing Lazarus. It pricked his ire.

Or sparked jealousy.

It was not his place to feel jealous. He would direct Markwith and others like him toward Miss Price. That was their agreement.

Lazarus looked about for Miss Price, but didn't see her. The set had finished, but it was possible she was already dancing another. Or perhaps, some lucky gentleman had taken her for a circuit of the garden.

At the voting table, he carefully wrote his choice on a piece of parchment and slipped it into the large box. Then he spent the next quarter hour suggesting others vote for Miss Price. After that, he mentioned to all his friends, and some of his acquaintances, that they should vote for Miss Price if they hadn't already.

Satisfied that he'd done enough and feeling parched, he made his way back toward the doorway to the men's side of the club. He slipped through the curtained threshold and immediately caught a flash of green silk.

Miss Price had been wearing green.

Lazarus stepped into an alcove and stopped short, for tucked inside was Miss Price. "What are you doing here?" he whispered urgently. "You can't be in this part of the club."

She looked up at him, and though they were in shadows, he could make out her dark eyes. "I know, but I'd heard there was a secret passageway to get to the men's side, and I thought I could find it."

"To what end?"

As she lifted a shoulder, a sheepish expression crossed her features. "I just wanted to peek."

"You'd be caught. A woman, especially one who looks as lovely as you tonight, stands out."

She glanced down. "You think I look lovely?"

Her emerald medieval gown was stunning, the oval neckline offering an exquisite frame of her collarbones. A pearl necklace shimmered against her smooth skin. But it was her dark locks that beckoned him. He longed to touch them and judge whether they were as soft as they looked. Seeing her hair down made it easier for him to envision her in a state of undress. Which was not something he ought to be doing.

"You are objectively beautiful," he said, thinking his voice sounded rather tight. He blamed it on the tension of being here with her. Not only was she not where she was supposed to be—on the men's side of the club—they were together in a dark alcove where Lazarus could be expected to steal a kiss or a caress.

God, he was tempted.

Miss Price smelled inexplicably of sun and citrus, like a bright summer day. He closed his eyes briefly and inhaled her scent, letting it wash over him and saturate his senses.

Temptation was fast turning into desperation.

"You need to go back to the ball," he said.

"You can escort me."

"Not from here, I can't. You'll be lucky if you can steal back into the ballroom without being noticed."

"You make a good point." She exhaled. "I didn't really think this through. It's just that I needed a respite. It's been a very busy evening. I've never danced so much."

"I'm pleased to hear that." And yet that annoying prick of jealousy returned.

"Well, it hasn't been ideal. I'm still terrible, but at least I've only run into someone twice and stepped on someone's toes once. And I forgot the steps once too. Or perhaps it was twice." She sounded so adorably concerned and yet not at the same time. It was as if she knew she should care that her dancing was horrid, but ultimately didn't. He had the sense that she tried to hide the latter from most people. Not him, however.

It seemed they were honest with one another.

"I should tell you that I spoke with your brother," Lazarus said, embracing honesty. "Rather, he approached me and asked if I was courting you. I felt it necessary to tell him I am not, that I am helping you gain admirers."

"I'm sorry you were in that position," she said. "I know you and Evan are friends. I will speak to my mother posthaste and explain that you've been helping me, that your interest isn't real."

"That sounds almost callous," he murmured, thinking his *interest* in this moment was achingly real.

Her bare hand—gloves were not a part of her costume—flattened gently against his chest. Lazarus sucked in a breath at the contact. She could have no idea what her innocent touch was suddenly doing to him. All manner of torrid thoughts shot through his brain and an accompanying heat flooded his body. His cock began to swell.

This was *terrible*.

"You aren't callous," she said, her gaze meeting and holding his. "I have you to thank for the change in my fortune. I will have at least two callers tomorrow, so it may be that our ruse is nearly complete."

Panic streaked through him. They couldn't be finished. She'd barely begun to help him with his reading.

"But don't think that means I won't continue tutoring you," she said quickly. "I am committed to helping you, no matter how long it takes."

Lazarus imagined her wed to someone else, but continuing to meet with him in secret. That would be incredibly risky. He wouldn't want to ask that of her.

She really needed to get back. "You must go," he urged.

"Yes." She took her hand from his chest and walked from the alcove. He stepped out just as she slipped through the curtains.

He made to follow her, but stopped himself. Then he heard her name called from the ballroom.

She'd been voted queen!

Lazarus moved into the ballroom, but stayed on the

periphery. If they'd called her name even a moment sooner, they might not have heard it. Someone would have gone looking for her, and calamity would have struck, for she had been tucked away with him.

She moved toward the dais where Lord Lucien stood. He helped her onto the stage, then looked out at the ballroom once more. "And our king is the Viscount Somerton!"

Bloody hell. It wasn't supposed to be *him*. Why was it him?

"Aren't you going to the dais?" someone to his left said.

Lazarus made his way across the ballroom and joined them on the small stage. "Evening, Lord Lucien," he muttered.

"Try not to look as if you're heading to the gallows," Lord Lucien said while smiling.

Lifting his lips, Lazarus faced the ballroom.

"Much better," Lord Lucien whispered. "Time for the coronation!" he announced. "Look at how well they match. It appears as if they planned this with their coordinated costumes."

They did indeed. This wasn't going to help Miss Price with potential suitors, not if they saw her as already taken.

As Lord Lucien stepped to the back of the dais, Lazarus joined Miss Price. She was smiling broadly.

"This is a surprise," she said, her cheeks flushed with pleasure.

"Quite." Lazarus continued to worry at how this looked. He didn't want them to be seen as a couple or for people to assume their betrothal was a fait accompli. He needed those gentlemen who said they would call on Miss Price tomorrow to actually call on her.

But what was he to do? Announce that he had decided not to pursue a courtship with her?

If only he hadn't reentered the ballroom after her. As

soon as he heard his name being called, he could have fled the club and avoided this entire situation.

In hindsight, he should have retreated as soon as Lord Lucien said his name. However, the people around him had been aware of his presence. His flight would have raised questions. And perhaps not reflected well on Miss Price.

"Take your thrones, if you would, please," Lord Lucien instructed.

"Does it matter which?" Miss Price asked, surveying both seats.

One was slightly taller and wider. "I suppose the larger one is for the king," Lazarus said.

"Indeed," Lord Lucien responded in a low voice. He held a painted wooden crown. "Please sit so I can put this on your head."

Lazarus waited until Miss Price took her throne then he sat down beside her. This was ridiculous.

"I crown thee King Somerton of the Realm," Lord Lucien said loudly as he put the crown atop Lazarus's head. He looked over at Lord Lucien, now holding the queen's crown. It was much daintier. Still, how were they supposed to move about with these on their heads? They would surely fall.

Lord Lucien placed the crown on Miss Price's head. "I crown thee Queen Gwendolen of the Realm."

"Does that fit atop the circlet?" Miss Price asked with a laugh. She tipped her head, as if she could possibly see the crown, and everything tilted.

"Careful," Lazarus warned.

She reached up and touched the crown. "I hope this doesn't fall. I'm liable to hurt someone." Based on her smile and the sparkle in her eyes, she was joking. But Lazarus didn't want her to think of herself as a walking hazard.

"You won't," he said. "Just keep your head up. Look down

at everyone as if they are your subjects. Which they are for the remainder of the night." He grinned at her.

Adopting a haughty expression, she surveyed the crowd gathered before the dais and looked down her nose at them. Then she giggled, and the effect was ruined.

Lazarus laughed too. "You had it until you couldn't hold your humor."

"This is all so silly. But also rather…wonderful." She looked sideways at him. "I'm glad to be sharing it with you."

They were on dangerous ground. Lazarus needed to flee, but as king, he'd likely be expected to stay. Dammit, this wasn't how things were supposed to go.

"There's my mother," Miss Price said softly. "She looks so happy." Turning her head toward Lazarus, she met his gaze with warm gratitude. "Thank you."

She couldn't know what he'd done to ensure she was queen. "You deserve this," he said.

"I don't know if that's true, but I deeply appreciate it. This is something I never dreamed of."

"And now, we shall recommence the dancing," Lord Lucien declared. "A waltz led by our king and queen."

Now he was to waltz with her? Lazarus groaned inwardly even as his body thrilled to the idea of holding her close.

He stood and offered her his hand. "My queen," he murmured.

She put her bare hand in his, and the connection was a strike of lightning. Somehow, he managed to keep from physically reacting. However, unlike lightning, which would have driven him to the ground, he wanted to pull her close and put his lips on one of her delectable collarbones.

As he guided her from the dais, she put her foot down onto the first step. Then her other foot caught her gown, and Lazarus clasped her hand more tightly, holding her upright. "All right?"

"Yes. I am not used to this type of gown. The skirt is a bit too long, and there's a train. It's a hazard, if you must know." She flashed him a smile, and Lazarus nearly tripped himself.

When they were safely off the dais, he led her to the center of the dance floor. "How is your waltzing?" he asked.

"As accomplished as you think it is," she said with a wry smile as they assumed their positions.

Lazarus pressed his hand to her back. "Just keep your eyes on me and hold tightly. I will guide you completely."

"What about my feet? You can't lift me and carry me about."

"I would if I could."

She laughed, and he couldn't help grinning. "I'm bound to step on you, so I'll apologize now."

"Don't think too much. Take small steps. I'll propel us. And no one will see your feet, because, as you pointed out, the skirt is too long. So don't worry what people might see."

"You've an excellent point, except we're the only ones here. Everyone is watching." She glanced about at the empty dance floor. "Why is no one else dancing?"

"I presume it's just supposed to be the king and queen for now." Again, Lazarus worried this was going to ruin everything for Miss Price.

The music started, and Lazarus swept her into the dance. She kept her gaze locked on his, and it didn't take long for him to realize he had to count the steps in his head lest he become completely lost in her eyes and her arms.

How had this happened? He hadn't even planned to speak to her tonight, and here he was, king to her queen, holding her in his arms as the entire ballroom looked on.

Thankfully, other couples now entered the dance. He felt her relax in his arms. Then she stepped on his foot.

She blushed faintly. "Sorry."

"Don't apologize. Now listen, after the dance, I am not

going to speak to you again. I'm going to flirt with other women and try to implicitly convince people that we are not courting."

Her magnificent eyes rounded briefly. "Do people think we are?"

"I think some will jump to that conclusion since I have danced with you before, we promenaded in the park, and here we are king and queen of the medieval festival in matching costumes."

"That does look…suspicious."

"You must try to say things that indicate you are enjoying meeting a great many gentlemen. Anything you can say that will indicate you are not spoken for will help immensely. And if you can manage to see those two gentlemen who said they planned to call tomorrow, reiterate how much you are looking forward to that."

She nodded. "I will." Her gaze softened. You've been so incredibly kind and supportive. If I manage to receive any offers, it will be entirely because of you."

"Nonsense. I may have helped, but once gentlemen see past what they think they know about you, they won't be able to deny that you are a sparkling diamond, and they'd be fortunate to have you choose them." Lazarus realized he was talking about himself. She *was* a diamond, and he never would have seen her if he hadn't taken the time to do so.

He really needed to put distance between them. And yet he would be alone with her tomorrow when they met for another reading lesson.

The music ended, and he escorted her from the dance floor. "Thank you," she said. "For everything. I'll see you tomorrow."

Her eyes sparkled with enthusiasm, but he knew it didn't match his. She was eager to help him with reading while he was thinking of all the ways he could touch her when they were alone tomorrow. He was worse than a rogue. But he was going to keep himself in check.

There was simply nothing else he could do.

"Enjoy the rest of your evening, Miss Price." He bowed and took his leave.

Then he spent the remainder of the ball flirting with every woman he met. He'd never felt more hollow.

CHAPTER 6

*G*wen arrived before Somerton at Tamsin and Isaac's house the day after the Phoenix Club ball. Tamsin accompanied her to the library to await Somerton's arrival. On the way, Gwen told her about being the queen of the medieval ball at the Phoenix Club.

"Oh, I wish I'd been there," Tamsin said. "Was it spectacular?"

"It was beyond my imagination." Gwen was still giddy—not just from being the center of everyone's attention, but because her mother had been so happy. That was all Gwen had wanted. To see the pride and joy in her mother's eyes had meant everything. "And today, I had *three* callers."

Tamsin beamed at her. "That's wonderful, Gwen! It seems this plan with Somerton is working."

"Yes, I can hardly believe it." Gwen went to set her bag down on the table before turning to face Tamsin.

"Tell me about the callers," Tamsin urged, moving toward the seating area.

They sat together on the settee, and Gwen told her about

each one, starting with Mr. Thaddeus Markwith. Before she could finish, however, Somerton arrived.

"I'll tell you about the last one later," Gwen said to Tamsin as they stood.

"The last what?" Somerton, garbed in a bottle-green coat, brown-and-gold waistcoat, and dark brown breeches that would have revealed a host of imperfections on any other man, asked jovially as he strode in the library.

"My callers today." Gwen grinned at him. "Thanks to you, I had three!" She laughed, unable to contain her glee. "My mother was beside herself. She didn't even care when I told her you weren't really courting me."

"I'm pleased to hear it. Should we begin?" He glanced toward Tamsin.

"Sorry, cousin!" Tamsin said to the viscount. "I'll see myself out." She turned and left the library, closing the door behind her.

When they were alone, Somerton surveyed her a moment. "Three callers, eh?"

"Yes, can you believe it? I cannot."

"I absolutely can," he said. "I suppose you don't need my help any longer."

"I don't know that I would go that far, but this is a huge improvement from where I was a week ago. I can't thank you enough." She moved toward him and was going to hug him, but stopped herself.

He narrowed his eyes briefly. "What?"

"I was going to hug you, but I realized that wouldn't be appropriate."

"Is it any more intimate than the waltz?" he said with his signature flirtatious smile.

"Are you flirting with me?" she teased.

His features sobered, but he didn't appear any less handsome. Gwen wasn't sure he could even if he rolled about in mud. "Probably. And I should not." He looked away from her, and she sensed a change in him.

"What's wrong?"

"I'm concerned that since you won't be needing my help much longer that we won't be able to continue meeting like this. For my...problem."

Gwen touched his sleeve, and he met her gaze once more. She saw the flicker of anxiety in his expressive green eyes. "I am committed to helping you—now and as long as you need it."

The moment between them stretched, and Gwen's pulse beat faster. There was something about the viscount that always made her feel...different. At least, not the way other gentlemen made her feel. Was that because he was a rogue? Whatever the reason, having his attention was exciting. Even if it was all a ruse. Just being in his presence was enough to make one's heart skip.

He arched a dark gold brow. "Will your betrothed mind you secretly meeting with me?"

She cracked a smile at his sarcasm—at least she assumed it was sarcasm—and stepped back from him. "I do not have a betrothed, so let us not put the cart before the horse. Come, let's get started. We only have an hour."

Somerton held her chair at the table as she sat down. Gwen angled herself toward him as he took his seat. "How did your writing go?" she asked.

"Slowly. I copied the first portion six times. Three each night."

Gwen was impressed. "How long did that take you?"

He looked up at the ceiling, his face scrunching as if he were calculating. "I don't honestly know. It did become faster as I went."

"That's excellent! That's exactly what we want, for this to become easier." She pulled a piece of parchment from her bag. "Today, I would like to work on reading first, and then we can spend some time reviewing your speech. How does that sound?"

He leaned back against the chair. "I am entirely at your command, as ever."

Something about the way he said those words and the manner in which his gaze seemed to…devour her made her shiver. She had no trouble seeing how he was able to steal kisses from nearly anyone. Although, Gwen was fairly certain he wouldn't need to steal. She would give them freely.

Did that mean she wanted to kiss him?

She had to admit she was curious. She'd never kissed anyone, and she had to imagine the experience with Somerton would be sublime.

She needed to stop thinking such things! There were nice gentlemen showing her interest, if not yet courting her, and she was tutoring Somerton—nothing more.

"Miss Price?" he prodded, jolting Gwen from her wayward thoughts. "Woolgathering?"

"I'm afraid so," she replied with a shake of her head, as if that would clear her mind. She needed to focus on the matter at hand—helping the viscount. Setting the paper in front of him, she said, "We're going to practice reading. I've chosen a new poem for today, which I've copied onto this parchment in a specific way. I've underlined words I think you already know and broken other ones into parts so they may be easier to read. I don't know if this will work, but I thought it was worth a try."

Somerton nodded as he focused on the paper before him. "You put a great deal of planning into this."

"Of course."

He looked over at her, his expression…humbled? "Thank you."

"It's my pleasure. I'm glad we're able to help one another.

You've been so very wonderful. Last night was particularly brilliant. I do think it may have changed everything for me to be queen of the ball." She cocked her head. "Did you have anything to do with that?"

He shrugged. "I certainly didn't stuff the box with votes for you. I may have suggested to some people that you would be a good choice."

Her heart skipped. He'd done so much for her. "For a rogue, you are very nice."

His brows dipped. "I'm not *that* nice. Remember that I am helping you because you are providing something for me in return."

"There's nothing wrong with that," Gwen argued. "We are both benefiting, as agreed upon. I hope you know I consider you a friend."

"I consider you my friend too. But you mustn't forget who I really am, Miss Price—a rogue conducting a transaction." His gaze held hers, and again, she shivered. "There may come a time when you will want to sever ties with me," he continued. "And I won't ever blame you for doing so."

He spoke so frankly. It was almost as if he were making her a promise.

Abruptly, he moved his attention to the paper before him. "Shall we begin?"

"Yes." They'd already spent too much time talking and not reading. That was her fault. She found him very distracting today.

Somerton took a deep breath and started reading. Gwen put all other thoughts from her mind, though she couldn't quite shake the lingering feeling that their friendship was more than a transaction, regardless of what he said. And she couldn't imagine breaking off their friendship, not for any reason.

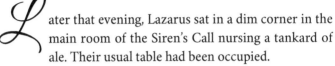

*L*ater that evening, Lazarus sat in a dim corner in the main room of the Siren's Call nursing a tankard of ale. Their usual table had been occupied.

His meeting with Miss Price had gone well, though he'd experienced some frustration when they'd worked on the memorization of his speech. He'd thought he'd mastered the first several lines after copying them so many times, but he'd struggled.

Miss Price had been unwavering in her support, her calm demeanor keeping him from giving up. Until their time had expired. They planned to meet again the day after tomorrow. In the meantime, he was to continue his writing exercises. He also planned to use the technique she'd employed with underlining certain words and rewriting others, breaking them down into pieces.

He'd already rewritten half the speech doing that. It had taken him all evening. He'd decided he'd earned a tankard of ale at the Siren's Call and a respite with friends. Only, they weren't here, and as it happened, Lazarus was perfectly content to be alone.

A pair of gentlemen came from one of the gaming rooms, and Lazarus saw that it was Shefford and Bedingfield, another fellow who sometimes joined them. Scanning the room as Bedingfield was speaking, Shefford laughed just before his gaze settled on Lazarus.

Shefford said something to Bedingfield, who continued toward the door. Pivoting, Shefford approached Lazarus's table. "Why are you skulking in the corner by yourself?"

Lazarus arched a brow at him, his hands cupping his tankard. "Skulking? I'm not Droxford. I wanted an ale."

"Well, finish up and come with us to the Rogue's Den. Bedingfield is hailing a hack."

Cramming himself into a hackney coach and spending the evening in debauchery did not appeal to Lazarus. His brain was overtired from all the work he'd done today, and he just wanted to…do nothing.

"Thank you for the invitation, but I'll pass this evening."

Shefford slid into the chair opposite him. "What's the matter? You do seem like Droxford—before he wed, anyway. You look almost, dare I say it, morose." He grimaced as if he'd just delivered terrible news.

"Nothing is the matter. I've had a long day, and I'm tired. We rode in the park quite early, or don't you recall?"

"I do, just as I recall the wonderful nap I took after bathing." Shefford grinned. "You should have slept."

"Yes, well, I had other things to do." Lazarus was surprisingly annoyed by Shefford's needling. Perhaps he was morose after all. Though, why should he be?

"Come to the Rogue's Den," Shefford cajoled. "You'll feel much better. I guarantee you will sleep wonderfully."

Lazarus did consider it, but he just wasn't interested in a night of bed sport. He blamed his mental fatigue. "I appreciate your concern, but I think I'll go home when I finish my ale. You and Bedingfield have a grand time."

Shefford exhaled and stood. "Of course we will. Join us if you change your mind."

He turned and left the club, and Lazarus lifted his tankard for a drink.

Jo appeared at his table, a dark brow arched in question. She took the chair next to him without asking. "I assume you just declined Shefford's invitation to join them wherever they are going. And am I right in thinking it's the Rogue's Den?"

Lazarus fixed her with a wry stare. "Do you know *everything* that happens here?"

She laughed. "Nearly. My mother likes it that way. Why

didn't you go with them? I don't know that I've ever seen you pass up an evening of hedonism."

Was everyone going to stick their nose into his business? "I just didn't feel like going."

Her long, dark lashes fluttered as she narrowed her eyes and studied him. "Is it a woman who's twisted you up?"

"I am not 'twisted up.' I'm tired. It's been a long day."

She briefly tapped her fingers on the table. "You did not deny the existence of a woman. You know, it would serve you right to be having romantic difficulties. You've broken a few hearts, at least. Perhaps it's your turn to experience that disappointment."

Lazarus flinched inwardly. "I hate that I've done that. It was never my intent."

"You can't help it if you're impossibly charming and so attractive it makes one's teeth ache as if they've eaten too many sweets." She gave him a sardonic smile, but there was genuine warmth behind it. Jo was a good friend and an excellent listener.

"Should I change the way I dress? Stop bathing? Let my hair grow into an unpleasant mess?"

"That would certainly help. May I also suggest you grunt instead of smile and try being surly instead of gallant. I'm sure your friend Droxford would give you lessons, though I hear he's almost genial now."

"He's completely enthralled with my cousin. It's quite nice, actually."

Jo sucked in a breath, her eyes rounding. "Are you in favor of love now?"

He rolled his eyes. "I've never been *against* it. I just haven't found it myself, nor do I see it as necessary." His parents had not shared a great love affair, but they'd been perfectly content with one another.

Lazarus noted the door opening and saw Evan Price walk in. Becky immediately engaged him in conversation.

"Is Miss Price the reason for your moodiness?" Jo asked.

Having picked up the tankard for a drink, Lazarus now returned it—heavily—to the table. He frowned at Jo.

"Why are you looking at me like that? I've heard the two of you are practically courting, that you were king and queen of the Phoenix Club ball last night. You made quite a stir. Some say you are completely gone for her."

Damn. That was not going to help Miss Price's cause. He needed to put distance between them—at least publicly. In fact, it might be time that she made it publicly known that she was not interested in courtship because he was too much of a rogue. Everyone would believe that story.

"You know a great deal," Lazarus said evenly. "Were you at the ball last night?" He knew her mother was a member of the Phoenix Club. Jo was not since she was unwed. However, she could attend the balls with a family member who was.

"No, but you must be aware that people come in here and talk. I know things that would make your eyes pop out of your head and roll across the floor."

The image was absolutely ghastly, but also rather amusing. Lazarus's mouth ticked up in a smile. "You are frighteningly easy to talk to." A thought struck him. "Do you collect information on purpose?"

"What a horrid thing to suspect," she said. "As you said, I'm simply easy to talk to. Just because I know some people's secrets doesn't mean I would ever share them. I am nothing if not discreet. To be honest, I hear a great many things at the literary salon I attend most weeks. There are several members of Society who attend."

Lazarus's interest was piqued. He shot his gaze to hers. "What literary salon is this?"

"You're interested in books?" She gaped at him. "I'm shocked."

It should not have insulted him since he generally disdained reading. He had to in order to hide his own secret. For some reason, he considered telling Jo about it, in part because he was feeling defensive. But also because she did have an uncanny ability to put one at ease and make one want to share.

However, he could not bring himself to disclose his shameful secret. Sharing it with Miss Price had been hard enough, and it had gone so well that he dare not tempt fate again. "I am interested in attending a literary salon. Could you garner me an invitation? Or two?" This wasn't just for him. He wanted to take Miss Price. She would be delighted.

"For you and your mysterious lady friend?" Jo teased. "I'm sure I could get you an invitation—and you could bring a guest. There are two ladies who host. Mrs. Fletcher-Peabody on the first and third Mondays and Mrs. Davenport on the second and fourth. If there is a fifth Monday, there is no meeting."

"Could I go on Monday?" That was in just two days, so perhaps Jo wouldn't be able to coordinate that.

"I don't see why not. I'll send confirmation by Monday afternoon. You'll understand why it may not be sooner as this is rather late notice."

"Of course. I appreciate your assistance." His mind began working as to how he could get Miss Price there. She would need to be disguised. Perhaps she could be heavily veiled and take on the role of his great-aunt who lived near Bath. But she would want to speak, which meant she'd have to make herself sound like an older person. Would she even want to do all this?

Of course she would. Miss Price was a deep lover of books, and she was most intrepid.

"Here comes Price," Jo said. "I won't tell anyone that you're harboring a tendre for his sister."

"I'm not," Lazarus protested, unsure if she was teasing him again or not. Because it was true. If not a tendre, he was harboring *something* for his sweet tutor. If he hadn't already been thinking he needed to end his public association with her, this realization made it necessary.

Jo gave him an enigmatic smile. "I'll send a note by Monday." Then she left as Evan bore down on Lazarus's table.

Yes, it was time for Miss Price to put an end to speculation that she and Lazarus might engage in a courtship. He would discuss that with her at their next meeting.

And he would ignore the pang of sadness that accompanied the end of their ruse.

CHAPTER 7

"Gwen, I've wonderful news!" Gwen's mother swept into the drawing room with a broad grin and excitement dancing in her eyes. "I've hired a dancing master at last. He will be here shortly."

Setting her book in her lap, Gwen blinked at her mother. "You've hired a dancing master since this morning, and he's due any time?" How was that possible?

"I offered him the position and asked if he could start immediately. He just sent a note saying he could be here at two."

But Gwen had an appointment with Somerton at three!

Gwen's mother regarded her with concern. "Is something amiss?"

"I was going to call on Tamsin this afternoon, but I can do that after." She closed her book and stood. "I suppose I should ready myself for the dancing master."

"You needn't sound as if you're marching to the gallows," her mother said wryly.

"No, especially when it's the dancing master who should probably feel that way," Gwen responded with a laugh.

Her mother's mouth tipped into a slight frown. "I wish you wouldn't say such things. Overall, your dancing is much improved. The other night at the Phoenix Club, your waltz with Lord Somerton looked exceptional."

Gwen wanted to say, *All credit to Lord Somerton*, but did not. "I have been trying."

"Of course you have, dear." Her mother smiled sympathetically. "And this dancing master will be the final step in your mastery. He has worked with a great many young ladies. Indeed, he's highly sought after. I wasn't sure we'd be able to secure him."

That usually meant he was above sixty years of age, French, and smelled of cheese. That had been two of Gwen's past three instructors. "I look forward to meeting him," she said gamely. She would do anything to please her mother, including take lessons from a hundred aging French gentlemen who enjoyed their fair share of livarot.

"Go and fetch your dancing slippers, and I'll ensure Mr. Tremblay is shown here to the drawing room."

"He is not French?" Gwen's other instructors had all been "monsieur."

"His family was, yes, but he was born here and considers himself an Englishman, apparently."

Lake came into the drawing room. "Mrs. Price, the new dancing master has arrived."

"I'd best hurry," Gwen said, picking up her book and rushing upstairs to her bedchamber.

Not five minutes later, she returned to the drawing room, where her mother stood with Mr. Tremblay. Not only was he not French, he wasn't old either. Gwen would judge him to be above thirty, but not by much.

And my goodness, but he was handsome. With shining golden hair and pale, almost crystalline, blue eyes, he looked like a portrait of some lovesick girl's fantasy. Or a sculpture, for his angled cheekbones, full lips, and cleft chin were most appealing. And his form was perfect for dancing—wide shoulders, narrow waist, and long, athletic legs. It was no wonder he was in high demand. Gwen wondered if he was any good at dancing at all, or if that even mattered to his students.

It mattered to her, of course, because she wanted her mother to be proud of her accomplishments. She would work doubly hard with Mr. Tremblay, and not because he was perhaps the most attractive man she'd ever laid eyes on.

More attractive than Somerton?

The question flashed in her mind. Had she thought him the best-looking man she'd ever seen? He certainly could be. He was the sort of man who, when he regarded you, you hoped everyone around noticed his attention.

Gwen realized she'd especially liked that over the past week during their faux almost courtship. Particularly at the Phoenix Club ball. To be his queen had been nothing short of exhilarating.

"Good afternoon, Miss Price," Mr. Tremblay said with a perfect bow. "I'm most pleased to make your acquaintance." His smile dazzled her, and Gwen didn't think she could look away.

She dipped a curtsey. "Good afternoon, Mr. Tremblay."

"Allow me to present my musical assistant, Mr. Nott. He will play the harpsichord or pianoforte—whichever you have."

"The pianoforte is just there." Mama indicated the instrument set in the opposite corner of the room from the doorway. "I'll observe." She picked up a copy of *La Belle Assemblée* from a table and sat in a chair near one of the three windows that looked down on Grosvenor Street.

"Shall we begin with the quadrille?" Mr. Tremblay asked.

"I haven't danced that yet," Gwen said. It was new this Season and quite the rage.

He grinned, and again Gwen was struck by his masculine beauty. "Then I have arrived just in time to save you from disgrace." His eyes narrowed slightly as if he were flirting.

"That is good news for me, then."

Mr. Nott, a small man with a fine bone structure and dark, wiry hair, went to the pianoforte. He readjusted his spectacles on his nose, then arranged his music. He looked toward Mr. Tremblay, presumably waiting for his signal to begin.

"I find the best way to learn a dance is for me to stand behind you and guide you through the movements. We'll do that a few times, and then, depending on how well you're learning the steps, we'll progress to me partnering you."

Gwen nodded, appreciating him describing what they would do. She found this part interesting—the method of teaching and learning. It reminded her of how she approached her lessons with Somerton. It was important to determine how best someone might glean what they needed to know. And she'd ascertained, just from the short time she'd spent with the viscount, that everyone learned differently.

Mr. Tremblay pushed the settee out of the way to give them more room then came to stand behind Gwen. He put his hands on her waist without any warning, and she jumped. "Are you ticklish?" he asked with a laugh.

"Perhaps." She was, but it was his surprising touch that had provoked her reaction.

"Begin, Mr. Nott," Mr. Tremblay instructed. Then he spoke in a flurry, his hands guiding her as they apparently danced the quadrille. To Gwen, it was a hopelessly confusing mash of nonsense.

She found it very hard to concentrate. Perhaps because

Mr. Tremblay's mouth was very near her ear. She could feel his proximity as much as hear it. And then there were his hands. They moved about her abdomen, pressing on her rib cage so that his fingers lightly grazed the underside of her breast. Then they slid down to her thigh, as he directed her leg movements. As he brought his hand back up, his touch was like a caress over her hip.

Gwen did not like it.

And while he did not smell of cheese, he did carry a rather strong scent of sandalwood and bergamot, as if he'd doused himself in it before coming into the house. Had he not bathed in some time? Or did he simply like to ensure he had a pleasing smell?

Gwen began to think Mr. Tremblay was a study in excess. Even his clothing was too much—from his bright green-and-blue-striped waistcoat to the large, jeweled pin sparkling in his frothy, overwrought cravat.

She stepped on his foot, and he at last released her. Though she hadn't done it on purpose, she now knew how to get him to stop handling her. Mr. Nott stopped playing.

"My apologies, Mr. Tremblay," she murmured. "I am not the fastest learner when it comes to dancing." She wondered if she could ask Somerton to teach her. As her mother had pointed out, he'd somehow made her look good waltzing.

"Quite all right, Miss Price. You are here to learn. Let us begin anew."

Gwen hesitated, as she didn't particularly want his hands on her in the manner he was using. But what if it helped? If Gwen could master the quadrille, her mother would be thrilled.

Taking a deep breath, she braced herself as he clasped her waist. By the end of the lesson, she was only marginally closer to dancing the quadrille, and she'd managed to step on his toes four times practicing the waltz. Meanwhile, her jaw ached from clenching it as she'd endured his physical direction.

After arranging their next lesson for later in the week, he departed with his musician. Gwen let herself sag with relief, but then realized it was now three and she was late for her appointment with Somerton.

"You look tired, dear," her mother said. "Perhaps you shouldn't visit your friend today. Just send a note."

"I'm fine, Mama. Although, I'm not sure Mr. Tremblay is the right dancing master for me. That was rather intense."

"He seems very dedicated. You are likely overwhelmed because he introduced a new dance. Perhaps next time, we'll tell him to just focus on the reel and cotillion." She gave Gwen an encouraging smile. "Let's give him one more chance, at least. It's not as if we have a great deal of choice, and he *is* in high demand."

Gwen didn't want to argue with her, both because she wanted to please her mother and because she was already late. "All right. I must be off." The driver had likely been waiting with the gig for a quarter hour.

"Before you go, I wanted to ask about the callers who were here on Saturday. Have you given more thought as to who might have piqued your interest?" Her mother watched her expectantly.

"Not yet. I liked them all." They were all gentlemen who enjoyed more than inane conversation, which made them more than acceptable. "I just need to become better acquainted with them."

"Of course. I must say, I'm relieved Lord Somerton isn't under consideration. While it was quite fortuitous to have his attention, I am not sure he would have been the best match. Because of his reputation," she added. "I only want you to have a happy, successful marriage."

Gwen knew her parents had fallen in love, and her mother wanted that for Gwen. She also wanted Gwen's marriage to be highly regarded. It wasn't that she was pushing Gwen toward a title, but a gentleman with an excellent reputation and, if possible, a decent amount of wealth. She wanted love, comfort, and security for her daughter, and how could Gwen argue with that? So long as he wasn't a rogue, Gwen would be agreeable.

Finally able to extricate herself, Gwen dashed upstairs to change her shoes and fetch her hat and gloves. Thankfully, Tamsin's house wasn't far, which was the only reason her mother allowed her to go alone in the gig, and Gwen arrived quickly. Still, she was exceedingly tardy. She hoped she and Somerton could still have an hour so they wouldn't lose any of their precious time together.

$\sim$

*L*azarus was beginning to grow concerned. He couldn't imagine why Miss Price would be so late. And Tamsin didn't know either. Droxford was working in his study, while Lazarus was in the library with his cousin.

"I hope nothing is amiss," Tamsin said from the settee, her brow gently creased.

Could she have forgotten? Lazarus couldn't see that happening.

At last, Miss Price burst into the room, her cheeks flushed. "I'm so sorry I'm late!"

Tamsin stood. "Are you all right?"

"Oh, yes. I had a lesson with a new dancing master. Mama was able to find someone to take me on, and she asked him to start immediately. My apologies." She looked to Lazarus with a faint grimace.

"I'm only pleased to see you are well." Lazarus had been genuinely worried.

Miss Price looked from Lazarus to Tamsin. "Can we still have an hour, or will that intrude on everyone's plans?"

"It's fine by me," Tamsin said. "I've correspondence to attend to." She smiled at them, then departed the library.

"And you?" Miss Price asked, facing Lazarus.

"I have an hour." He could take the rest of the day and night, but he'd get to that when he told her about the literary salon. He'd received confirmation from Jo that they were indeed invited to attend this evening.

But first, he needed to talk to her about their ruse.

"I wanted to speak with you about a few matters before we begin our lesson," he said.

She deposited her bag on the table and removed her gloves. "This sounds serious."

"Part of it is, I suppose." He smiled to put her at ease. It wasn't bad news. On the contrary, it was a marker of their success. "Since things are going so well for you on the Marriage Mart, I think it's best if we put an end to our public scheme."

Setting her gloves on the table, she removed her hat next. She smoothed a few stray locks behind her ear. "What do you mean?"

"I've paid a good amount of attention to you, and the Phoenix Club ball has provoked deeper speculation as to whether we will make a match. I don't want to deter other gentlemen from seeking to court you, and I'm afraid any perceived attachment between us will keep some of them away."

She rested her hand on the back of the chair. "I suppose I can't argue with that reasoning. I did speak with one of my callers from Saturday after church yesterday."

Despite the stab of jealousy cleaving into his chest, Lazarus summoned a smile. "That's wonderful. Exactly what we were working toward. Then yes, I think it's time we call a halt to our faux almost courtship or however you would describe it. I confess, it worked more quickly than I anticipated." Much to his chagrin.

"What will we do? You'll just stop paying attention to me?"

"No, as that won't help you either. You must tell people that you've decided we wouldn't suit. I'm too much of a rake for your tastes."

Her eyes rounded slightly. "Well, that's not very charitable of me to say. Can't I just way we don't suit?"

Lazarus shook his head. "I want it to be clear that this is *your* decision. And don't worry about me or my reputation." He chuckled. "I'll survive."

"Yes, I suppose you will," she murmured. "It's not terribly fair, is it?"

"Because a woman would not survive such a reputation." He pressed his lips together. "No, it isn't fair."

She frowned at him. "I still don't like it. I would rather say I decided we wouldn't suit."

"You could, but referencing my already known and widely accepted reputation won't cause anyone to think twice. Indeed, they'll applaud you for your good sense."

Taking her hand from the chair, she moved toward him, her sprigged skirts swaying. "It feels as though I'll be disparaging you, and I hate to do that."

Lazarus could easily have lost himself in the dark warmth of her gaze. "You must. And it's not as if it isn't *true*." He waggled his brows at her, offering his most wolfish grin. "I *am* a rake."

Miss Price sniffed. "You've behaved with nothing but

decorum and propriety with me. I do wonder if you are as much of a rogue as people say."

He fixed her with a heavy stare. As much as he enjoyed her kind thoughts about him, she had to accept who he was. "I am every bit that rogue," he stated firmly. "If you must know, I've simply been on my best behavior with you. Don't disillusion yourself about who I really am. If you were not my friend's sister or a young lady I've agreed to help, I would have stolen a half dozen kisses—and perhaps more—by now." Indeed, he was at this moment contemplating the contour of her lips and the curve of her hip.

Her nostrils flared, and her lips parted. The pink in her cheeks had faded since her arrival, but now reappeared. "I didn't realize."

"Now you do." It occurred to him that he wasn't laying the groundwork very well for his next topic. Would she agree to attend the literary salon with him now knowing he was a dastardly rogue? "But be assured I would never overstep with you. You can trust me."

"I've always known that," she said without pause.

"Good. Because I've something else to share, and this is much more delightful." His lips curved up.

She smiled in return, her eyes dancing. "Do tell me."

"I've secured an invitation to a literary salon this evening being given by Mrs. Davenport."

A surprised but clearly elated gasp leapt from her lips. "Her grandmother was one of the original members of the Blue Stockings Society."

Lazarus had no idea what that was, but delighted in her excitement. "I take it that's a good thing."

"Oh, yes! This is wonderful! But how can I go? My mother is already engaged this evening."

"I will take you. The invitation is mine, and I may bring a guest."

Her features fell. "Surely I can't just go with you."

He laughed softy. "Of course not. You must wear a disguise. I thought you could be my great-aunt. She lives outside Bath and could be 'visiting' me. She adores literary discussion, you see, but doesn't like to go out much because her face is quite marked by having the pox as a child."

"Is that true?" Miss Price asked incredulously.

"God, no. Except the part about not going out much. But that is because, generally speaking, she doesn't like people."

"Oh." She giggled. "So no one will suspect I'm not her?"

"No one who will be there even knows she exists. You will need a thick veil. Can you manage that?"

She nodded. "And gloves, of course. I'll be sure to wear a gown that comes to my neck."

"Very smart. Can't have any of your youthful, glowing skin showing." Why had he described that? That hadn't been at all necessary. It really was taking effort not to allow his mind to travel a wayward path with her.

Her lips twisted into a slight pout. "But how do I leave my house? It's true my parents will be at a dinner party, but the servants will know I've left."

"Can you say you're going somewhere with Tamsin as your chaperone?" Having a friend who was married was deuced convenient—for young ladies. Men such as Lazarus could go anywhere at any time with anyone. One's choices on those details might cause gossip, but to simply leave the house and go for a walk was not scrutinized. It wasn't really fair.

"I can do that," Miss Price said with a nod. "I'll say we're going to a musicale. I suppose I should check with Tamsin to make sure she isn't going to show up at the same dinner as my parents." She laughed. "Though, that seems highly unlikely."

"Excellent. I'll pick you up then."

Gwen sucked in a breath, but her eyes were glowing with anticipation. "I feel so scandalous," she whispered.

"All so you can simply enjoy a night of literary discussion. I'm sorry we must take such extreme measures. If you enjoy yourself, perhaps in future, Tamsin could actually accompany you." Lazarus would ask Jo to coordinate that invitation as she'd done this one.

"I've no doubt this will be the most exciting event I've attended all Season." Her giddiness was palpable. "But will you enjoy it too?"

He would, if only because he was watching her. "I will. I may not have read as much as you, but I hope to change that. It isn't that I don't like literature."

Her features creased, and she moved closer to him. "I know. That was terrible of me to ask. We should probably get to our reading lesson. I was already so late, and now we've spent a great deal of time talking."

Lazarus could have spent the entire time they had together talking. But he had an objective, and there was no knowing how long they'd be able to continue meeting like this.

"One last thing," he said. "You'll need to make sure you sound older when you speak tonight."

"Perhaps I should just be quiet."

"Somehow, I don't think that would be satisfying for you." He laughed. "You finally attend a literary salon, and you're just going to sit silently?"

She laughed as she moved toward the table. "You have come to know me quite well."

Yes, he had, and he would be sorry when he didn't know her any longer. Because at some point, their association would end entirely. It had already been halved. Or would be anyway.

Lazarus would treasure what time they had left together, for he'd come to regard her as a singular person. Though they'd only had two lessons so far, she'd had a great impact on his life, and he would be eternally grateful.

CHAPTER 8

*G*wen was glad to see there was a footman at the door instead of Lake, but she'd expected that at this hour of the evening. Her parents had left an hour ago, and they wouldn't return until well after midnight. Perhaps as late as two.

Anticipation thrummed in her veins as she walked into the entrance hall at the appointed time of departure. Somerton had said he wouldn't send his groom to the door, that she must be ready to come outside.

Thinking she heard the approach of a vehicle, she went to the door. The footman opened it, and indeed, a coach had just stopped in front of the house.

Waving toward the footman, Gwen departed and hurried to the coach. The groom opened the door for her, and Gwen climbed inside.

She sat on the forward-facing seat and noted that the viscount was across from her. Did he not want to sit next to her? His coach was large enough for them to do so quite comfortably.

"Good evening, Miss Price. That is an excellent choice of

gown, though it still doesn't quite say 'reclusive Great-Aunt Beatrice.'" He smirked at her.

"It was the best I could do. At least it's dark blue. And I wore sturdy boots." She lifted her hem and held out one foot, wiggling it for his perusal.

"Very clever. You didn't forget your veil, did you?"

"No. It was just too large to fit into a reticule." She lifted her skirt higher. "You may want to turn your head."

His eyes widened before he snapped his head to the side and closed them. "What are you doing?"

"I had to tuck the veil up my skirt." She pulled it from where it was tucked into her petticoat and settled her gown back down over her legs. "You can look now."

It took him a moment to return his gaze to hers, and when he did so, Gwen was intensely aware of a smoldering heat. What had happened?

She recalled what he'd said that afternoon about being a rogue and how if she'd been anyone else, he would have stolen a half dozen kisses or more from her by now. Indeed, she'd thought of that revelation many times in the intervening hours. She was torn between wishing she'd never known that and hoping he might yet kiss her.

Though, she shouldn't want that. Not from a rogue. Except it was precisely for that reason that she did. To be kissed by the Viscount Somerton had to be a transcendent experience. It was too bad she would never know for certain.

"Are you just going to drape that over your head?" he asked.

"Yes, why?"

"I thought you might have a hat or something. How will you keep it in place?"

"I have pins." She smiled at him. "Those fit in my pocket."

Placing the veil over her head, she adjusted it so the ends

hit her shoulders. Then she pulled the pins from her pocket and set them in her lap.

"You look as though you're going to a nunnery," he said.

Gwen laughed. "Do I? How would you know how someone would dress before visiting a nunnery?"

"Not to visit," he clarified. "To become a novice or whatever one does to learn to be a nun."

"I am definitely not doing that." She put one pin through the veil on top of her head and stuck it into her hair. "You are going to have to aid me this evening. I'm afraid I can't see well. When I tested it earlier, I walked into a chair in my bedchamber."

"I will be at your side all evening."

"Perchance asking someone who is already ungainly to wear a veil was not the best plan." She inserted another pin. "But I will persevere."

"Did you practice your speaking voice?" he asked.

"I did," she responded in a high, measured tone. "I tested several, and this seemed the easiest and most believable. Does it sound all right?"

"You sound like a bird who's drunk a flagon of wine."

Gwen snorted a laugh, which reminded her of her friends Persephone and Minerva. Both were great snorters. She applied the last pin and shook her head to ensure the veil was secure. "How do I look?"

"Not like a nun in training, but a fortune-teller speaking to the dead."

Sniggering, Gwen smoothed the veil down against her head. "Perhaps I'll try conversing with Shakespeare or Milton."

"You will be the toast of the salon." He leaned toward the window. "We are nearly there. Are you ready to become Miss Beatrice Villiers?"

Gwen nodded. "This is the most exciting night of my life.

Everything about it exceeds my imagination. I can't thank you enough."

"I'm so glad."

The coach came to a stop, and shortly, the door opened. Somerton stepped down and helped Gwen out. She then realized the worst part of the veil—she wasn't able to see him very well. His sultry gaze and brilliant smile were blurred, and she couldn't appreciate how handsome he looked in his black suit of clothing.

They walked to the door and were admitted into the stately terrace by a stiff butler. Gwen's pulse pounded so loudly, she could hear the echo in her ears. She took a deep breath and tried not to clutch Somerton so tightly.

"All right?" he murmured.

"Just excited," she whispered back. "And nervous."

The butler instructed them to go upstairs to the drawing room. Gwen went back to squeezing Somerton's arm as they started up the stairs. "Don't let me trip," she said, though if she angled her head down just right, she could see the stairs beneath the hem of the veil.

"I've got you," he assured her, putting his other hand over hers where she gripped his sleeve.

When they reached the top of the stairs, Gwen breathed a sigh of relief. Looking back over her shoulder, she decided going down would be trickier.

"Here we go," Somerton said softly as they approached the doorway to the drawing room.

Gwen made out the figure of a woman standing just inside. She had gray hair adorned with a cluster of feathers and wore a heavy, jeweled necklace.

"Welcome," the woman, who must be their hostess, Mrs. Davenport, said. "I assume you are Lord Somerton and his great-aunt?"

"Indeed we are." Somerton bowed. "I do appreciate you

including us this evening. Allow me to present my beloved great-aunt, Mrs. Beatrice Villiers. She is visiting from the country and was eager to attend a literary salon."

"We are always delighted to welcome like-minded people with a passion for literature." Mrs. Davenport seemed to focus on Gwen, but Gwen couldn't be sure. "Is it possible you attended one of the original Bluestocking Society salons as a young lady?"

"I did not," Gwen replied in her fake voice, hoping she sounded believable. She would not be able to discern anyone's reactions through the thick veil. "This is my first visit to London."

"Oh! Then I am glad you were able to come. Let me introduce you to everyone." Mrs. Davenport turned—that much Gwen could see—and went into the room.

Thankfully, Somerton escorted her. If she had to let go of him, she worried there might be disaster. They spent the next quarter hour meeting everyone—there were writers, booksellers, a painter, and a small contingent from Society. In fact, there was one name that was familiar to Gwen, so she was relieved to be hidden beneath the veil.

The last person she was introduced to was Miss Josephine Harker. Gwen couldn't tell for sure, but thought she might be close to her in age.

Mrs. Davenport moved to the center of the room and bade them all sit—there was a semicircle of chairs situated. Somerton guided Gwen to a chair and sat beside her. Gwen noted that Miss Harker sat on his other side. Mrs. Davenport introduced the evening's featured author, Miss Helena Stainesby, a woman of middle age who'd written a collection of several stories published in the *Lady's Monthly Museum*.

Miss Stainesby told them about her stories, which featured women in leadership roles, such as running their own farm, a circulation library, and a gambling den. At her mention of the last one, Miss Harker chuckled, and Gwen saw Somerton look toward her. He also smiled.

When she finished discussing her works, she launched a conversation about the changing roles of women and what they might look like twenty or fifty years from now. It was an engaging topic, and Gwen listened raptly until she could no longer keep quiet. Raising her hand to speak, she said she hoped that one day women would be admitted to universities so they could learn at the same level as men since they were just as intelligent.

This was met with agreement, and the conversation veered toward education. Gwen had no idea how much time elapsed, but Mrs. Davenport announced they would take a respite for refreshment. "Is there no alcohol as with the original Blue Stockings Society meetings?" she asked Somerton in a low voice.

"I don't know," he responded. "Would you like wine if it's available?"

"I'd best not drink or eat anything with this veil." She envisioned any number of mishaps as she tried to put the food or drink to her mouth while not dislodging the veil. "But you must help yourself. I'm just going to stand for a moment."

He rose with her. "I'll be right back."

Gwen watched him walk away through the haze of her veil. Smiling, she looked about the room. How she would love to attend every week. Perhaps Tamsin could garner an invitation and bring Gwen as her guest. Then, Gwen wouldn't have to wear a veil.

Miss Stainesby was standing nearby. Though Gwen was hesitant to move, she was also eager to tell the woman how much she admired her and that she looked forward to reading her stories.

It was only a short walk, perhaps five or six shuffling

older-woman steps. Surely she could make it that far without assistance.

Two steps in, she caught her foot on the leg of a chair and wobbled. The chair was pushed up against a piece of furniture—a table or a cupboard, Gwen couldn't exactly tell—and of course that wobbled too. Struggling to keep her balance, she stepped around the chair and gripped the back of the chair, sweeping her body around to face the center of the room. There! She'd done it.

But now she was stuck, as she ought not chance moving again.

"Bloody hell, you're on fire!"

Gwen wasn't sure who'd said that, but she immediately smelled something burning. Then she was bathed in liquid from the top of her head and down her back. "What the devil?"

Too late, she realized she hadn't modulated her tone.

Then she was plunged into darkness as a garment was thrown over her head. The smell of burnt fabric filled her nostrils as someone smacked at the back of her head and shoulders.

"It's out," Somerton said, sounding relieved. "Come, Great-Aunt Beatrice, let us survey the damage." He took Gwen's arm and steered her toward the doorway.

"There's a retiring room at the end of the corridor on the left," Mrs. Davenport said near the door. "Are you all right, Miss Villiers?"

Gwen now understood that she had been on fire. Rather her veil. And Somerton had thrown whatever beverage he'd obtained at her, then draped a garment over her. Was it his coat?

"She'll be fine," Somerton said before Gwen could respond. Then they were out of the drawing room, and he was hurrying her toward the retiring room. When they arrived, he ushered her into the room, but upon hearing voices, Gwen realized it was not empty.

"Pardon us," Somerton said. "Would you mind giving me and my great-aunt some privacy? She's just suffered a mishap with a candle and her veil, and I'm afraid she'll need to tidy up."

"Of course," someone replied, and a moment later, Gwen heard the snap of the door closing.

And then there was light—or more light than there had been—as Somerton removed the garment. "Are you all right?" he asked, sounding most concerned.

He moved behind her, and she felt him fussing with her veil and then running his hand over her shoulder and the upper part of her back. That felt rather nice, actually.

"Your veil has a large hole, and from the right angle, someone standing beside you can see your ear and probably the side of your face. I threw my coat over you to ensure no one glimpsed that you are not a pockmarked septuagenarian."

Gwen pushed the veil up so she could see. "This is so much better." She pivoted to face him. "Did I really catch my veil on *fire*?"

"Yes." He stared at her, his expression a mix of concern and consternation.

"I was just trying to walk to Miss Stainesby so I could speak with her." Gwen pursed her lips. "I knew I shouldn't have tried, but it was only a handful of steps!" She lifted her hand to touch the veil where it was damaged. "What did you toss on me? It feels sticky."

"Ratafia. That was all that was available. I didn't really want it, but Mrs. Davenport insisted you needed something to drink. So I took it, and I'm glad I did."

There was a tall mirror in the corner. Gwen went to stand in front of it and survey the damage. Turning her head, she saw the singed veil. "You are correct that this will allow people to see me." An idea struck her. "I can just take it off and turn it so the hole is in the back, though it is rather damp. Will that allow people to see I am not an elderly woman?" She began removing pins.

When she was finished, she looked in the mirror once more. Her gaze met Somerton's. He was standing behind her —not too close, but the intensity of his stare in the glass made it feel like he was directly at her back. Indeed, she imagined she felt his hand moving over her again, his caress stirring something forbidden inside her.

Gwen turned to face him. "Will you help me adjust it so the hole won't reveal anything?"

Somerton stepped toward her, his eyes dark and his jaw tight. He lifted his hands and rotated the veil atop her head.

Now he was very close. So close she could smell his tantalizing fragrance—pine and spice. It stirred her senses, as did his proximity. She'd been this close to him before when they'd waltzed and when they'd worked together on his reading. But this felt different.

"Did you mean what you said this afternoon?" she asked, her voice now sounding rather low and gravelly, quite the opposite of her Great-Aunt Beatrice voice.

"What?" His gaze held hers as his hands remained poised at her head.

"That if I weren't your friend's sister, you would have kissed me a half dozen times."

"Yes. At least that many." He uttered the words without hesitation and with great certainty.

"Perhaps you could just let me have one?"

His hands came onto her head and skimmed down her face, cupping her cheeks. "Gwen, do you know what you are asking?"

"Yes."

"And you know who I am. *What* I am."

"Yes. That's why I want you to kiss me."

He groaned, his eyes closing for the barest moment. "You tempt me greatly."

Gwen turned her head slightly and brushed her lips against his palm. "You tempt me. I'm only asking for one kiss. Please?"

His eyes darkened to a turbulent storm. "This is not part of our agreement." He brushed his thumb over her lower lip, and Gwen wanted to lean into him. Her body trembled with desire.

She wanted his kiss so badly, but recognized she'd put him in a terrible position. He was trying very hard not to be a rogue, and here she was begging him to be. "I am asking too much."

"Ask me one more time, and I will grant your wish."

Without hesitation, she said, "Please, Somerton, kiss me."

"Lazarus," he rasped. "My name is Lazarus."

His lips swept over hers as his hands moved back to cup her head. Gwen sparked to life, as if she'd been lying dormant over winter and the sun had awakened her once more.

She put her hands on his shoulders, one of them still grasping the hairpins, as his mouth whispered against hers. Eager to feel him, Gwen pressed her body closer to his.

Lazarus licked her lip and slipped his tongue inside her mouth. Gasping with delight, Gwen clutched at him more tightly as he deepened the kiss, his head angling as their lips moved together.

He lifted his head briefly, but only for the barest respite, as he claimed her mouth once more. He kissed her with a passion that surpassed any flowery words she'd ever read in a love poem. Indeed, she wasn't sure she could find words to describe what was happening.

"Oh, good God, what are you *doing?*"

Lazarus stepped back from Gwen, and she brought her hand to her mouth, both because her lips were quivering from his kiss and because she was horrified they'd been caught. She'd broken several rogue rules, and she was most certainly going to have to pay the price.

Gwen saw that it was Miss Harker who'd seen them. She cast an accusatory glare at Lazarus. "Somerton, you are an absolute scoundrel. You know better!"

His gaze dipped, and he appeared more than sufficiently reprimanded. Gwen sent Miss Harker a worried look. "It wasn't entirely his fault." Gwen had practically begged him to kiss her. That had to make her a roguess. Or something.

"He is wholly to blame," Miss Harker insisted. "Although you should know better also. But then, you came to this event in a disguise in his company without supervision."

Put like that, she made Gwen sound utterly devoid of intelligence—or propriety. Gwen wondered if she might be right. At least when it came to the viscount. He made her want to risk things she oughtn't. Because he made her feel beautiful and desirable. No one had ever made her feel that way.

Gwen mounted the only defense she had. "The viscount was kind enough to organize this invitation for me because he knew I would enjoy attending a literary salon."

"*I* organized it for you," Miss Harker said. She sent Lazarus another scolding look and clucked her tongue. "You're lucky it was me who found you. I wanted to see if all was well or if Miss Price needed to leave."

"You knew it was me under the veil?" Gwen asked. How did she even know who Gwen was when Gwen hadn't ever met her before?

"I did, because Somerton asked me to obtain an invitation for him and for you."

"I never said it was for her," Lazarus mumbled. "You assumed."

Why had she assumed? Unfortunately, Gwen did not have time to chase that thought at the moment. "I was just going to repin my veil so I could return to the drawing room," Gwen explained. "Somerton was, er, helping me rotate the veil so the hole caused by the candle is at the back of my head."

"I'll help you get it secured," Miss Harker offered, though it sounded more like a command. She glanced toward Lazarus. "You can wait outside or in the drawing room."

"She'll need help to get back. She can't see well with the veil."

"And I'm clumsy even without it," Gwen added. "With it, I'm a walking disaster, as evidenced by my scorched head-wear." She was fortunate nothing else had caught on fire, such as her hair.

"I'll be in the drawing room." Lazarus met Gwen's gaze, and she saw a flash of regret. It made her heart twist with disappointment. "We should leave soon."

Gwen nodded as he departed, her earlier joy replaced by a pang of sadness. What had been a thrilling adventure had devolved into a catastrophe. "I suppose I'm ruined now." There had been no discussion of marriage, which would be required since they'd been caught in a compromising position.

"You are not ruined," Miss Harker said firmly. "Sit." She gestured to a chair set at a small dressing table with a mirror.

"You don't plan to tell anyone what you saw?" Gwen handed her one of the pins.

"Why would I? If I wanted to be a horrible gossip, I would have already told all and sundry who you really were under the veil."

That was true. "How did you know who I was?" Gwen

asked as Miss Harker fixed the first pin through the veil into her hair. "I mean, why did you assume it was me?"

"Because I was needling Somerton about his association with you. I thought he might actually have feelings for you." She arched a brow at Gwen in the mirror. "Perhaps I was right."

"He wanted to kiss me, and I wanted him to," Gwen said. "That hardly signifies as 'feelings.'"

Miss Harker shrugged. "That's possible, given his reputation, but he gave me the sense that he at least liked you very much."

Gwen's mood rebounded upon hearing that. "How do you know him?" Gwen didn't think Miss Harker was part of Society, but perhaps Gwen just hadn't met her yet. She looked like a Society miss, with her fashionable dark coral evening gown that could have come from Bond Street.

Taking another pin from Gwen, Miss Harker replied, "My mother owns the Siren's Call, and I work there most evenings."

"You work at a gambling hell?" Gwen flinched as Miss Harker stabbed another pin into her veil—not because the pin hurt her, but because she'd probably just insulted her by calling her mother's establishment a hell.

Miss Harker smiled. "Yes. Owned and operated by women."

"Somerton is a frequent visitor?" Gwen asked.

"Somewhat." Miss Harker took the final pin and set it through the veil. "Pull that down and let's make sure it looks all right. We probably should have done that bit first. Particularly to guard against anyone else coming in." She shook her head. "This was ill-advised, and I'm sorry for my part in it."

Gwen pulled the veil over her face and surveyed her image in the mirror. "It looks good to me, but you are likely a better judge."

"It is passable," Miss Harker said. "It's fortunate the hole could be moved."

Smiling, Gwen turned to the side of the chair and lifted the veil so she could see Miss Harker more clearly. Just for a moment. "Thank you. Not just for helping me now and not telling anyone what you saw, but for securing an invitation tonight. This has been the most wonderful evening of my life."

Miss Harker's dark brow ticked up again and her wide mouth tipped into a smirk. "Because of Somerton or the literary conversation?"

Both, but Gwen didn't know Miss Harker well enough to share that. She wasn't even sure if she'd share it with her friends when they met tomorrow. Grasping the edge of her veil to pull it down once more, she met Miss Harker's gaze. "Would you like to come to tea tomorrow? I meet weekly with some dear friends. Perhaps you'd care to join us."

Miss Harker hesitated. "Why?"

Gwen just knew Miss Harker would fit in. Anyone who would help her attend a literary salon *and* keep her secret about kissing a known rogue was someone worth calling friend. "Because after the way you helped me tonight, we are already friends. I should like to return your kindness, and I will have trouble doing that that unless we are in the same social circle."

Laughing, Miss Harker fixed her with a curious stare. "You are unlike anyone I've ever met. I don't think we *can* be in the same social circle. Not really. While I do attend certain Society functions—with my father—I have not had a Season and never will. I'd be judged too old at twenty-five. And while you are undoubtedly delightful, I am not sure I'd feel as comfortable with your friends."

"Bah, of course you will. They are just like me. Except one is the daughter of a duke. And one is an actual duchess, but she won't be there tomorrow as she's recently become a mother. There will be a baroness and, this will make you feel more comfortable, a companion with absolutely no ties to Society save her friend—that's the daughter of the duke, Lady Minerva."

"Halifax?" Miss Harker asked. "The Duke of Henlow's daughter?"

"The very one."

"I know her brother—he also comes into the Siren's Call. But then I also know *your* brother. He's become a frequent patron this Season."

"That is not surprising. Because he's now very good friends with Sheff and Somerton."

"You call him 'Sheff'? You must know him well."

"Min is one of my closest friends. We met at Weston nearly two years ago. I've come to know her brother while we are all in residence there in August. The gentlemen don't stay the entire month as we do, but they are there a week or so. This past August, we socialized more because one of the gentlemen—the Duke of Wellesbourne, married one of our friends."

"That is the duchess, then," Miss Harker concluded.

Gwen nodded. "You'll come tomorrow?"

Miss Harker shrugged. "Why not?"

Smiling, Gwen lowered the veil and stood. She gave Miss Harker the time and her address. "Now, you really will need to guide me to the drawing room, or I will likely walk into the wall."

Miss Harker offered Gwen her arm. "I hope the kiss with Somerton was just that—a curiosity that will not be repeated. You seem a nice person, and I would hate for him to break your heart."

"But I thought you suspected he had romantic inclinations toward me," Gwen said.

"He may, but that doesn't mean he will make a good husband. Some people are not able to be monogamous. Perhaps that doesn't bother you, however."

The idea of an unfaithful spouse was unacceptable to Gwen. She'd be devastated if her husband was disloyal. After watching her own parents, she wasn't sure she could settle for less than mutual, unconditional love. Alas, she would probably have to. But keeping faith was a requirement upon which she would demand. "I think it would. Do some people not mind?"

Miss Harker lifted a shoulder—at least Gwen thought she did. "My own parents are not faithful to one another, but neither of them cares. They don't live together, and they rarely see each other. Honestly, I see no benefit in marriage."

"None? Not even the…physical aspect?"

"One needn't be married to enjoy that," Miss Harker said, sounding as though she was smiling. "But that is *not* advice," she added firmly.

They left the retiring room, and Gwen considered what Miss Harker had said to her—about Lazarus and about herself, cautioning her not to have her heart broken. Was Gwen remotely in danger of that? Wanting to be kissed by Lazarus and harboring a tendre for him were not the same thing.

She would do well to remember that. And to not think about kissing him again.

That last part was going to be difficult.

CHAPTER 9

*A*s Lazarus helped Gwen into his coach about an hour later, he tried not to think about how awkward things would now be between them. He hadn't spoken to her since leaving the retiring room because she'd been led about the drawing room by Jo, the two of them conversing with everyone they encountered. Lazarus was pleased to see Gwen enjoying herself, but was envious of Jo. He wanted to be the one escorting Gwen about.

Gwen.

At some point in the retiring room, Miss Price had become Gwen. As if he didn't know *precisely* what point that was. The moment he'd kissed her, the propriety between them had crumbled to dust. Or been driven away by an inescapable mutual desire.

Even now, an hour later and outside in the cool evening, Lazarus's body was heated, his cock stirring at the thought of sitting in a closed space with the object of his growing obsession.

With nowhere else to go, he climbed inside after her and took the rear-facing seat, as he'd done earlier. He'd decided sharing a seat with her was a bad idea, and now, after kissing her, it was an extreme risk.

She plucked the pins from her hair, one at a time, and tucked them into her pocket. Then she whisked the veil from her head and exhaled. "I am so glad to have that off. Since my encounter with the candle, there has been a persistent stench of burned gauze."

Her "encounter." As if she hadn't nearly suffered a terrible injury. "I might suggest you forgo veils from now on."

"I suppose I must," she said with a sigh. "I do hope I'll be able to attend another salon, though. That was even more exhilarating than I imagined." She met his gaze most earnestly. "Thank you. Truly."

"You shouldn't be thanking me," he said, almost growling as he scowled out the window. "You shouldn't even be nice to me. I've behaved abominably." He transferred his attention back to her. "I humbly beg your forgiveness, though I recommend you don't offer it."

"What a ridiculously contradictory thing to say." She laughed softly. "You behaved exactly as I asked you to. I should be begging your forgiveness. I should not have put you in that position. What choice did you have but to kiss me?"

He gaped at her. "I had every choice."

"You did try to say no," Gwen said. "But I was rather persistent. I am the one who is sorry. I hope you will forgive me. I imagine this makes you feel poorly about yourself, that you are worse than a rogue. Please don't let it. I know the rules—the rogue rules—and I broke them."

Lazarus could do nothing but stare at her.

She went on, "Let's see, I've broken: never be alone with a rogue, never flirt with a rogue, for I'm fairly certain asking one to kiss you is flirting with one. Never give a rogue a chance...perhaps not that one. I mean, the chances I've given you have nothing to do with a romantic relationship, and you've delivered quite brilliantly on every one of them." She fell silent. At length she said, "I've really only broken those first two, actually. I certainly haven't doubted your reputation," she said with a smile.

And why would she? It wasn't just his reputation. He *was* a rogue, which he freely admitted and easily demonstrated. The classification had never bothered him before, but he suddenly felt overburdened.

He had no one to blame for that but himself.

"Your scowl could rival Droxford's," Gwen observed. She was studying him closely. So closely that his body quivered to attention.

"I really am sorry," he said. "And no matter what you say, I will blame myself, so let us not speak of it again."

"I was just going to suggest the same thing. Let's put this behind us. We must if we are to focus on your lessons."

She wanted to continue tutoring him? He'd been worried about that since leaving the retiring room. How could they be alone together any longer after what had happened? He wasn't sure he trusted himself. She sure as hell shouldn't trust him. "Is that really wise? You'd be continuing to break your rogue rules."

"I already committed to that when we agreed to our arrangement. I will not abandon you now after what amounts to a…temporary lapse in judgment." She nodded. "Yes, we must accept that was all it was."

Except Lazarus was fairly certain there was nothing temporary about this situation. He'd already been desiring Gwen, and now that he'd kissed her, he wanted more. He wanted to feel the silken glide of her flesh against him while he explored every inch of her. He yearned to hear her moan and cry out as he drove her to the brink of ecstasy and beyond.

Now his cock was more than stirring. It was growing thick and hard. He was an absolute blackguard.

And he wanted her. He just needed to remind himself that he couldn't have her.

He could do this. He could rise above his baser instincts. Or alleviate them elsewhere.

Yes, he could go straight to the Rogue's Den after dropping Gwen at her house and find satisfaction in the arms of one, perhaps two, of the ladies there. What would usually entice him, however, now repulsed him. The thought of finding solace with anyone other than Gwen was extremely distasteful. At least right now. He hoped that would be temporary. If it wasn't, what was he to do?

"You're being awfully quiet," Gwen said, cocking her head. "I hope you aren't mentally castigating yourself."

"Among other things," he admitted.

"I don't regret it," she said softly, her lips curved into the gentlest of smiles. "I do appreciate you kissing me. It was divine."

Lazarus nearly groaned with want. "Yes, it was." His voice sounded very tight. Because he was coiled like a spring ready to explode. He needed relief, and he would find some with his right hand as soon as he got home.

"You'll want to turn your head again as I need to tuck the veil up my skirt once more."

Hell and the devil. Lazarus had forgotten that would be necessary. He snapped his head around so that he was practically looking at the squab behind him. If he saw so much as her ankle, he risked leaping on her and offering to "help" with the placement of her veil. Where would she put it? Between her thighs?

"I'm finished."

Lazarus exhaled and wiped his gloved hand over his dewy brow. This ride to her house was interminable.

"You're going to be sure to work on your writing and memorizing before you go to bed tonight?" she asked, yanking him from his thoughts.

"Yes." Just as soon as he found some satisfaction and could drive her from his mind. God, he hoped he could. He didn't remember the last time he'd been so fixated on a single person. Not an act or a desire, but a woman. He didn't think that had ever happened.

The coach arrived at her house, and a little of his tension eased.

"Thank you again," she said. She sat forward on the seat and lightly touched his knee. It was nearly his undoing.

Lazarus clenched his hands into fists lest he reach for her and pull her onto his lap. He would straddle her legs around him, pushing her skirts away, and arch up against her wet heat. Then he'd kiss her again, devouring all she would give him.

"Good night," he managed through the haze of lust that had swept over him.

Thankfully, she withdrew her hand—and not a moment too soon. "Good night."

Then she climbed down from the coach with help from the groom. Lazarus watched as she entered the house, and the coach started on its way.

Tonight had been an unmitigated disaster. Lazarus had already determined they should end their public association, but now he had to strongly consider ending their private one too. She might be able to put their kiss behind them, but Lazarus wasn't sure he could. He would try one more session with her in two days' time. However, if he couldn't focus on his reading and memorizing, there would be no point in continuing.

He hoped he could expel her from his mind and somehow exorcise his desire for her. If not, he was doomed.

$\sim$

A mix of anxiety and anticipation ran through Gwen as she awaited her friends. She was torn between telling them about what had happened with Lazarus last night, which also meant revealing that she'd gone to a literary salon in disguise, alone with a rogue and keeping the secret to herself. Well, and to Miss Harker.

But how was she to explain how she'd met Miss Harker in the first place? Gwen couldn't say she'd happened upon her at the Siren's Call. She now wished she'd asked her new friend to arrive early so they could arrange a story.

Except the thought of lying to her dearest friends made her almost queasy, hence her anxiety.

Lake appeared then and announced the arrival of Miss Josephine Harker. She was early! Gwen exhaled with relief.

Miss Harker entered the drawing room. She wore a smart walking dress of dark brown that complemented the chestnut color of her hair. She had striking hazel eyes that were similar to Gwen's mother's. Indeed, Miss Harker was an attractive woman, though Gwen imagined some would judge her mouth too wide or her nose a trifle sharp. Gwen found her features arresting and singular.

"I'm so glad you came," Gwen said. "Come and sit." She moved to the settee in the largest seating area and patted the cushion for Miss Harker to join her.

"Thank you for inviting me. I apologize for arriving a tad early, but I wanted to know how you plan to introduce me to your friends. Will you be telling them about last night, or do we need to fabricate another story?"

Gwen laughed. "Oh, my goodness, you read my mind. I was just regretting not inviting you to come early so we could sort this out."

"So, you do want to keep last night a secret?"

"Actually, I don't think I do. I would feel terrible lying to my friends."

"I think that's wise," Miss Harker said with a nod. "If they are your friends, they won't judge you."

"They most definitely are. There is no reason for me to keep anything from them." In the interest of honesty among friends, Gwen added, "I did worry they would think less of me for breaking our rogue rules, but you're right that they won't because they *are* my friends."

Miss Harker's brow furrowed. "Rogue rules? I'm afraid you're going to have to explain those, Miss Price."

"You must call me Gwen, for we are friends now too."

"And you must call me Jo." She smiled at Gwen. "Yes, we are."

Gwen launched into a description of the rogue rules beginning with their adoption nearly two years ago. She didn't want to specifically mention the scandal about Pandora and Bane, so she merely said the rules came about after a rogue treated one of them poorly. She then listed the rules, which she had committed to memory.

"I like the last one a great deal—ruin the rogue before he ruins you. That is *excellent* advice." Jo gave Gwen a reassuring look. "I don't think you need to worry about that with Somerton. He isn't going to ruin you. Not on purpose, anyway. You just can't go on with him as you were last night. How are you feeling about things?" she asked with marked concern.

Gwen didn't mention the graphic and lurid dream she'd had involving Lazarus and him helping her to put the veil under her skirt in the coach, only for the veil to completely disappear so that his hands were free to occupy themselves with her. "I'm feeling fine. I'm relieved we weren't caught. But I can't say I regret it." She also didn't reveal that she was nervous about their tutoring session the following day. Would things be awkward between them?

Lazarus had asked if it was wise of them to meet, and she'd assured him all would be well. But would it when she couldn't seem to stop thinking of kissing him again?

When Jo didn't respond, Gwen asked, "Should I?"

"Only you can decide, but I don't think there's anything wrong with sexual curiosity. Men don't seem to have a problem exploring that. Why should we?" She flashed a brief smile. "I know the answer of course. Society's rules don't allow women like you to do that."

Women like Gwen. What about women like Jo? Last night, she'd indicated that one needn't be married to enjoy the physical aspects of marriage. Did that mean she had done so? While Gwen was incredibly curious and could sometimes be intrusive, she couldn't bring herself to ask. "It's unfortunate. However, I can't imagine women being admired for their sexual prowess. And that hardly seems fair."

"Because it's not. We must be discreet, which I think we're more inclined to be anyway. We don't need to boast about such things to increase our self-worth." She winked at Gwen.

"You are the most fascinating person I have ever met," Gwen said.

Jo laughed. "I find that hard to believe."

"You shouldn't. I have spent my entire life in Bristol. I've been to Wales, to Bath, to Gloucestershire, and to Cornwall. This is my first visit to London. I've been quite sheltered." Not as much as Tamsin had been, but Gwen felt like an absolute bumpkin next to Jo. She was just working up the courage to ask about her sexual experience—whether she had any—when Lake announced the arrival of Min and Ellis.

As Gwen introduced them, Tamsin arrived, and Gwen

completed the introductions. When they were all seated and a tray with tea and cakes had been delivered, Gwen stood back up and went to almost close the door. Closing it entirely would raise her mother's curiosity, so Gwen left it just slightly ajar.

"Are we to share secrets today?" Min asked with a mischievous smile. "Or gossip?"

They didn't do a great deal of gossiping, but it wasn't completely unheard of. "As it happens, I've news to share, and it's best if I didn't air it to anyone outside this room," Gwen said.

Everyone, save Jo, looked at her expectantly. "Do tell," Tamsin prompted from the chair to Gwen's left.

Gwen glanced about. "You are probably wondering how I came to meet Miss Harker, rather Jo, as I'm now calling her."

"I know who she is," Min said, shooting a look at Jo. "Your mother owns the Siren's Call."

"Yes. And your brother is a frequent guest."

Min smiled. "That is how I know of you."

"He discusses such things with you?" Jo seemed surprised.

"Somewhat," Min said with a shrug. "We carp at each other, but we are rather close in spite of that. He does not tell me much about his visits to the Rogue's Den however. And I'm glad for that."

Jo laughed. "I would be too. It's sweet that you and he have a good relationship. I'm glad to hear it. I like Shefford, even if he's a little sensitive."

"Do you think so?" Min now appeared surprised. "How interesting that you gleaned that. You must know him rather well."

Lifting a shoulder, Jo said, "I'm not sure I would say so. I'm just an observer of people. It's hard not to be at the Siren's Call."

Min directed her attention to Gwen. "Did you meet Miss Harker at the Siren's Call?" She smirked.

Gwen laughed. "No. I met her at a literary salon last night."

"You went to a literary salon?" Tamsin asked, her eyes rounding briefly. "I would have gone with you!"

"I went with Lord Somerton." There, the secret was out. Well, part of it anyway. Gwen's pulse was still thrumming as apprehension gathered once more.

Tamsin, Min, and Ellis all gaped at her. "What do you mean you went with him?" Min asked.

"He heard about the salon from Jo—she attends them regularly—and asked if she could obtain an invitation for him and a guest."

"You can't just go to a salon with a gentleman!" Min said, horror etched in her features.

Ellis shot her a quelling glance. "She's not stupid, Min." She looked back at Gwen. "Please continue, and we shall all stop interrupting."

Gwen didn't mind, but thought it might be easier to get through the tale if she didn't have to keep stopping and regathering her courage. "Somerton took his 'Great-Aunt Beatrice' to the salon. I wore a modest gown and a thick veil over my head. As you can imagine, the veil made things especially challenging for me since I am awkward on my best day. It was the most thrilling evening I've ever experienced, and I pray I get to return." Gwen looked to Tamsin, "I'm hopeful we can go together—you can be my chaperone."

Tamsin nodded eagerly then pursed her lips briefly. "Why would Somerton take you to a literary salon?"

"He knows I like books and thought I would enjoy it. I may have mentioned to him that I was interested in attending a salon."

"That's very thoughtful of him," Ellis said. She narrowed her eyes at Gwen. "Has your association progressed to courtship?"

Min sucked in a breath. "Is he ready to renounce his rogue-dom?"

"I don't think, ah, no." Heat rose up Gwen's neck and into her face, but she plowed on. "I suffered a mishap last night—as you can imagine—and accidentally swept my veil into the flame of a candle." All three of them stared at her with wide eyes and open mouths. "The veil caught on fire, but Somerton extinguished it. We went to the retiring room to repair the situation because there was a hole in the veil that threatened to reveal I was not, in fact, his elderly great-aunt. While we were there, we, ah, became caught up. I may have asked him to kiss me."

"May have?" Jo asked sardonically, her brow arched.

"All right, I did ask him to kiss me. He was reluctant, but he eventually complied. That's when Jo walked in and saw us."

Three loud gasps filled the room as they all snapped their heads toward Jo.

"Don't worry, I wasn't ever going to expose them," Jo said.

"Of course not. Why would you be here today?" Ellis asked. She looked back to Gwen. "Why *is* Miss Harker here today?"

"Please, you must all call me Jo. Unless you decide to toss me out." Jo's lips curved into a small smile that said she wasn't at all concerned about that happening.

"I won't allow that," Gwen said firmly. "Jo was most helpful last night, and we became fast friends. I invited her today because I knew you would all like her as much as I do. She already has a favorite rogue rule."

Min's eyes lit with enthusiasm. "Oh, which one?"

"Ruin the rogue before he ruins you." Jo's eyes glittered with a mix of excitement and perhaps malice. "It really is wonderful advice."

Tamsin held up her hand and fixed her gaze on Gwen.

"Let me be sure I have this right. You asked my cousin to kiss you, he complied, and you were caught in this compromising position?" At Gwen's nod, she asked, "Then what happened? Are you now betrothed as Isaac and I were forced to become?"

"No, because Jo isn't Mrs. Loose-Lips." Gwen referred to the woman who'd seen Isaac hit a man who wanted to court and wed Tamsin. The man had been trying to touch her without her consent, and Isaac warned him to stop. When he did not, Isaac knocked him down, and Mrs. Loose-Lips, the woman who'd also caught Pandora and Bane in their compromising position, had made it clear she would share what she'd seen with everyone she met, thus prompting Isaac to declare that he and Tamsin were betrothed.

"Thank goodness for that," Ellis murmured.

"So you kissed Somerton?" Min asked.

"Yes," Gwen replied. "I broke at least two rogue rules, but I'm not sorry. I wanted to know what a kiss felt like, and now I do."

"Bravo," Jo said. "There is nothing wrong with kissing a man, provided you don't get caught. What if you married someone and they were terrible at kissing?"

Tamsin exhaled. "I didn't kiss Isaac until after we were married. It wasn't even on our wedding night. Fortunately, he is *not* terrible at kissing. Or anything else, for that matter." A faint blush bloomed in her cheeks.

"That is fortunate indeed, Lady Droxford," Jo said.

"You must call me Tamsin. If we're all to call you Jo, you must use our given names as well. I daresay we're friends already," she added almost shyly.

Min sent Tamsin an apologetic look. "I'm sorry you thought you couldn't share the truth with us. We must all promise to be honest—as Gwen has been today. We love each other, don't we? There will be no judgment."

They all nodded. "I promise," Gwen said. "I do feel better telling you about last night."

"I promise too," Tamsin agreed.

"I do as well, though I can't imagine I will ever have anything interesting to disclose," Ellis said. She was a confirmed spinster, even if she hadn't reached spinsterhood yet.

Jo sent Ellis a hooded look. "You never know what may happen. Also, I, for one, don't want to feel badly if I decide *not* to share something. There are just some things that aren't our secrets to share, and others can't be...articulated." She shrugged.

Min surveyed Jo with interest. "I suspect your experiences eclipse all of ours put together."

Letting out a short, sharp laugh, Jo shook her head. "I don't know if that's true. As I said, I observe a great deal. That doesn't mean it is *my* experience."

"You must hear a fair amount of gossip," Ellis noted.

"I do, but I discount most of it. People just like to hear themselves talk."

"Well, in the interest of sharing information, I should tell you something," Min announced. "Given my current reputation for being too discriminating, my parents are worried I have ruined my chances to wed by refusing so many suitors and making it clear I won't suffer anyone with even a hint of roguish behavior."

"What does that mean?" Gwen asked. "Are you no longer on the Marriage Mart?"

"It means her parents are furious with her behavior and want her to marry someone of their choosing." Ellis sent Min a sympathetic look.

"It can't be that bad," Tamsin said, ever the optimist. "You'll find the right person this Season."

Min shrugged. "I don't know if that will be possible. I am

not asked to dance very often, and I've had two callers. For the entire Season."

Gwen's jaw dropped. How could she have had more callers than Min? That made no sense.

"And I'm afraid I can't do much to fix things, even if I wanted to. My reputation has worsened, thanks in large part to gossip from other young ladies and their mothers. I think they believe my absence from the Marriage Mart will vault them into popularity." Min rolled her eyes.

"Are people really that cruel?" Tamsin asked.

"Yes," Jo replied. "I've heard plenty of gossip about Lady Minerva and her perceived arrogance."

"Arrogance?" Gwen couldn't think of a word that described Min less.

Min shrugged. "That doesn't surprise me. As Henlow's daughter, people have a predetermined idea of who I am. That has always been part of the problem with my time on the Marriage Mart. Most gentlemen I meet think they know all about me already. That, and they don't care to become acquainted with me. They see my father's title and connections, and that is what they really want."

"So true," Jo murmured. "I'm sorry for that."

Min looked over at Ellis. "We'll just be spinsters together, and that will be fine." She laughed, and Ellis smiled in return.

"I'll join you, as I've also decided to eschew marriage," Jo said. "We can form a club."

"Yes, please," Min replied with a grin. "We'll host literary salons. Can an unmarried young woman do that?" she mused.

"I just want to attend one," Tamsin said. She addressed Jo. "Can you obtain an invitation for me?"

"For all of us," Ellis said. "Tamsin, you can be everyone's chaperone."

Tamsin laughed. "I'd be happy to."

They talked of literary salons for a while, then Gwen suggested they have refreshments. Before they could rise, however, Ellis asked, "We got away from our initial subject—that of Gwen and Somerton. What happens next between the two of you?"

"Nothing," Gwen responded. "It was a single event and won't be repeated."

Min's lips curved into a sly smile. "Did you enjoy it?"

"Yes," Gwen said without hesitation.

"Brilliant." Min stood and went to the table with the tea tray. Ellis and Jo joined her, but Tamsin hung back to speak to Gwen.

"What about your meetings with Somerton at our house?" Tamsin whispered.

"They will continue. I'll see him there tomorrow."

"Perhaps you should leave the door open," Tamsin said with a faint grimace.

Perhaps they should. "It really was just an isolated occurrence," Gwen assured her. "We have put it behind us."

Tamsin nodded, appearing relieved.

Gwen was not certain it *was* behind them, but they needed it to be. Otherwise, yes, the library door should probably be left open.

CHAPTER 10

*I*t was Gwen's turn to arrive early at the Droxfords' home, so Lazarus braced himself to see her as soon as he walked into the library. He was both anticipating and dreading their meeting. He'd done little but think of her the past day and a half since the literary salon.

The butler greeted him, but said nothing further. By now, he understood that Lazarus and Gwen were having clandestine meetings in the library. However, he didn't acknowledge it in any way.

Lazarus hesitated just outside the library and summoned his most charming smile. Then he let it fall from his face. What was he doing? Did he think he could flirt this problem away? That would only make things worse.

Taking a deep breath, he walked into the library. Gwen stood near the table and turned to face him. She wore a simple, pale pink walking dress with a lace fichu. She looked feminine and alluring, and Lazarus had to work very hard not to rush over and take her in his arms.

"Should I close the door?" he asked, thinking that small act held more weight after their kiss.

"I had thought no, but I think you must. Else, the truth of our meetings—and your secret—may become known."

Lazarus wasn't sure it mattered, but he was still sensitive to his problem. Though his reading had improved—slightly —in the time they'd been meeting, he didn't feel confident enough for anyone to know that he required help to memorize and deliver a speech he'd written. He was beginning to wonder if he ought to try just speaking without memorizing it. If only he could have a person beside him who could murmur something to him if he lost the thread of what he was saying or had missed a point that he wanted to make.

He closed the door and went to the table, standing behind his chair so he was not close to her and there was furniture between them. He saw that she'd already put out parchment, pencil, and a book for their work together.

"I hope you have been well," she said, smiling tentatively. He could tell she felt strangely. He did too.

"I'm not sure we can act as if nothing happened," he said.

"We must try," she said gamely. Slipping into her chair, she motioned for him to sit. "Let's begin. Focusing on our work will ensure we aren't distracted."

Did that mean she was having difficulty not thinking of kissing? Lazarus should not contemplate that. Better to do as she said—focus on their work. He sat down and willed himself to relax.

"How have you been coming with memorizing the speech?" she asked. "Would you like to practice and show me your progress?"

The truth was that he'd been so distracted since the salon that he'd barely made any. "I suppose I could try."

"Let us practice reading first, and perhaps that will put you more at ease." She gave him an encouraging smile that made him want to kiss her. Hell, everything made him want to kiss her.

He needed to pull himself together. If he could not, his chance at improving his reading would be gone.

She opened the book and put it before him on the table. She'd written on the text, making the same sort of marks—underlines and slashes to break up syllables and sounds—she'd done on things she had copied.

"You ruined your book," he said.

"Bah, it's not ruined if it helps you."

"I'll buy you another. I know how dear they are to you."

Her gaze locked with his. "Teaching you is also dear to me."

She was dear to him. Lazarus brought one hand beneath the table and squeezed his fingers into his leg. It was torture not to touch her. To bask in her warmth and tenderness.

Forcing his gaze from hers, he looked at the book and began to read. Shockingly, it was easier than usual. Which wasn't to say it was easy. But he had a weird confidence he hadn't felt since his father had died. Perhaps it was the knowledge that he had a true ally—someone who genuinely cared about helping him and wanted to see him succeed.

He read for ten minutes or perhaps much longer. He wasn't sure. The words were flowing a little more easily. Until they didn't. He reached a word that made him falter, and he sat back in the chair, silently cursing.

"That was so wonderful!" she cried, her features alight with pride. "Do not be discouraged. You were reading marvelously! And you seemed to be enjoying yourself. That is the ultimate goal."

"But then I stumbled."

"*I* sometimes stumble when I read," she said. "You mustn't chastise yourself. You are making true progress. I hope you can see it. Please tell me you can, or I shall feel as though I'm failing you."

"You are not," he said quickly. "I could not ask for a better tutor."

"Thank you." There was pink in her cheeks again, as if she were embarrassed by his praise. Or was it something else? "Do you want to practice your speech now?"

"I suppose I can try."

Gwen pulled a piece of parchment from her bag. "I'll follow along with my copy in case you need any prompts." She held the paper, but watched him expectantly.

He felt suddenly nervous. "I should probably stand," he murmured, rising and pushing his chair back. He walked away from the table then back, loosening his shoulders as he moved. He took a position between the chair and the table and began to concentrate.

"Do you always close your eyes when you practice?" she asked.

Lazarus hadn't even realized he'd closed them. Opening his eyes, he fixed on her. "I hadn't noticed, but yes. I should try not to do that when I'm in the House of Lords." He'd look an idiot speechifying with his eyes shut.

"You can do it for now if it helps. We can work on one thing at a time."

"I'll try not to close them." Indeed, if he kept his gaze on her, he wouldn't *want* to close them. And yet, doing so might also distract him from saying anything beyond *"Kiss me again, Gwen. Please."*

"Begin whenever you are ready." She glanced down at the paper briefly before leveling her expectant stare on him.

It should have been unnerving, but he found it surprisingly comforting. Perhaps because she looked at him with such eagerness and confidence. And pride. She absolutely believed in him, even if he didn't believe in himself. To have someone in his life who seemed to truly understand him after so long without his father filled him with the strength he'd been lacking.

He felt a moment's pause, for he didn't wish to discount his mother, who had always shown him love and support. She just hadn't been aware of his reading difficulties because his father had managed his education and she'd been focused on their three daughters. Then, after his father died, Lazarus hadn't been able to tell her the truth. For the first time, he thought perhaps he could. Why had he ever thought he couldn't be honest with her? Because the shame he'd long carried had eclipsed everything else.

Setting aside his long-held emotion and focusing on the courage Gwen instilled in him, he somehow found the beginning of the speech in his mind and began to orate. Word after word flowed from him, and since he wasn't reading, it all sounded right and natural. After a while, he noticed she wasn't looking at the parchment. He stumbled then, the next words escaping him.

She prompted him with the next word, but didn't look down to see what it was.

"Have you memorized the speech?" he asked, incredulous.

"I may have done," she said with a faint shrug.

"Then why are you holding it in front of you?"

"Just in case I didn't have it memorized completely. You are not the only one who doubts themselves. You are quite normal in that, you see."

Lazarus knew in that moment he would never meet another woman like her. Someone who could see into his soul and somehow saw the best parts of him, who shared herself with him in ways that made him feel whole. It had been years since he'd felt that kind of understanding and connection. Not since his father had died.

"Do you need the next word?" she asked.

He recalled what she'd said and gave his head a light

shake. Picking up the thread, he went on, but only for a few lines because that was all he'd memorized. "That's all I have," he said.

She leapt up from her chair. "That's half, Lazarus!"

Her use of his name and her boundless excitement made him grin. She set the parchment down and moved around the table to where he stood. Then she hugged him, her arms curling around his neck. "I'm so proud of you," she said softly, her lips near his ear.

Lazarus froze. But only for the barest moment. Then he snaked his arms around her and held her tightly against him.

She pulled her head back and looked him in the eye, her lips parted. Giving him the slightest nod, she lifted her mouth to his.

Lazarus needed no further urging, nor did he want to hear the voices in his head telling him to stop. He kissed her eagerly, desperately, passionately. This was not a tentative embrace like the other night. This was a meeting of two people who wanted nothing more than to be in the other's arms.

He should not want this. He should not allow this. And yet, if the house were on fire as her veil had been, he would not have been able to stop.

She met the thrust of his tongue with her own and clasped the back of his neck, her fingers tugging gently on his hair. Lazarus pressed his hands into her back and clutched her hip, pulling her pelvis to his.

Their incoherent noises and soft moans surrounded him, plunging him into a seductive haze. The kisses ended, then started anew, then deepened as their bodies moved together, seeking and touching. Lazarus picked her up and set her backside on the table, moving to nudge himself between her legs as best her garments would allow. He kissed away from her mouth, exploring her jawline and her neck, moving down to the hollow of her throat.

Gwen clutched at his head, her fingers tangling in his hair. He brought one hand to the underside of her breast, cupping her. She arched toward him, eager for his touch. Lazarus was fast losing control, if he ever had it to begin with.

He should step away from her. Hell, he should run away from her. Instead, he lifted his head and kissed her again as he stroked his hand over her breast. She kissed him back with a passionate zeal that killed any inclination he had to stop.

Nipping at her lower lip, he flattened his hand against her bare skin, above and between the lace fichu that was tucked into her gown. How he wanted to slip his hand into her bodice and explore as much of her flesh as he could. But he couldn't risk disrobing her in his friend's library.

He shouldn't be risking any of this.

Reason finally took control, and Lazarus dragged his mouth from hers. He took a step back, his breath coming fast and his pulse racing. His cock throbbed with urgency, desperate for release—for *her*.

Gwen's lips were dark pink and kiss swollen, her eyes luminous with desire. Lazarus wanted her more than ever.

"Why did you stop?" she asked, her voice low and seductive. "I was enjoying that immensely."

"As was I." Lazarus took a deep breath to try to calm himself. "However, we must not continue. We weren't even supposed to start. I recall you saying we would put what happened at the salon behind us, and you were right to say that. Today was a mistake."

"It didn't feel like a mistake," she said with an utterly charming smile.

Lazarus nearly groaned with frustration. She was not

making this easy. But then, he doubted tearing himself away from her and doing what he must do next would be nothing but excruciatingly difficult and painful. "Nevertheless, it was a mistake. Even our meeting was a mistake. We will need to forgo future tutoring sessions."

Her eyes rounded, and she pushed herself off the table. "No. We can't do that. I'm committed to helping you."

As she moved toward him, Lazarus took another step back. "I do appreciate that. However, I am committed to not ruining you, which means we can no longer see one another."

"You won't ruin me," she said with such earnestness that he nearly believed her. He *wanted* to believe her. But he knew himself. And while he was a rogue, he was something else entirely with her. She consumed his thoughts, and if he didn't back away now, they risked being trapped together forever.

Would that be such a bad thing?

Lazarus nearly gasped at the tiny voice in the back of his mind. He had to have misheard it. Bloody hell, he was so far gone, he was listening to nonsensical utterances in his head.

"Gwen, please understand that this is not about you—it's entirely me. You know what sort of man I am. Apparently, I can't even help myself when it's in my best interest to do so." An ache centered in Lazarus's chest. He knew her tutoring was helping him. To walk away from it now seared into him and left him feeling...less. But what she'd done so far would have to be enough.

Her brow puckered. "This is my fault. I never should have asked you to kiss me. And today, I'm afraid I was swept away by the same impulse. If you weren't such an excellent kisser—"

Now, Lazarus did groan. "Please stop. We can't even talk about this." His body was already on tenterhooks in her presence. Discussing their mutual attraction and how much she liked his kissing was not going to help matters.

Her lovely face fell, as if he'd just told her that her horse died. "I've let you down, Lazarus. I'm so sorry."

"You have *not*." He wanted to touch her, to assure her she'd done everything right, but he couldn't dare. "You have given me something I have long been without—hope. My father started me on a journey to read, and you have helped me along that path. For that, I will be eternally grateful."

"Will you let me know if I can help you at all? Anytime. Anywhere."

Lazarus allowed a smile. Did she have any idea what that sort of invitation conjured in his salacious mind? "I will," he lied. He had no intention of seeking her out. He could not. She was on her way to finding a husband, and he would likely toast her wedding come June.

"I don't suppose you'll rescue me at Almack's again tonight if I need it?" she asked hopefully. "We didn't go last week, but my mother thinks we must attend tonight since my fortunes seem to have improved."

Watching her dance with a parade of eligible bachelors would be certain torture. And yet, he was drawn to want to protect her, to ensure she enjoyed a wonderful evening. "I don't think I will be there," he said regretfully.

She nodded, then moved around the table to collect her things. "You should keep practicing reading every day. If you don't mind, I'd be happy to send you things to practice with the markings I've made."

"Would you?" The words leapt from his mouth before he even considered her offer. But it would be fine. Sending him things didn't mean they would see one another.

"Of course. In fact, I'll do it anyway, if you don't want me to," she added with a chuckle.

"I do want you to," he said softly. "Thank you."

Picking up her bag, she gave him a lingering stare. "Thank *you*. For everything. You have altered the course of my life."

Then she turned and was gone from the library. Gone from *him*. Forever.

～

*T*he following afternoon, Gwen donned her dancing slippers for another lesson with Mr. Tremblay. She was not looking forward to the next hour or however long he would be there. She would much prefer another tutoring lesson with Lazarus, especially if there would be kissing.

But there wouldn't be any more tutoring nor any kissing. Gwen had felt as though she were in a fog since leaving him yesterday afternoon. She would blame that for her mishap at Almack's last night, but since she was clumsy on any given day, she could not.

She'd tripped during a longways dance and managed to fall onto a rather short, slender gentleman, knocking him to the floor. Thankfully, he'd laughed and helped her up, but her partner for the dance, Mr. Brentworth, hadn't been impressed. She was fairly certain that was the last she'd see of him.

Before that, she'd danced with Mr. Markwith and believed he was interested in a courtship. He had to leave London early this morning to visit a family member in Kent, but said he would see her when he returned. Instead of feeling excited by his attention and interest, she was still feeling foggy—or something—about Lazarus.

She needed to move on from their exciting interludes. He was precisely the man she thought he was—an utter rogue—and thus, the type of man she'd vowed never to wed. Not that he would have been interested in marrying her.

Indeed, he hadn't been able to get away from her quickly enough. All because he couldn't manage his rakish tendencies.

She thought of what her mother had said regarding his reputation and that he would not make a good husband. Perhaps she was right—her opinion mattered to Gwen. And here Gwen was behaving inappropriately with a known rogue. Her mother would be horrified. Gwen couldn't help but flinch inwardly.

Knowing Lazarus wasn't a good choice didn't make the pain of losing their friendship any less. But if she could focus on the fact that she was better off without him, perhaps the ache would ease.

"Gwen, why are you staring at the wall with that forlorn expression?" her mother asked. She was already seated near the window with her magazine.

Shaking her head, Gwen blinked. "Just lost in thought. Thinking of a book I'm reading," she fibbed.

Mr. Tremblay and his musician arrived, and Gwen forced a smile while her body tensed. "Good afternoon, Miss Price. Are you ready to waltz?"

"I don't suppose we could start with a simple longways dance?" Gwen asked, and not just because it would mean he wasn't touching her for very long. After last night, she could use the practice.

The dancing master frowned, his forehead pleating gently as his bow lips pursed. "Is that really necessary? I should think you ought to move beyond that."

"Just a quick review would be helpful," Gwen said. "I, ah, sometimes have trouble with it."

"I see." He suddenly smiled brilliantly. "If we have time at the end, we'll give that a quick practice. But first, we must focus on the more challenging dances."

"Mr. Tremblay," Gwen's mother called. "Would you mind

starting with the cotillion? Gwen is more likely to dance that than the waltz or the quadrille."

Mr. Tremblay appeared slightly disappointed, but he covered it with another smile. "Very well."

Feeling relieved, Gwen followed Mr. Tremblay's instruction. The music started, and he guided her through the dance, touching her more than she expected, his hand lingering on her arm and grazing her back and hip. A few times, she misstepped, and he was quick to grab her and steer her correctly. It would not have been strange at all, except for the length of time he held her and the way his touches sometimes felt like caresses.

Then there were the overly friendly smiles. Indeed, they were almost...seductive. Everything he did made her distinctly uncomfortable.

When the music stopped, he applauded briefly. "You've done very well, Miss Price. Time for the waltz."

Gwen glanced toward her mother who was just returning her attention to the magazine she held. Had she seen any of the things Mr. Tremblay was doing?

Wanting to get through the lesson as rapidly as possible, Gwen gritted her teeth and stepped toward the dancing master. He clasped her hand and pressed his palm against her lower back. His fingertips were pointed down, toward her backside, and encroached on that space. Gwen endured five minutes of his groping and abruptly stepped away from him.

Mr. Tremblay instructed the musician to stop playing. "Is something amiss?" he asked Gwen.

"I'm afraid I've a headache. I'm going to have to lie down," Gwen said. "Please excuse me." She barely glanced at her mother before hastening from the drawing room.

Up in her bedchamber, she kicked off her dancing slippers and considered asking for a bath to wash away the dancing master's insidious touch. Instead, she paced the room and rehearsed what she would tell her mother, for she could not suffer another lesson with Mr. Tremblay.

A light knock on the door drew Gwen to stop. "Come."

Her mother stepped inside, closing the door behind her. "Are you all right? I thought you'd be lying down."

"I'm fine. I don't have a headache."

Lines furrowed across her mother's brow. "Why would you lie?"

"Because I couldn't tolerate another minute of Mr. Tremblay's wandering hands or his suggestive looks. I'm sorry, Mama, but he is too familiar. I do not like him, and I don't want to see him anymore."

Her mother looked aghast. "I'm so sorry. I didn't notice any of that."

Gwen stopped herself from responding that it was because she'd been reading her magazine. "I'm sure it was difficult for you to see from your vantage point. But you trust me when I tell you he verges on behaving inappropriately, don't you?"

"Of course I do, dear." Her mother came toward her and touched her arm, looking at her with the warmth and care that had always made Gwen feel loved and protected. "No more Mr. Tremblay," she said firmly. "Though, now we are back to searching for a dancing master."

"Do I really need one?" Gwen asked.

Her mother arched a brow, her expression wry. "After last night?"

Gwen laughed. "I will never be perfect, Mama, but I am passable. And gentlemen are asking me to dance and calling on me."

"Yes, and it is wonderful." She fell silent a moment, then her eyes lit as if an idea had struck. "I wonder if Lord Somerton might be persuaded to practice dancing with you. He was so kind to help by paying you attention. Perhaps he would lend his assistance to aiding you with the waltz. You danced it marvelously with him at the Phoenix Club ball."

The idea of Lazarus being her dancing instructor was both madly appealing and highly laughable. He would never agree, not after what had happened yesterday and at the salon. "I don't think he'd want to do that," Gwen said. "Anyway, he's done enough, and I'm sure he has better things to do." Saying that stung, renewing the ache Gwen had carried since they'd parted yesterday.

"We could at least ask," her mother said with a light shrug. "I'll see if Evan can speak with him—a favor between friends."

"Please don't, Mama." Gwen couldn't imagine what Lazarus would say, and she didn't want to put him in the awkward position of having to decline.

"Why not? He helped you before."

"I would just rather not. Besides, how would that even work? He would be seen coming to our house, and I've just spent the last few days telling people we don't suit."

Her mother cocked her head. "I did notice that and wondered why you thought it was necessary."

"Actually, it was Somerton's idea. He thought it would be most beneficial for me if I was the one who decided we didn't suit."

"That was most clever of him. He really has been incredibly helpful. But if you would prefer we not ask him to practice dancing with you, I will not. I hope you might reconsider, however. I'm sure we can come up with a scheme for you to dance. Perhaps you can meet at someone else's house. Someone with whom you are both well acquainted."

Gwen pressed her lips together lest she smile or laugh. "I will consider it, Mama, but I doubt I will change my mind."

"I am sorry about Mr. Tremblay," her mother said. "After

what you told me, I'm surprised he's been so highly recommended."

"I can't begin to imagine why." Perhaps he hadn't behaved that way with his other students. Gwen struggled to believe that.

"Well, that much is settled—you are finished with Mr. Tremblay." She gave Gwen a nod and a smile, then left.

Gwen went to her desk to finish the reading exercise that she'd started last night for Lazarus. It was a rather romantic poem by John Donne. She hoped he wasn't already familiar with it, but that was the chance they took by no longer meeting in person.

As she sat down to work, she thought of Lazarus dancing with her. If tutoring him had resulted in kissing, what would dancing do?

She was disappointed that she would never find out.

CHAPTER 11

"What do you think, Somerton?" Shefford asked from across the table at the Siren's Call.

Lazarus had no idea what they were discussing. He'd been consumed by thoughts of Gwen, as had been the case for the past day since he'd completely ended their association.

"He's off in the forest again," Price said in a stage whisper that Lazarus was clearly meant to hear.

"What's troubling you tonight?" Keele asked.

There was no way Lazarus would tell them the truth, especially with Price sitting to his left. "Just thinking about estate matters and preparing for the speech I'll be giving next week."

"Yes, I'm keen to hear what you'll be saying about our returning soldiers and their plight," Keele said. "It's an important issue that requires more investigation and discussion."

Lazarus nodded vaguely, hoping Keele wasn't going to engage him on the topic right now. He wasn't in the mood for political conversation. Or any conversation, really. He ought to just go home.

What he really needed to do was stop moping about and focus on his reading. He'd made good progress with Gwen, and there was no reason he couldn't continue, especially if she sent him exercises to further his improvement. His chest lightened a bit as he considered that their association wasn't entirely over, not if she sent him things to work on.

How pathetic that he would cling to such a paltry connection between them.

Perhaps a visit to the Rogue's Den would help him put thoughts of Gwen out of his mind. Except his fixation on her was not entirely due to physical desire. He had plenty of that, but he also just liked being with her. She gave him confidence and made him feel that his reading problem was not a deficiency.

"I think I'm going to retire," Lazarus announced. He lifted his tankard to finish his ale, then set it back on the table.

"So early?" Shefford asked. He scrutinized Lazarus a long moment. "What is going on with you of late? You don't spend as much time with us as you used to. Have you struck up a liaison with someone?"

Lazarus was glad he'd swallowed his ale, or he might have choked. "No. I've just been busy."

"Not everyone requires near-constant female companionship," Keele said sardonically, eyeing Shefford.

"It isn't near constant," Shefford muttered before taking a drink of ale.

Rising, Lazarus looked around the table. "Have a good evening and behave yourselves. Not you, Keele. You wouldn't know how to misbehave."

"Not true. I know how. I simply choose not to." The marquess smirked.

Chuckling, Lazarus moved toward the entrance area. Jo was there and watched him approach.

"Leaving already?" she asked.

"You sound like them."

"It's a valid question. You have been, dare I say, *sedate* in your behavior recently," Jo observed. "Your reckless kissing with a young lady at a literary salon notwithstanding."

"Well, you can be assured there will be no more of that," he said darkly.

"I'm pleased to hear you have mastered your impulses."

Hardly. "I have removed temptation. Miss Price and I are no longer associated in any way. I don't expect I'll ever speak with her again." Saying that made the pain of their parting sharper. It would be some time, he realized, before he would feel like himself. But perhaps the man he'd been before he'd come to know Gwen was gone forever. Only time would give him the answer.

"It sounds as if you aren't pleased by that," Jo said softly. "Is there a chance you care for her?"

"We had become friends, so yes, I care for her. I hope she is able to find the husband she deserves."

"And what kind of man is that?" Jo asked.

Lazarus did not want to contemplate who would make Gwen happy. He just knew it wouldn't be a rogue like him. "Someone intelligent and proper, who will hold her in the highest regard."

"Well, you are two of those things anyway," Jo said with a light laugh. "The third—propriety—is a tad overrated. Why wouldn't she want you just as you are?"

He stared at her. "What are you suggesting?"

She shrugged. "That you could be the husband she deserves—and perhaps wants."

"Has she said something?" Lazarus's breath arrested as he waited, desperately, for her response.

"No, but I don't think you should see yourself as someone she wouldn't want."

He exhaled. "She has appropriate suitors—men who fit *all three* parts of the description I gave you."

She moved closer to him, her gaze fixing on him with an urgent intensity. "But what about what *you* want?"

He wanted Gwen. But he couldn't have her, not in the way he'd always had women. She was the kind of woman one married.

"Those are some pretty deep furrows on your forehead," Jo said. "I can see you are thinking very hard. Perhaps you are conflicted. Is there any chance you might be in love with her?"

The idea of it had flitted about his mind, but Lazarus hadn't wanted to think about it. Love meant a deeper connection, commitment, whether you wanted it or not. Because when you loved someone, they held a part of you that you could never get back. And if you lost them, that part of you was gone forever.

Lazarus realized, whether he wanted it or not, he *was* in love with Gwen. And he was already fighting against the pain of losing her along with some small part of himself, a part he'd only just discovered. Because of her. "There is a good chance," he whispered, afraid to say it, but unable to keep it inside.

"Then fight for her." Jo looked at him expectantly. "At least tell her how you feel and give her the chance to tell you if she feels the same."

"She cannot. Feel the same, I mean." She would never love a rogue like him. He was not at all the kind of man she wanted to marry.

"Why not? She was kissing you back, if I recall. And I think she even said it was her idea."

"Wanting to kiss a rogue isn't the same as loving one." Honestly, Lazarus couldn't believe Jo was being this obtuse.

Jo made a face at him and speared him with an icy glare. "It *could* be. You are being horribly obtuse."

This made him laugh. "I was just thinking the same about you."

"I am on the outside observing you and Gwen. If you don't want my advice, fine. But I think if you don't fight for her or at least tell her how you feel, you will regret it to the grave."

Lazarus sobered. Regret was an emotion he understood. He would always wish he had more time with his father, that he'd told the man who'd been his champion and his hero how much he loved him and how grateful he was for his support and love.

"I'll think about it." His mind churned with what to say. And how to react when she inevitably told him he was a wonderful kisser, but not the sort of man she could marry.

"Think fast, or you will lose the opportunity. Gwen is a lovely person. She may surprise you in how she feels."

"Are you sure you don't know something?" he asked.

"I swear I do not. Only that she seems to like you a great deal. I see the potential for more, even if you don't."

Lazarus nodded. "Thank you." He bade her good night and left the Siren's Call, hailing a hack to take him home to Bruton Street.

Should he call on Gwen tomorrow? He envisioned opening his heart to her, and a cold sweat broke out along his neck.

He had appointments tomorrow, so perhaps the park instead. He would go and see if she was there. If he revealed himself in a public place, it would likely be less awkward. Or would it be more awkward?

Lazarus wiped his hand over his face. He needed to work on his bloody speech. He'd been unable to focus since yesterday. Really, since the salon the other night.

As soon as he arrived home, a footman gave him a letter that had arrived that evening while he was out. Lazarus recognized the handwriting—it was from Gwen.

Waiting until he was in his chamber, he tore it open. There was a reading exercise. Before it, she wrote:

> *Dear Lazarus,*
> *I hope this finds you well and working hard. I know you will continue to improve with your reading, and I look forward to seeing the results someday.*

How would that happen? Unless she was hoping they would find a way to communicate or spend time together. Probably as friends. He continued reading.

> *I apologize for the romantic nature of this poem, but I thought it would be good practice. It is also how I think of you. If you would like, please write back with how you managed. I would also appreciate any updates on your progress with memorizing your speech.*
> *Fondly,*
> *Gwen*

She'd sent a romantic poem? And it was how she thought of him? And she'd signed it "fondly."

A grin spread his lips as wide as they could go. Throwing off his coat, he went to the desk, eager to read this poem. He finished it in a shockingly short amount of time, and he was filled with hope.

Yes, he would look for her in the park tomorrow, and failing that, he would call on her the following day. He would not allow regret to steal any more from him. Nor would he allow love to slip away.

~

*T*he afternoon was pleasant in Hyde Park as Gwen walked with her mother toward the Ring. The weather had been cool thus far this spring, so the sun peeking from the clouds was most welcome.

As soon as they neared the Ring, Mr. Henry Wilton approached and asked if he could take Gwen for a promenade. Smiling, Gwen's mother agreed and turned her over to the gentleman with light brown hair and blue eyes. Mr. Wilton was of average height and a rather round face. He was not the most effusive person, but Gwen admired his intellect and interest in science and history.

"I trust you've been well the past few days," Mr. Wilton said as they began their promenade.

Gwen had last seen him at Almack's the evening before last. "Indeed. And you?"

"Quite. Yesterday, I received a most enlightening paper from a scholar who is mentoring me on the subject of the Roman occupation of Britain. It has been fascinating to read."

That reminded Gwen of Tamsin's father, who was a scholar of history. She seemed to recall that he particularly enjoyed studying the Roman period. "I've a friend whose father specializes in that part of history. Perhaps you'd care to correspond with him. He resides in Cornwall and does not travel to London."

Mr. Wilton looked over at her with marked interest. It was the most animated she'd ever seen him, in fact. "Cornwall, you say? The gentleman who sent me this paper lives in St. Austell. Mr. Penrose."

Gwen laughed. "That is my friend's father. She is the Lady Droxford."

"I had no idea," Mr. Wilton said. "What a very small world we live in as we are all connected in one way or another."

As they continued around the Ring, Gwen looked about and saw many acquaintances. She also saw Min and Ellis and waved at them. At length, she realized she was looking for Lazarus. Though it had been only two days since she'd seen him, she missed his presence. His laughter, the way he looked at her, the diligence with which he worked on his reading. The exceptional skill and passion of his kisses.

Do not think about that, particularly when you are walking with another gentleman!

Suddenly, Lazarus was there. She saw him standing off the track. He was with a beautiful young woman, which sent a pang of envy through Gwen. She wanted to be the woman he was standing and conversing with. Not just in the park, but everywhere.

Mr. Wilton continued talking about the Roman Empire, which normally would have drawn Gwen's interest, but she couldn't stop thinking of Lazarus. Or stealing glances in his direction—until they passed him. Had he seen her? He hadn't seemed to. And if he had, he would likely not have acknowledged her.

Feeling a bit morose as they returned to her mother, Gwen wished she could stop thinking of Lazarus. He wasn't interested in her the way she might be in him. Might? What did she want?

More. Gwen wanted more of Lazarus. More kissing. More time together. More attending literary salons and being king and queen at medieval balls. She even wanted more dancing, which was baffling.

But he was a confirmed rogue with no interest in anything beyond the kisses they shared and the agreement they'd made. They'd become friends, and she knew he held her in high regard, but in the end, he was still the man she knew him to be: someone not entirely serious who enjoyed the liberty and debauchery of a wealthy, titled, rakish gentleman.

Was he really that man, though? Gwen saw him as so much more, even if he didn't see it himself.

They arrived at her mother, and Mr. Wilton bowed. He said he looked forward to seeing Gwen soon, and she agreed.

"Do you like him?" her mother asked after he departed.

"Mr. Wilton is quite clever," Gwen said, her gaze straying to Lazarus where he was still talking to the young lady. She wore a stunning teal-blue walking dress and a pretty hat adorned with flowers and a peacock feather.

"Do you prefer Mr. Markwith?"

Gwen dragged her focus from Lazarus and looked toward her mother. "Perhaps. I haven't decided."

"One of them may ask to court you soon, so you should think on it." Her mother patted her arm with a warm smile. "It's exciting to think you may receive an offer of marriage very soon."

Yes, exciting.

Except it wasn't. Because Gwen realized the only offer that would truly excite her would have to come from Lazarus. And that was not going to happen.

"Let us walk a bit, Mama." Gwen looped her arm through her mother's and guided her toward where Lazarus stood. She didn't get too close. She just wanted to be where he could perhaps see her, and she could make eye contact. Had he received her reading exercise? She was so hoping he would respond.

At last, the woman he was speaking with left his side, rejoining another group a very short distance away. Lazarus appeared to be frowning, his head tipped toward the ground.

Gwen fought the urge to go to him, to ask what was wrong. He looked up, and she finally caught his eye. Smiling, she began to remove her arm from her mother's, intent on going to speak with him, until she realized she could not.

Not just because they weren't supposed to continue their association in public, but because he turned and stalked away from the Ring. He'd seen that she was going to move toward him and had removed himself.

She ought to be grateful, but was instead disappointed. It seemed she would need to learn to live with that. As well as seeing a woman on his arm, knowing that would never be her.

CHAPTER 12

*L*azarus arrived at the park just before five. He wanted to catch Gwen the moment she approached the Ring. Anticipation rushed through him, along with apprehension and anxiety. What if she really didn't feel anything for him beyond friendship?

Perhaps that was precisely what he deserved. After years of roguish behavior, he'd finally fallen in love. It would serve him right for it not to be reciprocated.

"Somerton?"

Lazarus turned toward the feminine voice. For a moment, he was nonplussed, as he didn't recognize the young lady who'd spoken.

She moved closer, her lips curving into an almost nervous smile. "We met at Lord Haverstock's fox-hunting party—he is my grandfather."

Back in November, Lazarus had attended the party, though he hated fox hunting. He suddenly recalled her. "Yes, I remember now. How pleasant to see you."

"I hope you will continue to think that after you hear what I need to say. I do apologize it's taken me so long to approach you, but I've only just come to London this week. I've been ill for some time."

"I'm sorry to hear that." Lazarus tensed as he wondered what she could possibly reveal that would make things unpleasant. "I hope you are well recovered."

"Not entirely, but I will be in a matter of months." She took a breath, and Lazarus could see her pulse working along her slender throat. "I will be cured when I deliver the babe you gave me."

The *what*? The world tilted sideways. Lazarus blinked as a crushing sound roared in his ears. He never dawdled like that with young unmarried women. He just did *not*. "That's not possible," he managed, his voice sounding as though he were drowning and could not get enough air.

"I assure you it is." Her lip quivered, and she glanced away briefly. "Do you not recall our night together?"

Lazarus searched his memory for any time he'd spent with her. He'd probably flirted with her, but he didn't actually recall. Lazarus would never have gone further with her—she was the granddaughter of the party host! He wouldn't even have dared a kiss.

He thought of the week-long party, but could not summon a single specific recollection of her. A few nights had been fairly boisterous. Was it possible they'd had an interaction and he didn't remember?

No, he hadn't been that deep into his cups. Except for one night. He and Shefford had gone to a pub in the village one night and drunk an astonishing amount of ale. Then the owner had pulled out a cask of whisky he'd smuggled from Scotland, and they'd proceeded to become mindlessly incapacitated. Had something happened after they'd returned to the house?

The following morning, Lazarus had felt absolutely horrid. He'd stayed in his room until well into the afternoon.

He didn't remember anything out of the ordinary, save the excessive amount of drink he'd imbibed. Perhaps Shefford remembered something.

"I do not recall any specific meeting between us," he whispered, his body shaking. "Are you certain it was me?"

Her eyes rounded, then narrowed. "Of course I am. You are the only man I've…been with. I suppose I shouldn't be surprised that I don't stand out to a man like you. I am likely just one of an endless list of conquests."

Conquests? Lazarus didn't go about debauching his way through house parties. He carried on discreet liaisons with widows, and the occasional married lady, though that had been when he was much younger.

"I am not a scoundrel, Miss…" Hell, he didn't even recall her last name. It wasn't Haverstock or even Haverstock's surname. If he recalled, her mother was Haverstock's daughter.

"Miss Melissa Worsley."

"I do not…become intimate with young unmarried ladies. Not ever." He couldn't help thinking of Gwen, how he'd considered it with her. But he wouldn't have done it, would he? His heart twisted. Gwen would hate him if she heard this news.

"Clearly you did," she insisted. "I am not mistaken, so please do me the courtesy of not asking if I'm certain again."

"I swear, I could not have done this. I am no blackguard." It was all Lazarus could think to say. He was a rogue, but he wasn't completely immoral or cruel.

She lifted her chin and stared into his eyes. "Prove it, then."

"How do you—" He was going to ask how he could do that, but he knew the answer. She'd presented herself to him after some months carrying a child. "Why didn't you inform me sooner?" The world around him still felt unsteady. It was as if the edges were fraying, or he was standing in a watercolor that wasn't yet dry.

"As I said, I was ill."

"Do your parents know of your condition?" he managed to ask.

"My mother does, but she has not told my father or my grandfather. Our hope is that you will agree to an immediate marriage."

Frustration clawed at him. His vision began to tunnel, making him feel trapped, which he was. "The babe will be born in an inordinately short amount of time."

"We will remove to the country and keep the timing of the birth vague," she replied with an alarming confidence. "I and the babe will remain there for a year or more. In time, people will not notice such things. And if my family does, they won't say anything for we will be wed, and the babe's parentage will be secure."

She had it all worked out rather neatly. This made Lazarus slightly suspicious. And incredibly queasy.

"If you refuse me, I will be ruined." She worried her hands together and looked down at the ground. "I hate that this happened. I am so angry with myself. I was just so smitten with you." She met his gaze once more, and there were tears in her pretty blue eyes. "But this is my fault. I should never have allowed myself to be alone with a man, let alone one with a reputation like yours. I just didn't believe you would take things as far as they went."

Dear God, was he a monster? "I didn't force you, did I?" Now the world was spinning. Lazarus would have grabbed a tree for support if one had been within reach.

She shook her head. "No, it was…nice."

Lazarus still didn't remember a thing. "Was I inebriated?"

Her shoulder lifted slightly. "You may have been, but I don't have much experience with that."

He would have staked his entire fortune on not being able to perform in bed under the influence of that much alcohol, but since he couldn't remember a thing, what did he know?

"We don't have a surplus of time," she said. "I can't hide the babe much longer." She moved her hand gently along her abdomen, and he could make out the gentle curve beneath her gown.

Coughing as he choked on nothing but air, Lazarus averted his gaze. Was that his child growing inside her? He simply couldn't believe it. But she was so certain. And her emotions so very real.

She squared her shoulders. "I don't want to force you, but I will if I must. I'll tell my father and my grandfather, and they will force you to marry me. It will be a terrible scandal. Surely you don't want that."

He thought of his mother, his grandmother, his sisters, his cousin Tamsin… Gwen. He couldn't subject them to a scandal like this. And he especially didn't want Gwen to hear of his behavior. He could bear contempt from anyone except her.

His brain worked to grab something. Anything. "I can't leave London. I've responsibilities in the Lords." His speech was coming up soon!

"You must, or you will become the subject of great disdain —in the Lords and everywhere else." She paused, her gaze softening. "I can see you are greatly disturbed by my news, and I do understand. I sympathize. I was shocked when I learned what had happened, and it took me a long time to accept it. I suppose being ill was a distraction from the reality of the situation. However, we cannot ignore it, though I do apologize I wasn't able to inform you sooner. Now, you won't have much time to become accustomed to being a husband and a father."

A husband *and* a father. With a woman whose name he

hadn't even known, and he couldn't even recall bedding. He barely remembered flirting with her. Indeed, there was nothing remarkable about her that came to his mind.

"I'll give you time to consider everything I've said," she said softly. "I'll expect to hear from you tomorrow. No later than the day after."

"Thank you," he croaked.

"If you don't call on me before Monday, I'll have to tell my father and grandfather the truth."

He nodded. "I understand."

She pivoted and returned to a small group of people, none of whom he recognized. One of them was an older version of her, and she looked directly at Lazarus, her lips pursed. That had to be her mother.

Lazarus abruptly turned. He wondered if he might be sick.

His gaze met Gwen's some distance away. She smiled at him, then looked as if she might head in his direction.

He could *not* see her. They'd agreed to end their association, but even if they hadn't, he was in no condition to converse with her. He didn't want to stain her with his shameful presence.

Turning, he stalked toward the Grosvenor Gate, walking as quickly as possible without breaking into a run, which he dearly wanted to do. Indeed, he wanted to run straight out of London directly to Winterstoke in Somerset, where he would hide under the bed as he used to do when he was a boy trying to escape his older sisters.

How had this day gone from imminently brilliant to horrifically awful? He'd walked into the park hoping to see the woman he loved, to tell her how he was ready to put aside every bit of roguishness, except that which he would reserve entirely for her. He'd yearned to see his love reflected in her gaze, and her eager acceptance to his proposal of marriage.

But now that dream was gone. It had crumbled completely and irrevocably to ash. There was no way he could be with Gwen. The piece of him he feared he would lose was, in fact, all of him.

~

Though Gwen had been at the Phoenix Club ball for an hour, she had yet to see Lazarus. Perhaps he wasn't coming tonight. She hated that she now had to settle for seeing him from afar. It wasn't fair.

But what more did she want?

At least to help him with his reading and to prepare for his speech. She felt as though she'd let him down, and that was the last thing she would ever want to do.

She saw that Min and Ellis had arrived. They were just moving into the ballroom from the ladies' side. Min's mother was with them, but she immediately went to speak with someone. Gwen's own mother was a few feet away chatting with a couple of her friends.

Gwen caught Min's and Ellis's attention, and they made their way to her side. Min looked especially pretty in a pink gown decorated with rows of silk roses near the hem.

"Have we missed anything so far?" Min asked.

"I danced with Mr. Fortescue, and I'm proud to say I only made one tiny error."

They both looked at Gwen with sheer happiness. "That's so wonderful!" Ellis exclaimed. "You must be feeling quite accomplished."

"It seems your new dancing master has had an impact," Min said.

Gwen shuddered. "Hardly. I think I performed better this

evening out of spite. I want to prove to my mother that I don't need more lessons. I will definitely not be seeing Mr. Tremblay again."

"But why not?" Min asked. "He's so highly recommended. And devilish handsome," she added with a wink and a smile.

"Ugh," Gwen groaned. "He's also very free with his hands. I did not care for the way he 'instructed' me. He always found it necessary to hold me longer than appropriate, or his touch would stray to my backside or my hip or, once, the underside of my breast. It was most distressing. He seemed to be purposely provoking me because he was also flirtatious in his eye contact and the way he spoke to me. I do think he was disappointed when I did not flirt back."

"I did hear he was charming," Min said, frowning. "And charming can often mean flirtatious. But it sounds as though he's aggressive about it." Her nose wrinkled with distaste. "How perfectly awful."

"I've heard of more than one young lady falling in love with him." Ellis rolled her eyes. "Or so they claim. I suspect it's infatuation, not love."

"I'm sure you're right," Min agreed. She looked to Gwen. "You won't be having lessons with him any longer?"

"No. Thankfully, my mother allowed me to terminate them after I explained my concerns. I can't imagine I'm the only student who found him offensive." She shrugged. "I'm just glad I won't be seeing him anymore. I do wish I could prevent him from exerting his odious behavior on other young ladies, but it's not as if I can publicly share my experience so others can decide if they wish to hire him."

"That would be incredibly useful, though, wouldn't it?" Ellis mused. "A published record of people and places you could recommend."

Min nodded. "A numbered rating would be most helpful. You could give Mr. Tremblay a negative number."

They all laughed, and Gwen was most grateful for her friends. "I will also ask my mother if she will refrain from recommending him. Thank you for the laugh. I needed it."

"I did notice a slight furrow in your brow when we arrived," Min said. "What's troubling you?"

It wasn't that Gwen didn't want to tell them. She just didn't want to sound as though she were whinging. Furthermore, she couldn't tell them about the cessation of her tutoring lessons with Lazarus because they didn't know about those. Nor could she inform them since it involved a secret that wasn't hers to share. "I was looking for Somerton. I caught his eye in the park earlier, to wave and perhaps exchange a few words, but he turned away from me and left."

"Perhaps he had an appointment," Min suggested.

Gwen sighed, wishing things were different but not entirely sure what she wanted them to be. "I suppose that's possible."

Ellis met her gaze with sympathy. "You seem disappointed. Is there any chance you've developed a tendre for him?"

Oh dear. How had Gwen not seen that? There seemed more than a chance. "I think I may have," she whispered. "But there's nothing to be done about it."

"I should think not," Min said, briefly touching Gwen's arm. "He's a rogue, and there are nice, nonrogue gentlemen who are interested in courting you."

Min was right, but it didn't erase the feelings Gwen now realized she had for Lazarus. Feelings that were not reciprocated.

"He was very kind to help me in my moment of need." Gwen would always remember the way he'd swooped in and rescued her after the debacle with Eberforce at Almack's. He'd behaved like anything other than a rogue when he'd saved her from one.

"He was." Min adjusted one of the petals on her gown. "He's not the worst sort of rogue, just not a man you would wed, unfortunately."

Gwen wasn't sure she agreed. After all, he was Tamsin's cousin. In fact, several of them were related to "rogues," including Gwen and Min, whose brothers, particularly Min's, definitely resided in that category.

Lazarus had been attentive and sweet. And he'd revealed a part of himself to her that he'd kept hidden. How could she not feel a special connection to him?

Still, he'd broken things off with her entirely. He hadn't even responded to her sending the reading exercise. Then today in the park, he'd been with another young woman. Looking roguish.

Actually, he hadn't appeared happy. Gwen wasn't sure what was going on, but it hadn't seemed to be a flirtatious encounter. Or was that merely her hoping it wasn't?

"I can see he's affected you," Ellis said. "I'm sorry he's treated you callously."

Gwen sprung to his defense. "He hasn't. He doesn't know how I feel. I didn't even realize it myself until just now."

Min's brows rose. "You aren't going to tell him, are you? I don't think any good can come from that." Her gaze softened with sympathy. "Why not focus on the gentlemen who wish to court you?"

That was the sensible thing, of course. "I am trying to. As I said, I danced with Mr. Fortescue and I'm due to dance with Lord Mayhew, though I think he's a little old."

"He also has children," Min noted. "He tried to court me last year, but I wasn't ready to be a mother. I'm still not, so it's good I'm in no danger of that," she added with a light laugh.

"Don't look now, but here comes Lord Mayhew," Ellis said. Tall with angular features, Lord Mayhew was in his middle thirties. His wife had died two years earlier, leaving him with three children.

"We aren't due to dance yet," Gwen murmured.

The three of them curtsied as he arrived. He glanced toward Gwen with a faint smile, ignored Ellis entirely, and fixed his attention on Min. "Lady Minerva, would you honor me by dancing with me for the next set?"

"Certainly," Min said with a smile that said she was not enthused. Taking his arm, she looked back at Gwen and Ellis as she moved away, and quickly stuck out her tongue while wrinkling her nose.

They laughed. "Poor Min," Ellis said. "Now she's dancing with men she's already refused."

"I'm surprised he would ask her if she declined his suit last year."

"It's possible he sees her fortunes may have changed and thinks his chances are renewed." Ellis lifted a shoulder. "These are problems I thankfully never have to worry about."

At twenty-five, she was old enough to be on the shelf, but could one be on the shelf if one hadn't really ever participated in the Marriage Mart? Gwen asked a question that had long lingered at the back of her mind. "What will you do when—or if—Min weds?"

"Ask her to hire me as her paid companion?" she responded with a wide smile. "I imagine I will find employment, which I actually look forward to."

"As a paid companion?"

"I'd rather do something that requires more intellect. In truth, I would love to be someone's secretary," she said rather wistfully.

"You'd be wonderful." Gwen and she had conversed at length on a great many subjects. Ellis had a keen mind and perhaps read nearly as much as Gwen.

"Thank you. I can't imagine I'll ever have the opportunity,

but I would dearly love it." She held Gwen's gaze. "I think you should tell Somerton how you feel."

Gwen stared at her. "You do?"

"What's the worst that could happen? He tells you he doesn't feel the same. But at least you know for sure. That way, there is no room for regret."

"I'd also just like to…share how I feel with him. We'd become friends." She couldn't explain the ways in which they'd bonded. Helping him improve his reading had encouraged a level of intimacy that perhaps went beyond friendship.

Ellis smiled. "That's lovely. So you will?"

"I think so." But how to do it since they weren't supposed to publicly associate? Perhaps she could steal a moment or two with him tonight. If he even came to the ball. She would need an alternative plan.

Would he meet her at Tamsin's again if she asked? She could send a note first thing in the morning and request they meet tomorrow afternoon.

"I can see you are planning something already," Ellis said, her eyes twinkling.

Gwen laughed. "I can't help myself. Thank you for your counsel. I deeply appreciate it."

What exactly did she intend to say? She wasn't sure. Thankfully, she had all night and tomorrow morning to think of it. But as soon as she got home, she would draft another reading exercise so she could give that to him when they met. Or perhaps she would send it with the letter asking him to meet.

Just in case he said no.

What if he refused her request?

She wouldn't think about that. She would simply say she needed to see him, and could he please meet her at the Drox-fords' house at two.

If he did indeed decline her invitation, that would need to be the end of it. She wasn't going to write him a note saying she had romantic feelings for him.

Was she in love? Gwen had no idea what that felt like and wasn't ready to commit to something so…big.

Not yet.

Just admitting that she had a tendre for him was a huge step. He was not the sort of man she should want or who would want her.

Nevertheless, she wanted him, his roguery be damned.

CHAPTER 13

*A*fter leaving the park, Lazarus had spent a few hours in a dither. Closeting himself in his study, he'd drunk two glasses of whisky. Almost two glasses. He'd stopped because it wouldn't serve him to have a clouded mind. He needed a plan, and he needed it fast.

He realized he also needed help.

Which was how he found himself knocking on Droxford's door. Not only was he the best person to advise him—he would keep an even head—but he was likely the only one home this evening. Shefford and Price and likely Keele would be at the Phoenix Club assembly or someplace else. And Wellesbourne had his hands full with a new child.

Droxford's butler admitted him and a few minutes later showed him to the study where the baron was working. "Evening, Somerton," Droxford said, standing from behind his desk. "This is a surprise. Shouldn't you be at the Phoenix Club?"

"I don't go out *every* night." Actually, he did practically, so to act as though he didn't was a bit disingenuous. But he wasn't here to discuss his social activities. "I am in need of advice on a very…delicate matter."

Droxford's brows shot up. "I see. Let us sit." He gestured to a pair of chairs angled near the hearth. "Do you want a drink?"

Lazarus shook his head. "No. I've had enough whisky." He sat down on the edge of the chair, nervous energy coursing through him.

"It's a whisky problem, then." Droxford sat opposite him. "Whatever you tell me will be kept between us."

"Thank you. I appreciate that more than I can say." Lazarus exhaled as he ran his hand through his hair. Too late, he realized he'd ruined his valet's careful styling, but it wasn't as if he were going anywhere else. And surely Droxford didn't care if he appeared impeccable or not.

Hell, Lazarus was prevaricating in his own bloody mind. He met his friend's gaze. "A woman I met at a fox-hunting party says I got her with child. I don't remember taking her to bed. I don't even remember kissing her. And I definitely don't remember wanting to do either of those things, let alone actually doing them." He'd spoken more quickly with each statement, a sort of panic rising within him.

"That is…troubling. But you recall her from the party?"

"I do. She is the granddaughter of the host."

"I received an invitation to this party, I think, though I declined," Droxford said. "Lord Haverstock's fox-hunting party?" At Lazarus's nod, he blew out a breath. "I would not want to run afoul of Haverstock. His temper is quite nasty. I got into a rather vicious argument with him once about the impact of the war on the price of food, and he was most belligerent in his ignorance."

Lazarus only knew him socially. That was because until recently, Lazarus hadn't been seriously engaged in his position in Parliament. Hearing this made his stomach knot. "That is not encouraging."

"Does he know about the babe?" Droxford asked.

"No, nor does her father. Her mother does, however." Lazarus thought of the woman's icy glare in the park that afternoon. Perhaps the entire family had horrible tempers.

"This party was, what, last November?" Droxford flattened his lips. "Why is she only telling you now?"

"She's been ill. Or so she says."

"You don't believe her?"

"I'm not inclined to believe any of her claims. Drox, *I don't remember fucking her.*"

Droxford's brows rose again.

"My apologies," Lazarus murmured. He'd forgotten that Droxford didn't really curse. He'd never once, as far as Lazarus could recall, uttered any version of the word *fuck*.

"I don't mind swearing. I just rarely do it because my father beat it into me that such words came from the devil's mouth." Droxford sniffed. "So, you don't recall bedding her, and you think she may be lying. I do find it odd that she waited so long to approach you, ill or not. Surely her mother could have spoken to you."

Lazarus hadn't considered that. "She's given me until Monday to make my offer of marriage. If I don't, she'll tell her father and grandfather."

"Nothing like a little extortion to make one's story more believable." Droxford scowled. "Why would she not tell them straightaway?"

"She is trying to cover up the pregnancy entirely. She suggested we remove to the country after we are wed—with due haste—until well after the child is born so we can be vague about the timing of its arrival."

"She has a plan," Droxford noted.

"I thought the same thing."

"And you are her pawn." Droxford's brow creased into deep furrows. "Are you prepared to marry her?"

"I don't want to." Lazarus felt hopeless.

"But would it be the worst thing? You will need to marry at some point, yes?"

"Yes. But not her. I don't know her. I don't even find her attractive." Because as of recently, no one appealed to him aside from a sable-haired, dark-eyed beauty who tripped over her own feet and whose laugh sounded like a sunbeam. If they had sound.

"Let us talk through what will happen if you refuse to marry her. She will tell her father and grandfather. I can guarantee her grandfather will try to force the marriage. He may even bend the prince regent's ear and try to convince him to compel you."

Lazarus felt queasy. "He can't make me marry her."

"No, but he can end your life as you know it. You won't be invited anywhere. Your position in the Lords would be compromised—in that you would become largely ineffective as many members will refuse to associate with you. And of course, your family would be affected."

His mother. His sisters. Their husbands. Their *children*.

"Your wife," Lazarus whispered, horrified that this terrible situation could touch sweet Tamsin, who'd so recently found happiness.

"Perhaps," Droxford said with a grimace. "I won't lie. I think you may just need to marry this woman. Unless, are you certain you didn't bed her?"

"No, I'm *not* certain." Lazarus leaned one elbow on the arm of the chair. "I went to a pub with Sheff one night, and we got so drunk, I don't remember a thing. I don't even know how we ended up back at the estate. I was completely worthless the following day. And I think we left the day after that."

"Does Sheff remember anything?"

Of course Lazarus should ask. He'd thought of Shefford in the park earlier and should have gone directly to his apartment at the Albany. "I'll find out." Lazarus would hunt him down later.

"I propose you take the next couple of days to try to determine the truth. She is definitely expecting?" Droxford shook his head. "I hate asking that."

"I know. I hated thinking it. She was careful to show me her abdomen."

"Well then, you try to discern if it really could have been you. Perhaps Sheff will be able to provide you with an alibi."

God, that would be lucky.

"But you also need to consider what you'll do if presented with proof that you did, in fact, bed her. You've no idea what Sheff remembers."

Lazarus's momentary excitement vanished. He couldn't marry Miss Worsley. Not just because he didn't want to, but because he was in love with Gwen. He wanted to marry *her*.

But if he refused to wed Miss Worsley, and her family told everyone he was the father of her child, Lazarus wouldn't be able to marry Gwen. She wouldn't want him. He wasn't even sure she wanted him now. He was already a *rogue*. Miss Worsley's allegations made him out to be a complete blackguard. He wouldn't be fit to be anyone's husband.

How had he ever thought he was good enough for Gwen? He'd behaved poorly with her, giving in to his baser desires. Never mind his past transgressions, which perhaps included fathering a child on an innocent young lady.

"I can see this weighs heavily on you," Droxford said with

sympathy. "I'm sorry this has happened. I hope Sheff is able to help."

"I hope so too." Lazarus got slowly to his feet. "I appreciate your counsel, Drox."

"I wish I could do more. Hopefully, all will turn out right." He clasped Lazarus's shoulder in a rare show of support or perhaps even affection.

"Thank you for your discretion. You're a good friend."

"We are all in need of discretion at one time or another," Droxford said cryptically. "That's what friends are for."

Lazarus nodded, then departed in search of Shefford. He prayed his friend hadn't been as inebriated that night and could remember what happened. If he didn't, Lazarus feared he was ruined.

❧

Though Gwen had not received a response to her invitation from Lazarus, she went to Tamsin's anyway, hoping he would come. She hadn't included the reading exercise in the note to Lazarus because she hadn't finished it yet. But it was now complete and tucked in her pocket.

Tamsin received her in the drawing room upstairs. "I got your note, of course," she said without preamble, bringing Gwen to sit with her on the settee.

Gwen had also dispatched a missive to Tamsin that morning saying she needed to meet Lazarus at her house that afternoon. "Thank you for letting me descend upon you with little notice. And for not being angry with me for not even really asking." She grimaced faintly.

"There is no need to thank me," Tamsin assured her. "Your note said you needed to speak with Somerton about a matter of urgency. Is everything all right?"

"I hope it will be," Gwen said. "I find I don't want our association to be over. In fact, I'd rather it continued. Perhaps in a more…intimate manner."

Tamsin's eyes rounded. "Oh! Has something happened since you kissed him at the literary salon?"

"I've realized I have developed a tendre for him," Gwen confessed. "I'm rather smitten, to be honest." She felt warmth in her cheeks, but didn't care. It wasn't from embarrassment, but from the excitement of sharing that with one of her dearest friends. "How did you know you had feelings for Droxford? I know it wasn't before you wed, given the manner in which you had to marry."

"Actually, I had started to fall for him by then," Tamsin said with a shy smile. "I didn't realize it at the time, but my father's proposal that I wed followed by my acquaintance with Isaac showed me an enticing future I hadn't considered. I know Isaac appears brusque and brooding, but to me, he has always been drily witty and exceptionally caring. Almost from the moment we became acquainted, he made me feel protected and important. He was the first person outside my family and my closest friends who really saw me, if that makes sense."

"It does, actually. I feel that way about Lazarus. He doesn't care that I can't dance or will likely spill a drink on his favorite waistcoat. And when he planned that special evening, taking me to the literary salon…" Gwen couldn't help grinning. "Well, that was definitely when I began to feel differently about him."

Tamsin grinned too. "That's so lovely."

But Gwen sobered rather quickly. "I just don't know if he feels the same. I mean, he's a rogue. He's never given any indication that he wants to marry."

"Neither did Isaac. Even after we were wed," Tamsin added wryly. "If you recall, he wanted a marriage in name only. I can't imagine my cousin would want that, however. Particularly since you've already kissed. You are way ahead of where Isaac and I were."

"I know you and Lazarus aren't close, but have you never heard him discuss marriage?" Gwen asked. Her mother's counsel, that Lazarus wouldn't be a good husband, lingered in the back of her mind, but while Gwen wanted to please her parents, she also couldn't deny her own feelings. "I assume he'll have to wed at some point. Doesn't he need an heir?"

"Yes, and while my grandmother has laughingly said he's sowing his oats, she did indicate at Christmas that it's time he settled down. My aunt—his mother—agrees and had hoped he would take a bride this Season." Tamsin lifted a shoulder. "You never know what will happen. Are you planning to tell him how you feel? Is that why you wanted to see him today?"

Gwen nodded. "But I'm so nervous. What if he laughs at me?"

"He won't! And if he does, I'll kick him. Repeatedly." Tamsin patted Gwen's hand and gave her an encouraging nod. "Perhaps he feels the same about you and he will make his mother and our grandmother happy by marrying you."

"I'm not sure I dare believe that," Gwen whispered.

The butler appeared in the doorway and announced the arrival of Lord Somerton. Gwen's insides curled into tight, little knots. Her heart beat a rapid pace.

"Show him to the library," Tamsin said. When the butler departed, she looked to Gwen. "You've gone pale. Pinch your cheeks before you see him. Or think of kissing him. That'll put some color in your face." She smiled, and Gwen laughed.

"Thank you."

They stood together, and Tamsin said she would be here afterward, no matter what happened.

Then Gwen went downstairs to the library, walking alternately fast and then slow as she couldn't quite decide if she was excited for the coming conversation or dreading the result.

As she walked into the library, her breath caught. Had he somehow become more handsome since the day before? His blond hair was elegantly styled and his clothing superb. He looked as if he'd walked straight off a fashion plate.

But he wasn't smiling. Indeed, his face looked a bit drawn. Was something wrong?

"You received my note," Gwen said tentatively, feeing incredibly nervous.

"Yes. That is why I am here, though this is not something we should be doing. However, you said it was urgent."

"Did you receive the writing exercise I sent you the other day?" she asked hopefully.

He exhaled. "Yes. I apologize for not responding. It was most helpful. You are a wonder." He smiled faintly, and Gwen relaxed a little.

She pulled the new exercise she'd made from her pocket. "I've another one for you." She moved closer to him and held the folded parchment out.

He reached for it, clasping the proffered edge, while she held the other side. Their gazes met.

"Thank you," he murmured, taking the paper and tucking it into a pocket in his coat. "Is this why you wanted to see me? You could have sent it like you did the first one. I promise I'll respond in future."

"I appreciate that," she said. "But that isn't why I wanted to see you. I, um, I missed you."

His jaw seemed to tighten.

When he didn't respond, she gathered her courage and went on. "I saw you in the park yesterday. I thought you saw me, but then you turned and walked away."

"I did see you." He sounded almost...weary? "You looked as if you were going to come and speak to me, but I told you we can't be publicly associated any longer. How would that look if you approached me at the park?" He didn't sound angry, but there was some underlying emotion weighting his words.

"I realize that, which is why I wanted to see you. I don't want to not be able to speak with you or spend time with you. We'd become close, hadn't we?" She waited for him to say something or for his expression to change. When he remained stoic, Gwen began to worry that this would go very badly. Perhaps the worst that could happen was about to.

"I miss that closeness," Gwen said, knowing this was her only chance to tell him how she felt. "My mother has asked me which gentleman I am hoping will offer for me, and I realized that the only one I want is you."

Lazarus's nostrils flared. "You can't want that." His voice was low, nearly a growl.

"Why not?"

"Because you know what kind of man I am."

"Yes. The man I am in lo—"

He snaked his arm around her waist and pulled her against him. "*Don't* say it. You can't feel that way about me. I won't permit it."

She looked up in the firestorm of his eyes and ached at whatever he was battling. Was it that he didn't think he was good enough for her?

"What about what I will permit?" She pressed against him and put her arms around his neck.

He muttered something that sounded as though it may have been a curse just before his mouth claimed hers in a blistering kiss. Gwen's soul sang as his tongue swept along hers. She clutched him tightly, never wanting to let go. If this moment could last into eternity, she would be happy.

His hand moved lower, to her backside, bringing her pelvis in direct contact with his—nearly, for he was taller than her by several inches. This was nothing like the awful ways in which Tremblay had groped her. Lazarus caressed her and held her with a mix of care and unfettered desire. She felt both wanton and safe, as if this was exactly where she wanted and needed to be—in Lazarus's arms.

He kissed along her jaw then he abruptly stepped away, his breath coming fast. "I'm sorry for overstepping."

"I clearly didn't mind. I invited you to kiss me. Indeed, I invite you to do whatever you wish with me." *Please, do that,* she internally begged.

He wiped his palm over his mouth. "I can't be with you like this. Or in any other way."

He'd said "can't," not that he didn't want to. "Why not?"

"Because you deserve far better, for one. Beyond that, there are...reasons I can't explain." He took a deep breath. "Perhaps in time, things will be different."

"Are you asking me to wait? I will." She would wait as long as he asked. That had to break a rogue rule—or several—but she didn't care. She was gleefully throwing them all aside for a chance with this magnificent rogue. And that *definitely* broke a rogue rule: never give a rogue a chance.

"No, I can't ask that—or anything else of you."

"I wish you would explain," Gwen said. "You can tell me."

"There's nothing to tell." Now he sounded cold. "I am a rogue, and you know that. You are far better off without me. Choose one of your other gentlemen. They will all make you far happier than I ever could."

"I don't agree," she said quietly.

He moved toward the door. "If you ask to see me again, I won't come." He kept his back to her. "I do appreciate your reading exercises, though I will understand if you choose to stop sending them."

"I won't. I will always help you, Lazarus." Gwen's heart was breaking. This was worse than she'd expected. He wasn't even saying he didn't care about her, just that he wasn't good enough for her. That should be her choice, not his.

But there was something else. Something pulling at him. Something he would not reveal.

He left without saying anything more. Gwen wobbled on shaky legs to sit in a chair. She didn't cry, though she was devastated. She just felt…hollow.

Tamsin came in and rushed to sit near Gwen. "What happened? You don't look happy."

"He urged me to choose someone else."

"He doesn't reciprocate your feelings, then?" Tamsin's brow creased.

"He says he isn't good enough for me, but he also mentioned there were reasons he couldn't be with me. Though, he did not explain what those are. I suppose he just means that his reputation prevents him from doing so." Gwen shook her head. "I don't know."

Tamsin touched Gwen's hand. "I'm so sorry. What can I do?"

"Nothing. I don't think there's anything to be done." Gwen summoned a grateful smile for her sweet friend. "I think I need to take a respite from the whirl of the Season. For a few days. Or perhaps a week."

"Isn't there an important ball tonight?" Tamsin asked. "A friend of your father's?"

Blast, that was true. "After tonight, then." Gwen was suddenly tired of all the effort it took to be marriageable. She wanted time with her books. "I wonder if we could also attend a literary salon on Monday. I'll send Jo a note."

"Actually, I just received one from her while you were

speaking with Somerton. I have an invitation to attend on Monday. I will only go, however, if you accompany me."

Gwen's answering smile was genuine. "That would be lovely."

She may not have won Lazarus, but at least she had books. Beautiful, trustworthy, faithful books.

CHAPTER 14

Gulping air as he strode away from the Droxfords' house, Lazarus tried not to think of the gut-wrenching look of disappointment on Gwen's face as he'd told her that he couldn't be with her. He'd considered telling her the truth, but what would that solve? Absolutely nothing. True or not, the existence of the allegation would ensure Gwen never looked at him with affection again.

Or love.

God, she'd tried to tell him that she loved him. He nearly doubled over as he walked.

How was it possible that he'd finally found love, where he'd least expected it, and couldn't embrace it with both hands? Fury raged through him—entirely directed at himself.

Even if he hadn't actually bedded Miss Worsley, he'd put himself into a position where it was not only possible but likely. If he were an upstanding gentleman with a pristine reputation, this would not be happening.

He'd blithely sauntered his way through life thinking his behavior wasn't that bad. He toed the line, but never crossed it. But now he may have done the unthinkable, and worse, he didn't even remember.

Lazarus made his way to Piccadilly. He dearly hoped Shefford would finally be at home. He hadn't been last night, nor had he been at any of their regular haunts. And he hadn't been home earlier today either. It would be just Lazarus's luck if he'd left town for a few days, which would not be unheard of.

He could only pray that Shefford recalled something of that night last November. If he did not, Lazarus wasn't sure what to do next. Aside from marry Miss Worsley and become father to her child. The world felt as if it were closing in around him.

Shefford's valet opened the door. He appeared unsurprised to see Lazarus for the third time in less than a day. Indeed, Lazarus didn't have to utter a word before the valet said, "His lordship is present now. I informed him you would be calling at some point this afternoon. He'll receive you in his study."

"Thank you, Spears." Lazarus practically ran to the study, not that he needed to since the apartment wasn't terribly large.

"Ah, there you are again," Shefford said. He wore a banyan over a pair of pantaloons, and his hair was wet, indicating he'd just bathed.

"Here *you* are," Lazarus huffed. "Finally."

"What the devil has you so distressed?" Shefford, who reclined on a chaise with a newspaper, gestured for Lazarus to take a chair.

Instead of sitting, Lazarus paced. "Do you recall that fox-hunting party we attended in November?" He glanced toward Shefford, who set his paper on the floor next to the chaise and swung his legs down to sit upright.

"Haverstock's, yes?"

"His granddaughter confronted me in the park yesterday and accused me of fathering her unborn child." Damn, but it did not get easier to share that information, and each time he said it, Lazarus felt even more disgusted.

Shefford's jaw dropped. "The hell she did."

"Do you remember her? I barely did."

Furrows lined Shefford's brow as he considered the question. "Red hair?"

"Blondish, I think." Lazarus hadn't been able to tell beneath her hat. He also hadn't been looking at her closely. His mind had been too occupied with trying to make sense of her claims.

"Did she say when this happened?"

"No, but it could only be the night we went to the inn. I remember the other nights of the party, and I was not with her. On the second night, I had an enjoyable interlude with Lad—" Lazarus cut himself off for the sake of keeping the lady's identity secret. "Never mind who. I was occupied that evening, at least for a time, in the orangery. But I don't remember the night we went to the inn—that was the second to the last night."

"That was a hell of an evening." Shefford wiped his hand down his face. "We drank a ridiculous amount of ale, then the innkeeper brought out that smuggled whisky. You did drink more of it than I did."

Lazarus hoped that meant Shefford remembered more of what happened. "What did we do that night?"

"Besides drink? There were a pair of eager women at the inn, and we spent some time with them."

Lazarus froze, his mind working furiously. He vaguely recalled a high-pitched, feminine laugh and rouged lips. He'd said something about her not leaving rings of red on his cock. He groaned at how terrible that sounded. Honestly, so much of his past behavior was incredibly repulsive to him now. Not the least of which was potentially getting a young lady with child.

But perhaps he really hadn't. It would be a relief to discover that was true, but it still didn't excuse the fact that he couldn't say for certain.

"How long?" Lazarus asked. "All night?"

"No. I slept for a while. I've no idea what you did, but you were still quite groggy when we departed before dawn. That was when we returned to Haverstock Hall."

"So, we weren't even at the house most of the night," Lazarus said, relaxing slightly for the first time since he'd encountered Melissa at the park.

Shefford shook his head. He rested his elbow on his knee and put his chin on his hand. "And I have to say, I can't think you were in any condition to fornicate when you returned to your bed."

"I had the same thought, but it helps to know this timeline."

"What will you do?" Shefford asked.

"She's given me until Monday to make an offer of marriage. If I do not, she'll tell her father and grandfather she is with child and that I am the father."

Shefford lifted his head and took his elbow from his knee. "They don't know? Furthermore, why didn't she tell you before now?"

"She said she's been ill, but her mother knew and could have informed me." Lazarus recalled Droxford's excellent point on that matter.

"Why would she accuse you of this?"

"All I can think is that the real father is someone she can't marry. A footman or someone inappropriate."

"A married man," Shefford said with an incredibly derogative tone, his lip curling.

Lazarus suspected he understood the reason for his

friend's disdain. His father carried on with other women to an excessive degree. It was possible, if not probable, that he'd impregnated an innocent such as Miss Worsley. "I hope that isn't what happened to her," Lazarus said softly. "I do sympathize with her situation, but I truly don't think I am the father."

"I can't imagine you are; however, if she tells people, you will then have to fight against rumor and innuendo."

"Don't we already do that by the nature of our reputations?" Lazarus asked, finally dropping into a chair. He'd barely slept last night, and he was exhausted.

"I suppose, but no one is out there saying we are fathering children out of wedlock with the granddaughter of a viscount."

Lazarus flinched as if he'd taken a physical blow. "I may be rakish, but that is beyond the pale."

"Since it's likely you didn't even do it, you can't marry her."

"I don't *want* to marry her. But I suspect if I tell her this, she'll insist it was me. She needs to marry in haste, and why not snare a viscount?"

"While I also sympathize with her predicament, this is an awful way to keep herself from ruin. She made a mistake."

"What if she didn't?" Lazarus said, feeling sorry for the young lady. "Plenty of women are coerced. Or worse."

Shefford pressed his lips together. "I would hope that hasn't happened here, but perhaps you should find out. In the meantime, I am happy to speak on your behalf. I will also send word to the innkeeper and ask him to provide an alibi for you. In fact, I'll send someone who can make the trip there and back with extreme haste."

Lazarus sagged against the back of the chair. "You would do that for me?"

"Of course. We must also see who at Haverstock Hall can

recall anything from that night. I forget if you had your valet with you or if one of their retainers assisted you that week."

"It was one of theirs. Could your man interview him?"

"Of course. I'll instruct him to interview as many people as he can." Shefford grimaced. "He won't return by Monday, however."

Even so, this was more hope than Lazarus had possessed an hour ago. "I'll have to ask her for more time. I'll also tell her I don't think she's remembering what happened correctly."

"That's a polite way of calling her a liar," Shefford said with a smirk.

"I hate doing that, but I did not do this. Perhaps I can offer to help her call out the true father."

"Unless it's someone she can't marry. She would much rather wed a viscount, and her family will want that too. You said her mother knows." Shefford narrowed his eyes briefly. "Have you considered speaking to the mother and telling her you know this is a ploy to entrap you in marriage?"

Lazarus blew out a breath. "I had not. I was too focused on the shock of it all. I am grateful for you and Droxford having level heads."

Shefford arched a brow. "You spoke to Droxford?"

"Last night. I was, to borrow your phrasing, distressed. I hadn't even thought to find you yet."

"You went to Droxford first?" Shefford laid his hand against his chest. "I'm wounded."

"No offense intended, but he is the most upstanding of our set and possesses an extremely level head."

"He's made his share of mistakes, but you are correct in that he is better behaved than we are."

"Perhaps it's time we corrected that." Lazarus stood, feeling weary. "If I can survive this disaster, I am definitely changing my ways. You should consider it. Where were you last night and today?"

"Behaving badly. Don't ask me to change," Shefford said, rising. "I'll just endeavor not to get drunk enough that I can't remember what I was doing." His lips lifted in a quick, humorless smile.

Lazarus realized that Shefford didn't ever drink to that level of excess, at least not that Lazarus could recall. How had he never noticed that before?

"Anyway," Shefford continued. "I don't give a fig about my reputation, as you well know." He flashed a genuine smile then. "I'll send for my man immediately."

Lazarus stood. "Thank you. Who is this man, anyway?"

Shefford shrugged. "Just someone I employ from time to time. What will you do about this young woman? What's her name?"

"Miss Melissa Worsley."

"Will you speak to her or to her mother?" Shefford asked.

"I suppose I'll send a note to her mother."

"I'd be careful about what you put in writing. But you also don't want to be seen calling on them." Shefford frowned. "Bloody awful situation. I'm so sorry, Somerton."

Lazarus would put as little as possible in writing, and not just because it was a chore. "I appreciate your help. And commiseration. Your memory of the evening is most reassuring. Perhaps tonight, I will sleep." Or not. He would probably lie awake thinking of how he'd hurt Gwen.

"I'll let you know as soon as my man returns," Shefford said. "Please keep me apprised of any developments. I will do whatever necessary to keep you from the parson's trap."

Lazarus nodded, then took himself out. While he felt better overall, he was still bothered by the whole situation. That a young woman sought to entrap him was galling, but he also felt badly for her. Was she so cornered that she'd decided lying and manipulating someone was her only escape?

~

*G*wen was not in the mood to attend a ball with her parents that evening. The host was a good friend of her father's, however, and she was required to accompany them. She'd been reminded of this when, after returning home from Tamsin's, she'd attempted to tell her mother that she had a headache.

Badger, Gwen's maid who went by Badge rather than be called a generally disagreeable animal, set the last jeweled comb in Gwen's hair and surveyed her in the dressing table mirror. "All finished!" she declared in her thick Yorkshire accent. "You just need your gloves." After fetching the long, white accessories, Badge handed them to Gwen. "Why do you look so worried today?" Badge, who was in her middle thirties and was as much a mothering figure as Gwen's own mother, smoothed her fingertips across Gwen's brow.

"I have a bit of a headache." Gwen had no intention of telling Badge about Lazarus.

"You should have said something," Badge gently admonished. "I would have mixed a tonic for you. I still can, if you like."

"I am not sure there is time," Gwen said, pulling on her gloves.

A rap on the door drew them to turn. Badge went to answer it.

Gwen could hear the conversation she had with the butler. Gwen's presence was requested in her father's study, which was odd, since they were due to leave for the ball shortly. Couldn't her father say whatever he needed to in the coach?

Badge turned from the door, and Gwen said, "I heard. I'll go down directly."

A few minutes later, she arrived at his study. Inside, he was seated behind his desk, and her mother was in a chair nearby. They both looked very serious.

Gwen's insides did a number of somersaults. She slowly stepped inside.

"Close the door," her father said.

Doing as he directed, Gwen pulled the door closed and moved to stand in front of his desk. "Is something amiss?" Her heart beat wildly as she tried to imagine why her parents looked so...unhappy. Upset? Disappointed. She'd no idea.

Her father's hair had been a lighter shade of brown than anyone else's in the family, but what was left of it had gone mostly gray as it had receded back from his forehead. His eyes were a flat brown like Gwen's, and his features were strong and artistically pleasing like her brother's. He'd been painted several times, as artists found him to be an attractive subject. Indeed, he and her mother had been painted together more times than Gwen could count.

"We've received a disturbing letter just a short while ago," he said, frowning deeply. "From Mr. Virgil Eberforce."

What could that cad have to say that would interest her parents? "Did he ask you to compensate him for the waistcoat I apparently ruined at Almack's?"

"No. He alleges you have been visiting your friend Lady Droxford in order to conduct a liaison with Lord Somerton. Is that true?"

Gwen wished she were sitting down. How on earth had Eberforce worked that out? Liaison was not an accurate characterization of why they'd been meeting, though Gwen wouldn't have minded that.

"Of course it's not true. I was visiting my friend, which I did this very afternoon." Had Eberforce seen her and Lazarus arriving around the same time? But it sounded as if he had observed them several times. How, and why had he even been paying attention?

Gwen had a horrifying thought—was there any way he would have been able to see into the library? If he had, he would have seen they were kissing. Not just today, but the other day as well.

No, that was absurd. He would have had to be in the rear garden with a direct line of sight into the library. She couldn't even recall if the draperies had been open to allow someone to see in. Of course they had. There'd been sunlight. Why had they been so reckless?

Her father studied her intently. "Eberforce says you and Somerton call at the Droxford residence around the same time and have been for the past fortnight or so."

"That is merely a coincidence, then. I visit with Tamsin. I had no idea the viscount was there," she lied. She saw the flicker of uncertainty in her father's eyes and wished she'd thought to say she had seen him there once. That would perhaps have been more believable.

"It doesn't matter," her mother said, drawing Gwen to turn her head toward where she was sitting. "Eberforce has been saying cruel things since that mishap at Almack's. True or not, he will spread this information, and it will reflect poorly on you."

"That isn't fair," Gwen said. Except she had been meeting Lazarus secretly. But for good reason! They hadn't been conducting a liaison. Not really. And definitely not at first.

"Regardless, that is what will happen. And given Somerton's reputation, people will likely believe it." her father said. "I've sent word to Markwith that we'd like to negotiate a marriage settlement as soon as possible. I understand he will return Monday."

Gwen felt as though she'd been plunged into an icy river

and was fighting to keep her head above water. "Why Mark-with?" She even sounded as though she were struggling to breathe.

"I thought you perchance liked him best," her mother said with a faint smile. "I'm sorry it's come to this, my dear. It's time you wed."

Gwen couldn't agree more. Only, she wanted a different groom. "Can't we just say that Eberforce is lying because he's holding a grudge? Intelligent people will know he's being spiteful." Over a waistcoat! He would destroy Gwen's reputation for a ruined garment.

Her father cleared his throat. "Be that as it may, I don't think you can weather that scandal. If it were some other gentleman, we would have an easier time of it. However, Somerton has a particular reputation, and he paid you attention until recently. It will not be a stretch for some people to believe this." He narrowed one eye at her. "You are telling us the truth, aren't you? There is nothing between you and the viscount?"

How Gwen wished there were. "There is nothing between us," she said quietly.

Her mother looked at her father. "I told you that was highly unlikely, dear."

Gwen wanted to ask why. Because she wasn't the type of woman Lazarus would want? Well, as it happened, she wasn't. At least not for more than a fleeting moment. It seemed he really was the rogue he claimed to be. Gwen had fallen completely under his spell. She'd forsaken the rules she'd vowed to follow, and now she would pay the price with a hasty marriage to a man she didn't love. She would also make her parents happy in doing so, and wasn't that what she wanted most?

Perhaps not.

"In any case, you will no longer be calling on your friend

Lady Droxford," her father announced as he stood. "Hopefully, you will be wed by June, and then you can visit whomever you please."

Gwen's mother rose and looked at Gwen with an encouraging smile. "Markwith will be a wonderful husband. I can see how much he enjoys your company."

"And he has ten thousand a year, so you will be quite comfortable," her father added. "I daresay you will also be happy. It seems the two of you share many things in common. I must say I am pleased to see you with someone who possesses a sharp intelligence and appreciation for academic endeavors."

What he meant was that Markwith would support Gwen's reading addiction, which many gentlemen would not. That he seemed genuinely happy for her was nice, but Gwen didn't want to marry Markwith. She didn't love him.

Gwen looked at the floor and prayed she wouldn't cry. "Does it matter that I am not in love with Mr. Markwith?"

"Your emotions may yet decide otherwise," her mother said. "I did not reciprocate your father's affection until we were nearly wed—long after the betrothal." She gave him a sweet, love-filled smile.

Her mother's experience did not give her hope, however. Gwen was already in love and couldn't imagine feeling that way about anyone else. And certainly not in the next several weeks before she would apparently wed Mr. Markwith.

How could this be happening?

Gwen's headache intensified. She wished she'd asked Badge to make that tonic.

"That is settled, then," her father said. "Let us depart." He gestured toward the door, and her mother waited for Gwen to precede them from the study.

So, she was just supposed to carry on with the evening as if her life hadn't been decided without her input? Why did she even need to go to the infernal ball if her engagement was all but finalized?

Because her father wanted them all to go. Even her brother would be there.

Taking a deep breath that did nothing to calm herself, Gwen opened the door and left the study. She'd already felt raw after seeing Lazarus earlier. Now she was numb.

She would need to set aside the love in her heart and look to a future she didn't want.

CHAPTER 15

For perhaps the first time ever, Lazarus was attending a ball with the sole purpose of speaking with someone about a parliamentary matter. Droxford would be exceedingly proud.

He arrived relatively early, hoping to complete his errand and be gone before he ran into someone troublesome. Such as Miss Worsley or her mother. Or Gwen. Though, truth be told, he wouldn't mind observing the latter from afar. Or pining, such as the case may be.

Shefford happened to be there too and approached him with a nod. "I sent my man on his way. I hope you were able to find some rest."

"Thank you," Lazarus said. Rest was beyond him at this point. He had tried working on the reading exercise Gwen had given him that afternoon, but his mind was too preoccupied. It hadn't been another love poem, unfortunately, but a passage from a scientific pamphlet. She'd explained that it would be good for him to read a variety of things. He could not fault her logic.

Indeed, he couldn't find anything to fault with her at all. She was perfect in every way.

"You here looking for someone?" Shefford watched him. "You keep scanning the ballroom."

"Yes, I need to speak with Morganfeld about a matter he's discussing in the Commons." Lazarus was concerned they would be delivering speeches on the same thing, and he hoped they might complement one another.

Gwen appeared in the ballroom suddenly, flanked by her parents. Lazarus hadn't seen them enter. Her beauty made Lazarus's chest ache with want. Her dark hair sparkled with bejeweled combs that caught the candlelight. She wore a green gown trimmed with ivory lace, with an embroidered bodice.

He wanted nothing more than to go to her, but he needed to avoid her as if she carried a deadly disease. Perhaps he should look for Morganfeld elsewhere.

"I'll go in search of Morganfeld in the gaming room," Lazarus said.

"I'll join you," Shefford said. "I'd rather be in there than here."

"Why *are* you here?" Lazarus asked as they made their way from the ballroom.

"My father was supposed to attend, but is unable to do so. He asked if I would come in his stead. He owed Jordan a favor." Jordan was the host.

"He wanted a duke to grace his wife's ball?" Lazarus asked.

Shefford nodded. "The duke's heir will have to be good enough."

As they departed the ballroom, Lazarus glanced back toward Gwen. She'd seen him, and now their gazes connected. He saw the longing he felt reflected in her eyes.

None of this was fair! He could only hope that in a few days, the Miss Worsley situation would be behind him, and he could perhaps consider courting Gwen.

But should he? She still deserved someone better than him.

Lazarus went to the gaming room, but Morganfeld wasn't there either. It was likely he hadn't arrived yet. If he didn't show up at all, Lazarus would be frustrated. But Lazarus wasn't sure he would wait much longer. Being in the vicinity of Gwen and unable to talk with her was absolute torture.

"I'm going to play for a bit," Shefford said. "Join me?"

In his current state, Lazarus didn't have the patience or attention to gamble. "I'm going outside."

He strolled out the exterior door into the cool evening. No, it was bloody cold. What had he been thinking?

But before he could return inside, a flash of green hurried toward him. "Lazarus, I must speak with you," Gwen said urgently as she grabbed his forearm and dragged him toward the shadows.

"It's freezing out here," he said. Instead, he looked for another entry. There was a door near the corner of the house. "This way." He clasped her hand and led her to the door against every one of the voices of reason in his head that were screaming at him not to.

Turning the latch, he ushered her inside a dim landing. Stairs led up and down. The latter likely led to the kitchen. It seemed to be a servants' passage.

Lazarus pulled Gwen inside then closed the door. Two sconces on either staircase provided meager lighting. But it was enough for him to make out her flushed cheeks.

"You should not be following me," he said harshly. "Nor should I have brought you in here." He should have run back into the house and left the ball.

"I need to speak with you about an urgent matter." Her voice was tight, and he could feel the anxiety coming from her. Unless that was just his own. He had so much of it.

God, did she somehow know about Miss Worsley? But no, how would she? Lazarus forced himself to breathe. "What's happened?"

"Eberforce sent a note to my parents saying you and I are conducting a liaison, that we've been meeting at your cousin's house."

"*Bloody fucking hell.*" Lazarus clenched his jaw shut, but it was too late, for he'd already let the curse out. "My apologies." Could things get any worse? And could his behavior deteriorate further?

"Do not apologize. Those are my exact sentiments."

Lazarus tried to ignore the thunderous thumping of his heart. It wasn't entirely due to this vexing news. He was also keenly aware of Gwen's proximity and the fact that they were alone and would likely not be interrupted. Desire pulsed through him with a steady, insistent rhythm. "What did you tell your parents?"

"That it's not true, that Eberforce is just being spiteful."

"Which he is. But how on earth does he know we've been meeting?" Lazarus set his hand on his hip. "And why would he say we're having a liaison. Unless…is there any way he saw us kissing?"

"I had the same questions, but I can't see how he would be able to access Droxford's rear garden, and that is the only way he would have been able to see into the library."

Lazarus saw that her heart was also beating fast. Her chest was rising and falling rapidly. Was she as affected by him as he was by her? Or was her physical reaction entirely due to her concern over that giant arse, Eberforce?

"I will find a way to deal with him," Lazarus promised, thinking he would again need to consult with his friends.

Except, it wasn't his place to do so. He wasn't a family member, and he wasn't her husband. While he was also implicated, his reputation would not suffer as Gwen's would. A powerful yearning tore through him. "Unless your father plans to put an end to his baseless gossip. He would be better suited," Lazarus added rather lamely.

"He will not. And it isn't baseless. We *were* meeting, even if we weren't actually having a liaison."

No, but Lazarus would have liked to. Even now, he couldn't help thinking how much he wanted to back her against the wall and kiss her. He'd raise her skirts and stroke her thigh, then her sex. She'd moan for him, and he'd bring her to a fierce climax. Then he'd lift her so she could wrap her legs around him while he opened his fall and—

"Lazarus?"

Christ, had she said something? "I'm sorry. I was thinking of ways I'd like to put Eberforce in his place," he lied.

"I was telling you my father's plan to respond to Eberforce's information which Eberforce will surely make public. He may be spreading his rumors this very moment." She pressed her lips together, and Lazarus hated how this was affecting her. She was supposed to be attracting a husband, and this would be a terrible setback. Because of him—Lazarus's reputation would fuel Eberforce's rumor. It would be easy to believe Gwen would be seduced by the rakish Viscount Somerton.

"What is your father's plan?" Lazarus hoped it would save her from disaster.

"He has written to Markwith to negotiate our marriage settlement." She sounded as if she'd been sentenced to prison. Or transportation.

Lazarus let that sink in. She wasn't happy with her father's plan. Which was to marry one of her very excellent suitors.

But why *would* that make her happy when this very afternoon, she'd tried to tell Lazarus that she loved him?

"I'm so sorry," he whispered, cupping her face and moving to stand before her so their bodies nearly met.

"I don't want to marry Markwith," she said, her voice nearly breaking.

"No, I can't imagine you do. Nor do I want you to. This is all my fault." Lazarus stroked her cheeks with his thumbs. "I allowed us to grow too close."

"Nothing you could have done would have changed anything. Unless you'd never rescued me at Almack's, and I hope you don't regret that. Your actions that night and ever since have been the greatest things anyone has ever done for me. To think that I was actually the queen of the Phoenix Club ball and attended a literary salon—because of you. You have made dreams I didn't know I had come true. " She looked into his eyes, her lips parted. "Please don't regret any of it."

"*Never.*" Lazarus lowered his head and kissed her with a savage intensity that he feared would consume him if he didn't unleash it. His body sang with passion and hope as he cupped her head and brought one hand down her throat, caressing her warm flesh as she pressed her body into his.

She clasped his neck and returned his kiss with a ferocity that made him tighten his hold on her. He couldn't get enough of her, and he never wanted to let her go.

He steered her backward into the darkest corner at the base of the stairs that went up, his mouth devouring hers with an ever-increasing lust. He had never wanted to possess anyone the way he did Gwen. She'd completely overtaken his mind, his body, his heart, his very soul.

Kissing along her jaw, he nipped at her earlobe. "Gwen, I am desperate to touch you. May I?"

"Yes, please. Touch me."

Lazarus clasped her hip as he licked the flesh beneath her ear. "I want to lift your skirt."

She pulled at the garment herself, and Lazarus skimmed his hand beneath the fabric along the inside of her thigh. She shivered, her flesh pebbling.

"Part your legs, my love," he whispered, kissing her neck as he stroked her.

Widening her stance, she dug her fingers into his nape. "Yes, touch me," she breathed.

Gently, he swept his fingertips along her sex. He lifted his head to look at her, but her eyes were closed. "Look at me, Gwen."

Her dark lashes fluttered, and her eyes opened, though the lids were heavy. Lips parted, her breath was coming fast, echoing his own excitement.

"I should not touch you like this." His hand barely grazed her as he urged himself to walk away from her.

She slipped one hand inside his coat and pulled at him. "I want you to touch me. I will die if you don't touch me. Please don't walk away. What if we never have another moment like this?"

Because she was to marry Markwith. And Lazarus might yet find himself coerced into marrying Miss Worsley. "Then I must tell you that I love you. I may be a rogue, but for the first time in my life, I am a rogue in love. I wish I could erase everything that has come before so that there is only you."

Her eyes glowed with emotion as her mouth curved up. "I don't want you to do that because then you wouldn't be the man you are today—the rogue I love." She smiled widely then. "Thank you for letting me say it."

He kissed her hard and fierce. "I couldn't bear to hear it earlier, for I don't deserve your love." If she knew what he was accused of, she would agree. Even if he wasn't the father of Miss Worsley's child, the fact that he could have been solidified his rogue status. He would never believe he could be worthy of someone as pure and perfect as Gwen.

She dug her fingers into his neck. "You absolutely deserve it. You have seen me as no one ever has. Please don't turn away from my love. I couldn't bear for you to do that."

He kissed her again, more gently this time, his tongue mating with hers. She moaned softly as he stroked her sex once more, his fingers moving softly, delicately.

Guiding them toward the stairs, he lifted her right leg and set her foot down on the third stair. "Put your foot here." Now she was more open to his touch and could be more stable.

"*Lazarus,*" she rasped as he opened her folds and rubbed his thumb against her clitoris.

She clutched him tightly, her hips rotating against his hand. Nonsensical noises and moans escaped her lips, and Lazarus kissed her so no one would hear her.

He increased his speed, urging her toward ecstasy. Breaking the kiss, he moved his mouth to her ear. "I want you to come for me. But you must be quiet. Can you do that, my love?"

"I will try, but I can't say I know what to expect."

For a brief moment, Lazarus considered ending this blissful interlude. This was not how she should experience ecstasy for the first time. But she was right in wondering if they'd ever have a moment together again. He wasn't going to let her go without giving her something beautiful to remember.

He put all his attention onto her sex, stroking and coaxing until she was panting, her pelvis moving in wild jerks. Kissing her again, he slipped his finger into her slowly, astonished by how wet she'd become. His cock ached to fill her, to claim her, but this was entirely for her pleasure. His could come later.

After pumping his finger into her, he withdrew it to work her clitoris, then he thrust into her again. Over and over, he pushed her to the brink. He felt her muscles clench, and knew she was on the precipice.

Then she cried out into his mouth, her body trembling madly. He held her close and guided her through her orgasm until her body began to calm. He withdrew his hand and moved her foot to the floor.

Her breathing began to slow. "This can't be the only time we have. It isn't fair. There has to be a way for us to be together." Her eyes met his. "Unless…you don't want to marry me."

"I do want to marry you, but I can't. Not yet." He couldn't tell her the truth, not right now. The potential rumor from Eberforce and her father's betrothal negotiations had further complicated matters. It seemed fate did not want them to be together. "If you can wait, things may change."

"*May* change? If we wait, I will be wed to Markwith."

No, Lazarus would do everything in his power to keep that from happening. Footsteps on the stairs below them jolted him into action. He took her hand and pulled her to the door. "You need to go. Just…don't marry Markwith. Not yet." Not ever. But how could he expect her to wait for him if he would end up being forced to wed Miss Worsley?

She kissed him on the mouth and met his gaze. "I will wait. I love you, Lazarus, and I don't want anyone but you."

Then she was gone, and Lazarus closed the door then leaned his forehead against the wood.

"All right there, sir?" a male voice asked from behind him.

"Yes, just taking a respite away from the noise of the ball," Lazarus said before opening the door and walking out into the garden. The night air felt even colder, or perhaps he was merely registering the loss of Gwen.

She might not want anyone but him now, but when she

learned what he'd been accused of, she would understand just how terrible his behavior had been. He had much to be ashamed of, and he hated that he'd dragged her into this. Lazarus hoped Eberforce wasn't here, for if he was, Lazarus might call the man out.

Making his way back to the gaming room, Lazarus walked inside, intent on departing the ball as soon as possible. However, Shefford intercepted him almost immediately and steered him from the room. "What the devil is going on with you and Miss Price?" he demanded.

Apparently, Eberforce's gossip was already making the rounds. "Nothing." That was a laughable lie, but Lazarus couldn't tell him the truth. He also couldn't reveal that he already knew about the rumor. "What are you talking about?"

"There is a rumor making its way through the ballroom that you and she are having a liaison, that you meet at Droxford's. But you're saying that's not true?"

"I am not having a liaison with Miss Price." Not for want of trying. If it were up to Lazarus, he would be deep inside her this very moment. Only it wouldn't be a liaison. He would make her his wife. The ache to have her, to claim her as his own, was overwhelming.

Lazarus wondered if Eberforce's name was publicly attached to the gossip. "Who is spreading this rumor?"

"It originated with that dolt, Eberforce."

"That right there should tell you it's rubbish," Lazarus said vehemently. "He's been insulting Miss Price since she spilled something on him at Almack's."

"It sounds as though he needs to learn a lesson about grace and generosity." Shefford scowled.

"Droxford would be most impressed with the pitch of your brows." Lazarus was surprised he could find humor in this moment. He dearly wanted to find Eberforce and plant him a facer. Or ten.

Shefford's forehead smoothed, and his brows went back to their regular position. "Speaking of Droxford, he's going to be livid that Eberforce has dragged him and his wife into this salacious nonsense. Though, I can't credit Eberforce with much intelligence, so I doubt he considered that."

Lazarus felt a pang of guilt. He was the one who'd dragged his friend and cousin into things. He should not have involved them in his secret meetings with Gwen. But then, when he'd initiated them, they'd been entirely about improving his reading and memorizing his speech. Lazarus could never have predicted that he would fall in love with his tutor.

Looking at Shefford with concern, Lazarus asked, "Is the rumor that bad, or are people discounting it since Eberforce started it?"

"It's too early to say, but I've heard it from two different people now. I daresay if you went into the ballroom, heads would turn in your direction. More than they already do, anyway."

Dammit. Gwen had likely returned to the ballroom. Was she suffering from everyone staring at her and whispering? His heart ached to think of her being subjected to that. And yet, if he went to the ballroom and they were there together —even if they weren't *together*—the gossip would grow.

"I need to leave," Lazarus said, moving toward the entrance hall.

"Yes, let's," Shefford replied. "I hear the Siren's Call luring us."

Lazarus had no desire to go anywhere but home, but perhaps Jo might know something about why Eberforce was doing this. Was he really just seeking vengeance over a bloody waistcoat?

As they left Jordan's house, Shefford looked over at Lazarus. "You've had quite the couple of days. Perhaps you should become a monk."

"That is the best idea you've ever had," Lazarus replied. Though he'd no plan to join a religious order, Lazarus vowed in that moment that he would remain celibate until he could be with the only woman he would ever love.

CHAPTER 16

*D*ucking into the ballroom, Gwen hoped her absence hadn't been noted. She'd told her mother she was going to the retiring room and had left with alacrity to avoid any discussion or her mother accompanying her. She still felt flushed and quivery after her encounter with Lazarus.

That had been truly scandalous, but she didn't regret a moment of it. Indeed, she would race right back into his arms if she could.

As she looked about for her mother, she saw Min and Ellis coming toward her. They looked...intent, especially Min.

"There you are," Min said without preamble. "We've been looking all over for you."

"I was in the retiring room, then I went outside. I was feeling a trifle overheated." It was as good an excuse as anything.

"You may wish you'd stayed outside," Ellis said ominously.

Gwen tensed. She glanced around them and realized

several people were looking in her direction. Had she not situated her gown correctly after her interlude with Lazarus? Panic streaked through her, as she glanced down at her skirts. They were exactly as they should be, hanging to the floor. Gwen swept her hands over her backside to make sure nothing was wrong there either. Thankfully, all felt right.

Min ushered them to the edge of the ballroom. She spoke in a low, urgent tone. "There is a rumor racing through the ballroom that you have been carrying on a liaison with Somerton."

Gwen's neck prickled at the notion that everyone was talking about it, but it wasn't as if she hadn't known it was coming. Honestly, her parents should have let her stay at home tonight. Except, if she had, she would not have spent that wondrous time with Lazarus.

"The gossip is that you've been meeting him at Tamsin's house, which you have," Ellis said with a slight grimace.

"But not to carry on an affair," Gwen said. "He was helping me with dancing and how to better converse with prospective suitors." She couldn't reveal the real reason and would let her reputation wither and die before she did.

"You don't seem surprised," Min observed.

Not surprised, but that didn't mean she wasn't tense now that the gossip had started. "Eberforce wrote to my parents about it this afternoon. He alleged the affair because he's observed us both calling on the Droxfords' around the same time. He can't have seen us actually meeting one another, however. Indeed, I don't know how he even knows we were there at the same times."

Min frowned deeply. "He lives on the same street as Tamsin. He likely saw you both arriving and leaving and made up a story that would be damaging to you. He is the absolute worst rogue *ever*."

"I would call him out if I could," Ellis said with a sneer.

"And if he were smart, he'd refuse and apologize," Min replied firmly. She glanced toward Gwen. "Ellis is rather good with a pistol, if you didn't know."

"You are both such dear friends," Gwen told them with a smile, though she was uncomfortably aware of a good number of people starting at her. "Do you know if people believe this rumor? Or do they know Eberforce started it? I'd like to think people would recognize that he has an ulterior motive."

Min gave her a sympathetic look. "I'm not sure they all know that about Eberforce. His treatment of you after the Almack's incident was not common knowledge. However, everyone is aware of Somerton's reputation, so as soon as they hear he was having a liaison with someone, they are, probably, inclined to believe it. I'm sorry, Gwen."

Should she tell them what Lazarus had said to her? That he loved her and wanted to marry her? She was nervous to do so, afraid Min would say he wasn't being honest, that he was a rogue. Instead, she decided to tell them what her father was doing to combat the rumor. "My father sent word to Markwith asking if he would like to negotiate a marriage settlement."

Min's and Ellis's eyes rounded as they gaped at her. "Is that what you want?" Ellis asked.

"No," Gwen admitted. "I don't love him." She glanced toward Ellis, who gave her a quick, faint smile of encouragement. That small action bolstered Gwen more than anything else could have in that moment.

"Are you going to marry him?" Min asked.

"I don't want to." But Gwen also struggled with defying her parents. She wasn't sure she could. And yet, she loved Lazarus and would do anything she could to be with him. She only hoped that would be possible.

A very pretty young woman with reddish-blonde hair

approached them. Something about her was vaguely familiar, but Gwen didn't think they'd met. The woman's lips lifted in a brief, tentative smile. "Miss Price?"

"Yes," Gwen responded as Min and Ellis looked toward the interloper.

"May I speak with you?" She glanced at Min and Ellis, but quickly refocused on Gwen, her expression expectant.

Gwen tried to think of how she might know this woman, but nothing was coming to her. Before she could think of how to respond, the woman added, "Please. It's urgent. I would not bother you if it were not deeply important. Please."

Her repetition of the word "please" along with the words "urgent" and "deeply important" gave Gwen pause. She could listen to this woman for a moment or two. "Certainly."

Min's jaw tightened and she took a step forward, as if she would block the young woman. Gwen looked to her and met her gaze. She gave her head a tiny shake and mouthed, *It's all right.*

Gwen moved toward the unknown woman with a pleasant smile and walked with her along the edge of the ballroom. "I'm afraid I don't know you."

"I am Miss Melissa Worsley. My grandfather is the Viscount Haverstock."

"My grandfather is also a viscount," Gwen said. "How coincidental."

"I didn't realize that," Miss Worsley murmured. "Do you mind if we step outside? I'll be brief." Miss Worsley walked out through one of the open doors, and Gwen had no choice but to follow her.

Actually, she did have a choice. She could abandon her and return to her friends. But she did not. There was a shadow in the woman's eyes that provoked Gwen's concern.

Outside, Gwen shivered in the night air. It hadn't felt that cold after she'd left Lazarus's arms.

Suddenly, she remembered where she'd seen Miss Worsley before. She was the young woman Lazarus had been speaking with at the park yesterday.

"I won't prevaricate," Miss Worsley said, her shoulders twitching as a cool breeze swept over them. "Forgive me for my frankness, and I do apologize for how this news will probably shock you. I am carrying Lord Somerton's child."

If Gwen hadn't been chilled before, she would be now. Ice frosted her veins and cloaked her skin. She wrapped her arms around herself, but there was no warmth anywhere. She tried to think clearly, but it was difficult. Then it struck her—why was this woman telling *her* this?

"Who are you?" Gwen said, though she knew the woman's name. What she should have asked was who she was to Lazarus. Except Gwen didn't really want to know.

His hesitation and inability to offer for her crystallized and now made sense. Miss Worsley and her child were his "reasons." He was going to be a father.

But he'd also said he loved Gwen.

The woman spoke. "I met Somerton at a house party last autumn."

Autumn? And he hadn't married her before now? Gwen felt sick. "I'm so sorry." Lazarus really was a rogue, and a rather despicable one at that.

"It has been difficult," Miss Worsley said quietly. "I've been ill. Indeed, I just told Somerton yesterday, and I did wonder at his hesitation. However, now that I hear he has been carrying on a liaison with you, I understand. I wanted to ask you to please let him marry me. I realize I am asking a great deal, particularly if you genuinely care for one another, but I need his protection."

Gwen was relieved to hear Lazarus hadn't known about

the babe until yesterday. "I don't understand why you didn't tell him sooner."

Dark pink stained Miss Worsley's finely sculpted cheeks. "I confess I didn't know until my mother worked it out. As I said, I was ill. I was also incredibly naive."

Though Gwen wanted to tell the woman that she and Lazarus were not having a liaison, she realized it wasn't really true. They might not have been meeting secretly to conduct a love affair at the Droxfords', but they were now. Or they had been. Gwen realized that was over.

He had to marry Miss Worsley. There was simply no other acceptable outcome. Even if he loved Gwen.

Despite his behavior, her heart ached for him. How could it not when she loved him so? He'd carried a tortured look in his gaze, which she understood now. He didn't *want* to marry Miss Worsley, and it seemed he might be trying to find a way out of doing so. He'd told Gwen that if she could wait, he might be able to marry her. What was he expecting would change?

"I'm dreadfully sorry for the position you are in," Gwen said. "However, I don't think I can help you. Somerton will choose his path." But she could encourage him to do the right thing. To not be a rogue.

"I understand. I'm only asking for you to step aside, to free him to wed me as he must."

Gwen could tell him there was no chance with her, that she would marry Markwith. The joy she'd felt a short while ago in his arms melted away like snow beneath the sun. Only, there was no sun here. No brightness at all. Just a deep and lingering sadness for the love Gwen couldn't have.

"If I can, I will advocate for you to him. I may not have that chance, though."

Miss Worsley nodded. "I appreciate anything you can do to aid my cause." She touched her abdomen, and Gwen could just make out the curve of her belly as her gown briefly went taut. "Our cause," Miss Worsley amended with a small smile.

A sob rose in Gwen's throat. Agony and jealousy and despair shot through her. She bit the inside of her lip as another chill made her body quiver.

"It is rather cold," Gwen said, her voice sounding hollow. "You must go back inside." While Gwen was eager to go back in too, she didn't want to enter the ballroom with the mother of Lazarus's child.

"I will. Good evening." Miss Worsley turned, her gown swirling about her ankles as she made her way into the ballroom.

Gwen looked about for another door. There was one farther down—toward the refreshments away from the dancing. As she walked briskly toward the door, she didn't know what was worse: returning to the ballroom to face the rumors churning about her and Lazarus, or returning to the ballroom knowing the man she loved had fathered a child with someone else. Either way, she would have to smile and laugh, and make hideous chitchat.

Once inside, she looked for her mother. There was no way Gwen was staying.

She located her mother, who saw her at the same moment. Her features flickered with both surprise and concern, and she immediately made her way toward Gwen.

Gwen did not move from the edge of the ballroom, however. That would bring her into contact with too many people. Gwen couldn't bear their judgmental stares.

"There you are," Min said, arriving at Gwen's side with Ellis. "Who was that woman, and what did she want?"

Gwen's mother was bearing down on her. "I can't explain now. We'll meet at your house tomorrow afternoon. I must go."

Both Min and Ellis looked alarmed. "We love you," Min

said. "Everything will be all right." They smiled and exchanged a brief greeting with Gwen's mother before departing.

"Mama, I am unwell." Indeed, Gwen still felt chilled to the bone. And horribly queasy. "I need to go home."

"I can see you are pale," her mother said with concern. "Let us go. I was going to suggest we leave anyway. The rumor about you and Somerton has overtaken the ball. I'd no idea it would spread like that." She looped her arm through Gwen's and steered her toward the nearest doorway to exit the ballroom. "I'm so sorry, my dearest. But everything will be all right."

Her mother's assurances and the echo of her friend's words did nothing to ease Gwen's turmoil. For one thing was absolutely certain: everything would *not* be all right.

~

*A*fter a mostly sleepless night, Lazarus ought to have dragged himself to church where he could have prayed for his debauched soul. Instead, he'd prayed for an impossibly quick return of Shefford's man.

In the early afternoon, his butler announced the arrival of Mrs. Worsley. Lazarus's insides turned to mush. He'd written to her yesterday, but he hadn't received a response. And now she'd come in person.

"Show her to the drawing room," Lazarus managed as he stood from his favorite chair in his study and paced about the room for a few minutes. Had she come to agree to his request for more time? He'd been purposely vague in the missive, saying only that he needed more time to respond and that he wasn't sure he believed what her daughter had disclosed to him.

Bracing himself, he strode upstairs to the drawing room.

He paused at the threshold and saw that Mrs. Worsley stood in front of the windows that overlooked the street below. She was petite and curvaceous, with a generous bosom. Her hair was the same reddish blonde as her daughter's, but her features were harsher, her nose longer.

"You've an excellent situation here in Mayfair," she noted with a smile. "Your house is splendid. My Melissa will be an excellent hostess here." She spoke confidently and, if he were honest, almost arrogantly.

"Thank you, Mrs. Worsley. May I presume you've come in response to my note?" He didn't invite her to sit. He hoped she wouldn't be staying very long.

"Indeed, I have, and I must decline your request. You must understand there can be no delay in your marriage. The ceremony must take place with due haste. This week, in fact."

"There must be a delay," Lazarus said, working to keep a tight grip on his patience. "I am not the father of your daughter's unborn child, and I will prove it."

Mrs. Worsley appeared indignant. "Of course you are."

"We were never together at the fox-hunting party. I'm sorry to say, but she has confused me with someone else." That was the politest he could think to say that Miss Worsley had fabricated his involvement.

Mrs. Worsley exhaled, and her cheeks flushed. "She has not confused you. I don't understand your insistence that you weren't together. My daughter is not mistaken. She is lovely and beautiful. She will be a wonderful viscountess for you. Furthermore, you need to wed. If you do not marry Melissa, your reputation will be ruined. Already, it is stained because you've apparently been carrying on with another unmarried young lady. If your marriage to Melissa weren't necessary, I doubt I would support you as her groom."

"That gossip isn't true," he growled. At least it hadn't been until yesterday. Did his previous kisses with Gwen at the salon and the tutoring session count?

"I suppose I'm relieved to hear that. I would prefer my daughter marry someone without the reputation of an *absolute* blackguard."

He gave her a tight, humorless smile. "And yet, you're perfectly happy to have her wed a mere rake, which I think you'll agree I am. Or rogue, if you prefer that term."

"I'm happy for her to become the Viscountess Somerton. That is the only outcome I will accept." She pursed her thin lips at him. "I do hope you will not force us to make this into a scandal."

"I am not forcing you to do anything. I think you'll find the coercion is coming entirely from one direction." His patience was nearing its end. He took a step toward her and studied her intently. "Who did this to your daughter? Because it wasn't me. He should be made to account for his actions."

"It *was* you," she insisted, though her eyes darted toward the window for the barest moment.

"Was it someone she can't wed? A footman or a married man? If someone took advantage of her, you can bring him up on charges—"

"Do not advise me on what we are able to do," she snapped, sneering at him. "You will be the one to marry her. I will expect you to call tomorrow. If you do not, my husband will be calling on you by nightfall. He knew your father, you know."

The mention of Lazarus's father turned his blood cold. "What is that supposed to mean?"

"Your father was a good and honorable man. He would hate to see how you've debauched women without a care."

Nothing she said could have hurt him more. His father's love had been a constant in Lazarus's life, even after he'd died. To think he would be disappointed in his son nearly drowned Lazarus in grief and regret. The sensation was nearly identical to how he felt when he thought of Gwen learning about this. And of course it would be—Gwen had believed in him and supported him in ways no one had since his father. It only made sense that he valued her opinion of him more than anyone else's. He would hate to see the pride and admiration for him in her gaze replaced with disgust and disappointment.

But he had already vowed to change the way he lived. Furthermore, nothing Mrs. Worsley said would convince him he'd taken advantage of her daughter. "I didn't bed your daughter," he said quietly. "And I think you know that."

Sniffing, she lifted her chin. "I think you know that it doesn't matter once everyone thinks you did. Please do what you must—call tomorrow and marry Melissa. You will not be unhappy."

Mrs. Worsley swept past him and left the drawing room.

Lazarus went to a chair and gripped the back. He needed to find the father of this child. Perhaps then he could force something—he could ensure Melissa married the man who'd used her and tossed her aside.

Only, he feared it wouldn't be happy for her. And for that, he was sorry.

But Lazarus was not going to pay for that man's sins. Even if his reputation made him an easy target.

CHAPTER 17

*A*fter telling her mother that she was going to spend the afternoon with her friends to hopefully cheer herself, Gwen was now on her way to Min's father's house in Grosvenor Square. Her mother had felt badly about taking her to the ball last night, saying she should have realized the gossip would be bad.

Gwen hadn't seen her father, for he'd left the ball at some point last night and gone to his club. Then today, she'd kept to her chamber until leaving for Min's.

The Duke of Henlow's London residence was one of the largest in the square, with several columns decorating the facade. Gwen had not yet reached the door before it was opened by a young footman in pristine maroon livery.

Inside the entry hall, the butler, who appeared stuffy but never failed to greet Gwen warmly, took her hat and gloves then directed her up to Min's sitting room. Located on the second floor, it was connected to her bedchamber. They preferred to meet there instead of the drawing room because they would not be disturbed.

Decorated in varying shades of pink with an abundance

of floral motifs, the sitting room boasted extreme femininity. Min hadn't had a hand in decorating it, however. It was due entirely to her mother. Min found it a bit overdone.

Everyone was already there—Min, Ellis, Tamsin, and even Jo. Gwen hadn't thought to invite her, but obviously someone had. They all rose when Gwen entered.

"We are so sorry this has happened, Gwen," Min said, rushing to hug her. The rest of them took turns embracing her, including Jo, who was last.

"I hope you don't mind that I'm here," Jo said. "Min invited me."

"Not at all. I am overjoyed, in fact. You are one of us now," Gwen added with a smile.

They took their seats, and Gwen knew she had to tell them about Miss Worsley. She'd tried to think of how to explain, but there was simply no good way. She'd also contemplated whether she should have told Tamsin first— separately—since Lazarus was her cousin.

Gwen took a deep breath before speaking. "I know you all think the gossip about Somerton and me is the reason for my distress, but it's more than that."

"Min and Ellis said you seemed upset after some young woman badgered you to speak with her," Tamsin said.

"Yes, my conversation with her was most upsetting," Gwen said softly. "Her name is Miss Melissa Worsley. Her grandfather is the Viscount Haverstock."

"My father knows him," Min said, wrinkling her nose. "And from the way he speaks of him, I'd say I'm disinclined to like him."

"Why is that?" Jo asked.

Min pressed her lips together. "Because my father speaks highly of him. That typically doesn't recommend a person."

Jo grimaced.

"Why did Miss Worsley wish to speak with you?" Tamsin asked. She was seated to Gwen's right.

Gwen angled her body toward her. "I should probably have told you this privately as it involves your cousin, and I'm afraid it's disturbing news."

Tamsin's features creased. "What did she say?"

Clearing her throat of the cobwebs that had suddenly formed, Gwen addressed everyone. "Miss Worsley is expecting a child, and she says Somerton is the father."

Everyone spoke at once, and Gwen heard none of what they said. She held up a hand. "Please let me finish, and then you can ask me questions, though I doubt I'll be able to answer them. She said they met at a party last autumn and that she only told him of the babe the day before yesterday because she'd been ill. She indicated she hadn't realized she was carrying. She blamed naivete."

"How does one not know?" Ellis asked. "Your courses cease. I would think one would notice that."

"Perhaps she was ill enough that she didn't realize?" Gwen suggested.

"Or she could have thought her illness was the reason she wasn't having them," Jo said. "I was very sick when I was younger—only a year or two after I started bleeding. I missed my courses for a few months."

"I can't believe Somerton would do that," Tamsin said quietly. "He can be roguish, but he has never dallied with young unmarried ladies. Never ever. My grandmother has mentioned her relief about that many times."

That was the man Gwen wanted to believe he was. "I've no idea what happened, but she claims he is the father."

"Why on earth did she want to tell you about it?" Min asked.

"Because she heard the gossip about me and Somerton and wanted to ask me to step aside so that he would marry her. When she informed him of the babe the other day, he did not immediately offer for her."

"That tells me it isn't his child," Tamsin said with a certainty that Gwen wished she shared. Why didn't she?

Because he'd known about the child and hadn't told her. Instead, he'd tried to push her away, then asked her to wait for him. He should have told her. That he didn't prompted suspicion and doubt.

"I don't think it's his child either," Jo announced, drawing everyone's attention. "I know something of Miss Worsley. I hear a great many things at the Siren's Call and at the literary salons. Last fall, she fell in love with her dancing master. Her parents had to pay him to never speak of it."

Gwen immediately thought of Mr. Tremblay. But that would be quite a coincidence. "Do you know the dancing master's name?"

"Mr. Tremblay," Jo replied. "He's very attractive. I've seen him myself. He is purportedly quite familiar with his students."

"I can confirm that," Gwen said. "My mother engaged his services, and I had two lessons with him before I told her I could not continue. He flirted with me constantly and touched me inappropriately. I believe most firmly that if I'd shown even a modicum of interest, we could have had an affair." She stared at Jo. "Do you suppose that is what happened between him and Miss Worsley?"

"I think it's entirely possible. What if the child she is carrying belongs to the dancing master?"

"Her family wouldn't want her to marry someone like him," Min said. "They'd rather she wed a wealthy, attractive viscount."

"With a rakish reputation," Tamsin put in, sounding disgusted. "What a horrible thing to do. I can only imagine how Somerton felt being accused of such a thing."

Gwen recalled the tension and distress he'd carried yesterday. He'd likely felt trapped. Here was this woman claiming he'd fathered her child, and he was in love with another woman he hoped to wed. Still, there was likely a reason he was in this situation. "Why would Miss Worsley accuse him unless there was a possibility that he could be the father? He had to have bedded her." She looked at Tamsin with concern even while her heart was crumbling into bits.

"He must have," Ellis said softly, her gaze falling on Gwen with sadness and sympathy.

Gwen couldn't keep the sob from breaking through her lips. She clapped her hand over her mouth.

"Oh, Gwen, you have a tendre for him," Min said. "This has to be so hard."

"It's more than that." Gwen struggled to draw breath. "I love him. And…he loves me."

There were several gasps, and Gwen fought against the tears that threatened to overwhelm her. Tamsin turned fully toward her and reached to clasp her hand tightly.

"Just last night at the ball, he said he loved me," Gwen said. "And he asked me not to marry Markwith."

"He didn't tell you about Miss Worsley?" Min asked.

Gwen shook her head.

"He wouldn't have wanted you to know," Tamsin said.

Min looked at Gwen with sympathy. "This makes him the very definition of a rogue—one we cannot marry and who cannot be reformed as Wellesbourne and Isaac have been."

"I need to see him," Gwen said with great conviction. "I need to know the truth about Miss Worsley—from him. And I may be betrothed to Markwith as soon as tomorrow."

Jo nodded. "Then you must see Somerton today." She cocked her head to the side and narrowed her eyes. Her brow creased as she appeared to be thinking.

Min shook her head. "She can't see him. Not with these rumors racing about."

"She'll need a disguise," Jo said. "And I will find out what I can about Mr. Tremblay and Miss Worsley. Someone has to know something."

"You would do that?" Gwen asked, blinking away the moisture that had clung to her lashes but not fallen as tears.

"If only because I'm dead curious," Jo said with a laugh. "But I imagine you would like to know the truth, as would Somerton, I'm sure. If he is not the father, this has to be eating at him horribly."

Gwen agreed. And when she thought about his behavior, it seemed this could be possible. She was incredibly eager to speak with him.

Min was frowning. "I still don't think it's wise for Gwen to see Somerton. Not with all that is happening."

"But that's precisely why I need to." Gwen would not be deterred. "Everything is moving quickly, and I can't afford to wait and see what happens." She looked to Jo. "Do you have a disguise in mind?"

"It depends on what Min has available. I'd prefer to dress you as a young man, if possible." Jo tossed a smile toward Min. "I don't suppose you have anything like that."

"I do," Ellis said, prompting everyone to swing their attention to her. She shrugged. "Sometimes, I dress up like a man and go for a walk. It's easier that way." She glanced at Min. "Min knows."

Min nodded. "You should see Somerton if you feel that strongly. I'm only concerned for your reputation and welfare."

"I know, and I appreciate that so much. But I do feel strongly—I love Lazarus." She decided she could use his name with her friends.

"Then you must do everything in your power to ensure a

future with him, especially since he apparently loves you too," Min said.

Jo gave Gwen a knowing smile. "He does. I've seen them together, and it's rather obvious. I've also seen him without her, and he's a mopey mess."

"He mopes?" Tamsin asked, incredulous.

"He's downright despondent," Jo confirmed. "But he's also a clueless man. I do believe I had to point out that he was perhaps having romantic feelings unlike any he'd ever had before."

This provoked everyone to laugh, including Gwen. How she would have loved to have heard that conversation. "He is *my* clueless man," Gwen said. "At least, I hope he will be."

Jo stood. "Let us assemble your costume. You need to be on your way. Presumably, you can say you were here all afternoon to account for the time you are with Somerton?"

"Yes, I'll do that." Gwen had indicated to her mother that she would be occupied all afternoon.

Ellis rose and went to the door. "Follow me, then. My chamber is at the end of the corridor."

Before Gwen could reach the door, Jo clasped her hand briefly. "All will be well. I'll find out what I can about Tremblay and Miss Worsley as soon as possible."

Gwen embraced her tightly. "I can't thank you enough."

Jo patted her back. "I'm glad to help. I can't thank *you* enough for including me in your group of friends. I've never...belonged to anything like this."

"We are a sisterhood," Gwen said. "And now you are one of us." She linked her arm through Jo's, and they made their way to Ellis's chamber.

～

*A*fter Mrs. Worsley left, Lazarus would have contemplated drinking a great deal of smuggled whisky, but since learning of Miss Worsley's child, he'd decided he was much better off not ever being inebriated again. Instead, he'd tried to distract himself with reading. Because that also made him feel closer to Gwen.

He sat at his desk and worked through the exercise she'd given him yesterday, reading it over and over until he did so with ease and relative speed. He realized he'd begun to memorize it, so it had probably lost its efficacy.

Perhaps he should try reading something else. And he could mark it the way she did. Why not?

He went to the bookcase and searched for something to use. His book collection was terrible. Winterstoke had a marvelous library, owing to his father, but here in town, Lazarus hadn't kept much. He'd sent entire bookcases to the country. Now, he wished he hadn't.

"Papa, you would be so pleased with my progress," he murmured. "And you would love Gwen."

Mrs. Worsley's mention of his father had carved a hole in Lazarus's chest. He wanted to make his father proud. And he realized now that his roguish behavior had countered that objective. Lazarus also realized that he'd sought solace in those actions to dull the pain of losing his father. He'd been focusing on the wrong things.

No longer. He would master reading and dedicate himself to a more substantial role in the Lords. And, if he were very fortunate, he would marry Gwen. Not that he deserved her. He'd behaved worse than a rogue.

He'd risked her reputation with their foolish scheme, not to mention his behavior at the literary salon and at the ball last night. He'd also risked his cousin's and friend's reputations. It didn't matter that his reasons hadn't been scandalous. They'd been selfish.

A knock on the door jolted him from his self-recrimination. Lazarus responded, "Come."

His butler stepped just over the threshold. "You've a caller, my lord. A young man who wishes to provide you with some information."

"About what?" Lazarus didn't have time for nonsense. What young man?

"He did not say."

"Did he give you a card?"

"No, but he said his name was Gawain Price."

Lazarus nearly laughed at the first name, but the surname made him freeze. "Thank you, Harris," he breathed, moving past the butler with a deft speed. He stalked to the entrance hall and saw the slender young man. His costume was ill fitting, and to Lazarus, he looked no more like a male than London was a quiet, sedate place.

"Follow me," Lazarus said, leading Gwen up the stairs. Where was he taking her? His study might have sufficed. Instead, he led her to the drawing room. And closed the door as soon as she was inside.

She'd moved into the interior, away from him so he couldn't immediately pull her to him. "I was afraid you wouldn't see me."

"With a name like Gawain Price, how could I not?" He took two steps toward her but paused. Her expression was a mix of eagerness and something much darker. "Why have you come? And dressed like that?" As much as he loved seeing her in splendid gowns, he had to admit the shape of her legs encased in breeches was a stirring sight. But then he suspected she could wear a grain sack and be every bit as appealing.

"I needed to see you today." She spoke softly, almost haltingly. "I don't know how to broach this topic, so I shall just come out with it. Will you please tell me about Miss Melissa Worsley?"

Lazarus exhaled, his entire body just…wilting like a cut flower left without water. "I was hoping you wouldn't ever need to find out about her." His voice was low, as agonized as he felt—not for himself, but for her.

"I wish you had told me." Lines creased out from her eyes, and he couldn't miss the sadness they held.

"I am horrified by my actions. I couldn't bear how you would see me, for the rogue I truly am."

"You bedded her, then? Her child is yours?"

Did she doubt it? Lazarus was overwhelmed with gratitude—and surprise that she would give him that benefit when he surely didn't deserve it.

"I did not bed her," he replied sharply. "We met at a fox-hunting party at her grandfather's house. Gwen, you must know that I would never—I have never—bedded a young, unmarried lady. And I would certainly never do so in her grandfather's house." And yet, he'd done improper things with Gwen, a young, unmarried woman. Whom he'd been purportedly helping to find a husband who wasn't him.

He wiped his hand over his face, setting aside the turmoil inside him so he could say what needed to be said. "I was very inebriated one night at the party. I'd gone to a pub with Sheff, and the innkeeper shared his smuggled whisky. I don't remember most of what happened afterward. I couldn't say with absolute certainty that I hadn't been with Miss Worsley —I just knew in my soul that I had not. That I *could* not."

"I know that too," Gwen said softly, again surprising him. "But I do wish you had told me. I know you are a rogue. I've embraced that about you, haven't I?"

She had agreed to meet with him privately, and she had accompanied him to a literary salon while wearing a disguise. And she'd thrown caution out the window when she'd kissed him, on multiple occasions. "I've corrupted you," he croaked. "I never meant to risk your reputation or cause you distress. This is all my fault. I'm so sorry."

"Oh, stop that," she said, her lips pursing. "I am not corrupted. I am merely in love. With a rogue."

An unstoppable smile lifted his lips. "I shall never tire of hearing you say that. How did you learn of Miss Worsley's claim?"

"She approached me at the ball last night."

Now, Lazarus moved close to her. "She did *not* dare."

"She absolutely did. She also dared to ask me to step aside so you would marry her, as if I were the only obstacle in her way. She'd heard the rumor about us having an affair."

"What did you tell her?" Lazarus's breath caught.

"That I wouldn't be able to move you to do anything. You will do as you choose. I did say I would try to use my influence to persuade you to do the right thing."

"I hope the right thing is choosing you, because that's what I want," he said, curling his arm around her waist and pulling her against him.

"And I choose you. However, you have a problem in that there will be a scandal if you don't offer for Miss Worsley. And we are currently embroiled in a scandal of a purported liaison between us. Furthermore, Markwith will return tomorrow, and I expect his proposal will be imminent."

"Then it seems we must obtain a special license and marry immediately or run away to Gretna Green. I've no preference."

She giggled, then quickly sobered. "We can't do either, and you well know that. You need the problem with Miss Worsley to go away before it becomes a scandal. I fear my parents will not want me to marry someone who is accused of fathering Miss Worsley's child."

"Shefford has sent a man to Haverstock Hall to interview the retainer who attended me during the party to learn what he recollects about that night. He will also speak with the innkeeper where Sheff and I spent a good portion of the night in question. I am hopeful both will be able to provide me with an alibi. Sheff remembers that night—he never drinks himself into oblivion—and says we returned to Haverstock Hall just before dawn. So, the opportunity for me to have been with her at all is quite scant."

Relief cleansed her expression for a moment. "Brilliant, but when will Sheff's man return?"

"Therein lies the problem, for the Worsleys want me to make my offer of marriage tomorrow, and I can't imagine Sheff's man will return until the day after that."

"This all sounds very promising, though the timing is not," she said. "I'm pleased to report, however, that we are working on another angle—determining the actual father of Miss Worsley's child."

Lazarus gripped her upper arms, excitement coursing through him. "How on earth can you do that?"

"As it happens, I met with my friends earlier, and Jo was aware of an interesting situation. Last fall, my most recent dancing master, Mr. Tremblay, was instructing Miss Worsley. She apparently fell in love with him, and her parents paid him to never speak of it." Gwen put her hand on his chest. "Now, I can speak from experience that Mr. Tremblay is attractive, flirtatious, and rather free with his hands. I believe if I'd wanted to have an affair with him, it would have been most welcome."

Fury tore through Lazarus. "What did he do to you with his hands?" He thought of the many ways he could break them.

"Nothing too terrible, just a stray fingertip here and a wandering caress there." She touched Lazarus's cheek.

"Goodness, but you look ready to commit something nefarious."

"I will ensure he doesn't touch a young lady without her consent ever again."

"My knight," Gwen whispered before brushing her lips against his. "Jo is doing her best to learn the truth of what happened between him and Miss Worsley—quickly. She is also responsible for my disguise today. Do you approve?" She stepped away from him and turned in a circle. Lifting the tails of the coat, she wiggled her backside. "I do feel rather exposed, or I would if the coat didn't cover me."

"I heartily approve. Of everything about you. How can you love a rogue like me?" She was too generous. Too pure. Too far above him.

Facing him, she pursed her lips for a moment. "How can I not? You have been the kindest, most gallant gentleman I've ever met. You've given me unforgettable memories I never dreamed were possible. I was the queen of a ball!" The joy in her features made him want to sweep her into his arms and spin them both around until they were dizzy with laughter. "You stepped in to save me, to protect me when no one else ever has. Not even my parents, whom I love very much. They've done their best, but I've always known that I fall short. I don't feel that way with you. You make me feel like I'm enough."

Lazarus could scarcely breathe. How could anyone think that about her? "You are perfect." He dropped to his knees before her and took her hand. "Marry me, Gwen. At the earliest possible moment, please be my wife."

"I will." A wide, beatific smile lit her face, and Lazarus knew he would never live up to her brilliance. But he would spend every moment trying.

She tugged at his hand, and he rose to take her in his

arms. Then he kissed her. Thoroughly. Passionately. With all the love in his heart.

Gwen pulled back and looked into his eyes. "I don't want to go yet. Where is your bedchamber?"

Lazarus swallowed. She couldn't be asking what he thought she was asking. "You must know that I am extremely against debauching unmarried young ladies."

She lifted a shoulder. "Since I will be your wife, I don't see the problem with it. But I don't wish to cause you discomfort."

Though Lazarus wasn't sure he could refuse her, he was overwhelmingly aware of his inappropriate behavior with her. If he was trying to reform himself, this was probably not the way to do it. And yet, they loved one another. They were also betrothed, and he would move heaven and earth to ensure they wed. "Forgive my hesitation, but I am trying to be a better man—the man you deserve and not the rogue I've been."

She took his hand. "You are the very best man I could hope for. That you want to change your behavior makes me absolutely giddy. However, I also can't refute the fact that I fell in love with who you *are*. So, to put you at ease, I insist you take me to your bedchamber." She gave him a smile that went from teasing to sultry in the blink of an eye, and Lazarus was lost.

He led her to the door, which he opened carefully. Looking to make sure no one was about, he guided her past the staircase to the back of the house where his chamber was located.

Opening the door, he gestured for her to move inside. She did so, releasing his hand and removing her hat as she looked around his bedchamber.

Lazarus nearly groaned at the image of her in his most

private space. He'd imagined her here, in his bed, but he'd never actually thought it might come to pass.

Latching the door, he moved toward her. He took her hat and sailed it somewhere to his left. He cupped her face and brushed his thumb over an errant lock of hair that had dislodged when she'd taken off the hat.

"Jo provided these clothes?" he asked, surveying her simply knotted cravat and mundane waistcoat. Everything was brown, save the white shirt and cravat.

"Not Jo, exactly, but I am lucky to have use of them. I was desperate to see you as soon as possible."

"I'm so glad you did. I'm sorry I didn't tell you about Miss Worsley. I was ashamed of my behavior. Though I was certain I couldn't have done what she claimed, the fact that I couldn't know with complete certainty is abominable. I've sworn off drinking alcohol like that. Never again will I lose my ability to see and think clearly. And remember what I've done."

She put her hands on his shoulders. "You mustn't chastise yourself too severely."

"I'm afraid it's too late for that. I had already planned to ask you to marry me—it's why I went to the park the other day. But before I could find you, Miss Worsley spilled her accusations. If not for my terrible behavior, we would have been betrothed before now. Before Eberforce was able to spread his ridiculous nonsense."

"Except no one will think it's nonsense once our betrothal is announced." She grimaced faintly. "I suppose they will likely think you were beholden to marry me. Not that it matters what people think."

Lazarus resolved to ensure the entire world knew precisely why he was marrying Gwen—because he was utterly and completely mad for her, and that his love knew no bounds.

Gwen's lips as they curved into a smile. "You'd planned to propose at the park?"

He nodded. "Would you have said yes?"

"Probably not. It seems I needed a scandal or two to persuade me." She laughed softly. "Of course I would have said yes. Now, help me with these garments, since you are far more versed with them than I."

There was something almost sinfully erotic about disrobing her from gentleman's clothes. Lazarus's cock, already hard, twitched as he thought of peeling the breeches from her hips.

"Let us start with our boots." He swept her into his arms and carried her to the bed where he set her on the edge.

He sat down beside her and pulled off his own boots, letting them fall to the floor. "Shall I help you?"

She tugged one off. "They are large, so they come off easily." The second one followed. "Stockings next?"

"Yes, but I find I'd like to remove yours, if you don't mind." Again, the act of removing the clothing from her was playing merry hell with his anticipation. He hurriedly removed his stockings then slid from the bed to stand before her.

"I don't mind," she said, sounding a bit breathless.

Lazarus slipped his fingers up beneath the hem of her breeches and found the top of the stocking. Then he pulled the garment slowly down her calf, exposing her flesh to his hungry gaze. Her feet were small and elegant.

She wiggled her toes. "Hard to believe this appendage can cause so much havoc on the dance floor, isn't it?"

A laugh burst forth from him, and Lazarus's love for her somehow grew. "It's not that bad." He moved to her right leg and performed the same task.

"You're correct. My right foot is far more egregious."

"Stop," he said, laughing again. "I don't like it when you denigrate yourself."

"Your laughter says otherwise. Anyway, it doesn't bother me that I'm clumsy, at least not with you. Because you've never cared."

He met her gaze as he moved to stand between her legs. "And I never will." He kissed her, his mouth opening over hers as she met his tongue with her own.

She clutched at his neck and shoulders as he thrust his fingers into her hair, dislodging her hairpins. Breaking the kiss, she reached up and plucked them free. "I'll need these later." She handed them to him, and he placed them carefully on the small table beside the bed. "You've a book there," she noted.

He nodded. "I read before bed now, even if it's just one page. Though, I've been somewhat distracted these past few days. I was actually looking for a book in my study when you arrived. I'd planned to make my own reading exercise."

Gwen grabbed his lapels and pulled him back to her. "Have you any idea how arousing that is?" She kissed him fiercely and pressed her palms against his chest.

Awkwardly, Lazarus kept kissing her as he worked to remove his coat, letting it fall behind him. Then he pushed hers from her shoulders and drew it away, throwing it behind him.

He paused, his gaze fixing on the fall of her dark waves as her unfettered hair fell past her shoulders. He brushed it back from her face with both hands and kissed her again. Bringing his hands down her neck, he unknotted her cravat and slipped the silk from her collar.

The shirt gapped open, revealing a tantalizing triangle of her flesh. He kissed down her throat and feasted on what was now exposed to him. He wanted to devour every inch of her.

Which meant he needed to get her garments off with utmost speed.

He went to work on the buttons of her waistcoat, slipping them open with an eager intensity. Then he realized, she was mirroring his actions and unbuttoned his waistcoat at the same time. They each shrugged their garments off, and Lazarus took them both so he could drop them somewhere out of their way.

Her shirt was too large, as all the garments had been, but the neckline was low enough that he could see her breasts were bound against her chest. She'd had help with this disguise. From someone who knew what they were doing.

Desperate to see and taste her, Lazarus pulled the shirt from the top of her breeches and drew it over her head. She lifted her arms, and he glimpsed the rise of her breasts at the top of the binding.

She reached behind herself and pulled the fabric, a light muslin, loose, unwrapping it around her front.

"Let me," he said softly, taking the end of the muslin and unwinding it around her. Using both hands, he worked quickly, until the fabric fell from her chest. He glanced at it briefly, thinking it would come in handy when their bed sport progressed, but there would be plenty of time for adventures together. He looked forward to every moment.

Her breasts were high and round, larger than he'd anticipated. He stared at the dark rose nipples and licked along his lower lip.

"You are unbelievably beautiful." He cupped her breasts, dragging his thumbs back and forth across her nipples. They lengthened and pebbled at his touch.

Moaning softly, she closed her eyes as he continued to caress her. She was so responsive, not at all shy or hesitant. Still, he wanted her to feel safe and secure with him.

"Gwen, are you certain you wish me to continue? You must stop me at any moment if want that."

Her eyes opened as she clasped his hips, pulling him tightly against the bed between her legs. "I will not stop you. I want you, Lazarus. Now. Please. Make me yours."

CHAPTER 18

*G*wen watched as he lowered his head to her breast. He held her as he kissed her nipple and the surrounding area. His left hand massaged and caressed her other breast, and the sensation of everything was almost too much.

Almost.

It was heavenly. The throb of desire within her had started as a dull, persistent ache these past few days. When he'd brought her here to his bedchamber, it had sharpened to an overpowering lust that threatened to consume her. With anyone else, she might have been frightened by the force of her need and her emotions, but with Lazarus, everything felt…right. And wonderful.

His lips closed around her nipple, and he tongued her, much the way he kissed her mouth. She clasped his head, gripping his hair as waves of pleasure swept through her. He lightly pinched her other nipple, and she gasped. There was no pain, just a deep and surging desire that pulsed straight to her sex.

His mouth and hands moved over her, arousing her so

fiercely that she panted with want. The breeches against her mound felt wet. They were also constricting, and she dearly wanted them off.

Moving one hand to her waist, she opened the buttons of the fall. He realized what she was doing and took over, freeing one breast as he made short work of the fall. Then he stepped slightly back as he pulled the garment over her hips.

She arched up to make the removal easier, and he groaned. His fingers closed more harshly around her nipple, tugging her flesh, and she cried out as her sex screamed for a similar attention. She wanted what he'd done the other night with his hand.

He swept his shirt off, baring the expanse of his muscular chest. She longed to touch him, to explore every bit of new flesh, but his hand was on her sex, gently rubbing her folds.

Suddenly, he scooped his hands beneath her and moved her onto the bed so her head was against the pillows. He settled himself on his knees, between her legs. She watched as he looked down at her, his gaze lingering on her breasts, then fixing on her sex.

Now, she felt the first bit of shyness. A shiver danced across her skin.

"Part your legs wider," he said with a dark, husky rasp.

She did as he said, opening herself to his deeper perusal. He put his fingertip on her clitoris—she'd read this word and now knew how vital it was to a woman's pleasure—then dragged it slowly down her crease before slipping it slightly inside her.

She needed more. Gwen lifted her hips, inviting him to put his entire finger inside her.

But he did not. He teased her with soft, gentle strokes. Then he dropped down, and his mouth replaced his finger.

Gwen cried out as she clutched his head, holding him to her in mindless abandon. Yes, this was what she wanted, and she hadn't even realized it was possible. He licked at her clitoris and her folds, then thrust his tongue inside her. What had seemed to take forever to build last night when he'd touched her roared upon her like a giant wave on the beach.

He stroked her clitoris as he feasted upon her flesh, one hand gripping her backside, as if to hold her captive to his mouth. As if she could have moved away. But she did move—wildly, her hips bucking as she sought her release. It was so very close. Now his finger was pumping into her as his lips and tongue drove her to the brink of ecstasy.

His finger curled, touching a spot inside her that sent her over the edge. Darkness claimed her, then a dizzying array of light as her body tensed, then broke apart. She may have screamed his name. She'd no idea what was happening except that it was pure bliss.

Gradually, she began to slow, but he didn't stop caressing her sex. He kissed her thigh, then her hip. Then he was gone completely.

She opened her eyes and saw he was unbuttoning his fall. It came loose and fell open, and he guided his shaft free. It was long and hard, and utterly beautiful. She touched the hooded end without thinking.

He put his hand over hers and guided it down along the length, then wrapped her fingers around him. Moving her hand back up to the tip, he showed her how to stroke him.

"This is what you like?" she asked, eager to please him and overcome with erotic curiosity.

"Yes."

"Aren't you going to take your breeches off?"

"Do you want me to?"

"It seems only fair," she said. "Take them off. Now, please."

He smiled. "Feel free to order me about."

"When you say I'm yours to command, you mean in the bedroom too?"

"*Especially* in the bedroom," he said with a seductive rasp.

She had to release him as he removed the garment. When he returned, she clasped him once more. "Can I put my mouth on you too?"

"Yes, but not now. I'll come in a horrid mess before I have any chance to put my cock inside your pussy, and I'm afraid that just won't do." His gaze locked on hers. "Unless that is what you prefer. I did say you could order me about."

Gwen licked her lips. "I want your cock in my pussy, then. Now." She decided to leave off the please.

He groaned. "Gwen, you continue to surpass every expectation I might have had. Bend your legs up, love."

She planted her feet on the mattress as he put his hand around hers once more, and together they guided him to her sex. He pressed inside, thrusting slowly. He took his hand away, and she did the same.

There was no pain, just an uncomfortable tightness as her body became accustomed to him. He stroked her clitoris, and she relaxed as her arousal returned.

Coming over her, he braced himself on one hand. "Wrap your legs around me."

She curled her legs around his hips, which brought him more deeply inside her. That spot his finger had found sang as his cock rubbed against it. Gwen cast her head back and moaned as an intense new pleasure rushed through her.

Lazarus kissed her, his tongue spearing deep into her mouth as his hips began to move. He withdrew almost completely then drove into her with a controlled precision. She could feel that he was being deliberate, that he didn't want to hurt her.

The friction of him moving inside her was more delicious than she could have imagined. She moved with him, delighted when his speed began to increase. But he was still tightly reined.

He stopped kissing her as they moved faster. She marveled at the feel of his muscles beneath her legs and moved her hand down his bare back to the curve of his arse. She clasped him as she jerked her hips up.

Groaning, he thrust harder and faster. She kissed his cheek and moved her mouth to his ear. "I want you to lose control. I want to feel you explode as I did. That is an order."

He sucked in a sharp breath. "You have to come with me," he growled. "If you can. Please, say you can. I want to feel you squeeze around my cock."

He reached between them and massaged her clitoris once more, his fingers moving with a fast and deft precision. Again, Gwen felt the pleasure and pressure build within her. She knew now to let go, and so she did, digging her heels into him as she moaned her release.

After a few more thrusts, he shouted, then she felt him tense, his entire body going rigid. His movements slowed, and she kissed his cheek, his jaw, his neck. He claimed her mouth, kissing her with a tender passion that made her want to smile.

He pulled his head up to look down at her. "You are magnificent."

"You are spectacular," she replied with a giggle.

He withdrew from her and rolled to his side, pulling her with him so they faced one another. "I can hardly wait until we are wed."

"It will be an interminable torture now that I know what awaits me nightly."

"Nightly, daily, afternoonly, whenever," he said, nuzzling her neck before kissing her throat.

"I can't stay much longer," she said. "I need to get back to Min's and then home."

"You won't be in trouble, will you?"

She shook her head. "My parents think I am at Min's all

afternoon. Which I am, of course." She smiled at him, and he laughed.

"Of course." He sobered. "Do you know what Jo is doing to find out about the dancing master?"

"I don't, but I know she'll send word—to both of us—as soon as she learns something."

"I'm so relieved by what she was able to share about him and Miss Worsley. Though, I do feel terrible for her. He seduced her, even if she was enamored of him, he should have shown restraint."

"I wonder what will happen. It seems her family won't want her to marry him, but what choice will they have?"

He brushed his lips across Gwen's forehead. "They'll send Miss Worsley far away to visit relatives that don't exist, and hope that no one ever discovers she gave birth to a child."

"And her child will be removed from her, never to be seen again, probably." Gwen's heart ached for the poor woman. "It's so unfair. And sad."

Lazarus sat up. "Come, let's get you back into your disguise. First, you'll want to tidy." He went to the washstand in the corner to wet a cloth, then delivered it to her.

"Thank you. That is most thoughtful." She splayed her hand across his chest and leaned up to press a kiss against his nipple. "Next time, I want to explore this area." She kissed his other nipple. "And this one."

"I can't wait." He kissed her again, and she felt another tug of desire. It seemed she would never tire of him, not that she doubted it.

They dressed—and touched and kissed so it took longer than it ought—then he escorted her downstairs. "Did you walk here?" he asked.

"I took a hack, and I can return in the same."

His eyes rounded. "The hell you will. I'll walk you back."

"We can't be seen together," she said.

"You're dressed like a young man, remember?" He shook his head. "I'll risk the scandal. As it happens, we're already supposedly having an affair."

"Not *supposedly.*" She waggled her brows at him as she laughed.

"No, not supposedly," he said darkly, sensually. "And I can't wait until you are publicly mine."

"Very soon, my love," she said. "Tomorrow, I hope."

She just prayed Jo would find the proof they needed.

～

*T*here was no way Lazarus could sit at home and wait to hear from Jo about Tremblay or for Shefford's man to return from Haverstock Hall. He arrived at the Siren's Call anxious and eager, but not as tightly wound as he could have been. Spending a blissful afternoon with the woman he loved and obtaining her hand in marriage would comfort anyone.

Lazarus clung to that amidst the sea of unknown currently buffeting him. He could see Gwen's smile, hear her joyous laugh, feel her electrifying kiss. And soon, she would be entirely his.

He was already quite hers, even if he wasn't yet her husband.

Scanning the common room, he didn't see Jo. He didn't feel like roaming the gaming rooms for her, so he approached Becky and asked where he could find Jo.

"She isna here," Becky replied in her thick brogue as she balanced a tray carrying four tankards of ale. "I expect her soon, though. Probably." She shrugged and took herself off to deliver the beer.

He exhaled with frustration, but decided he would wait. As he made his way to the usual table he occupied with his friends, Shefford came in and joined him.

"Before you ask, my man hasn't returned," Shefford said as he sat. "I was hoping he might have sprouted wings. Perhaps you did too."

Lazarus chuckled. "That would have been helpful."

Shefford cocked his head and studied him intently. "You are surprisingly relaxed. What's going on? Did you learn something new?"

"I have, in fact." Though, the primary reason behind Lazarus's not-horrible mood was due to Gwen. "But before I get to that, I will share that as of this afternoon, I am betrothed. I'm afraid you've lost another friend to the dreaded parson's trap."

Jaw dropping, Shefford paled. "You can't be marrying Miss Worsley? That makes no sense."

"God, no! I am wedding Miss Gwendolen Price. I hope her brother won't find that awkward."

Shefford sat back in his chair, his shoulders dipping. He almost looked defeated. "*I* find it awkward. But not because of Miss Price. She's lovely."

"She is, and I love her beyond measure."

"I confess I am shocked. I didn't think that would happen to you."

"Why not?" Lazarus asked, genuinely curious.

"You never seemed interested in that," Shefford said with a faint shrug.

"It isn't that I wasn't interested, I just wasn't looking for it, I suppose." Lazarus contemplated why for a moment and realized it was because until he'd met Gwen, he hadn't been completely himself. Not even with his friends. He'd opened himself up to her about things he kept secret, and by doing so, he'd apparently made himself vulnerable. He smiled.

"You look disgustingly happy."

Lazarus laughed. "Quite. But let me tell you the other

reason I am feeling relieved. Gwen was with her friends earlier, and Jo had the most interesting piece of information."

"Jo is part of their set now?" Shefford asked.

"I'm not sure, but she was there."

"That is baffling." Shefford gave his head a shake. "I can't imagine how they even know each other."

"My fault," Lazarus said. Becky approached their table, bringing them their usual ale. She exchanged a few pleasantries, but didn't linger.

Shefford took a long draught before fixing on Lazarus once more. "How is it your fault?"

"Jo arranged for me to attend a literary salon, and I brought Gwen. They met and became acquainted."

"You took Miss Price to a salon… *How?*"

"Er, it involved a disguise. She wanted to attend a literary salon, and I wanted to make her happy."

Shefford blew out a breath. "You *are* in love. What is this compelling piece of information that Jo possesses?"

"As it happens, Miss Worsley was in love with her dancing master last fall. His services were terminated, and he was paid not to speak of it. And we know this dancing master is at least somewhat of a libertine because he was employed by Gwen's mother for a short period recently, and he made unwanted advances on Gwen." Lazarus still wanted to beat the man.

Shefford stared at him. "How have you not hunted him down yet?"

"Jo said she would seek to confirm whether Tremblay— that's the dancing master—is the child's father." Lazarus paused, mulling Shefford's question. "You make an excellent point, however. Perhaps we should go find him now."

"We fucking well should," Shefford said, taking another pull on his ale.

Lazarus couldn't wait to interrogate the man. And plant

him a facer. Perhaps not in that order. He took a drink from his tankard before rising from the table.

However, he didn't move toward the door, because Jo had just walked in. He waved at her, and her gaze fixed on him. Nodding, she came straight for their table, the dark skirts of her walking dress flowing as she moved with swift purpose.

"Josephine, is there anything you don't know?" Shefford, who'd also stood, asked with a crooked smile.

"Plenty, but I can usually find out." She returned his smile, but hers was slightly mischievous. She sat at the table. Lazarus and Shefford retook their chairs.

"You spoke with Tremblay?" Lazarus asked.

She shook her head. "I wasn't able to find him. However, I did speak with his musician assistant. He's called Nott, and he plays music for Tremblay's dancing lessons."

Shefford, who sat opposite Jo, leaned forward. "And what did he say?"

"He confirmed Tremblay and Miss Worsley had an affair, and that Tremblay was paid to keep silent about it," Jo said looking at them both intently. "He was *not* aware that Miss Worsley was with child. I do wonder if Tremblay even knows he's to be a father."

Lazarus smacked his palm on the table. "I knew it wasn't me."

"How can you be certain it was Tremblay?" Shefford asked. He glanced at Lazarus. "Sorry to cast doubt, but we should be absolute in our investigation. Perhaps she had other lovers."

"I suppose that's possible, but she was, according to Nott, rapturously in love with Tremblay. She wrote him letters that Tremblay would read in a mocking voice to Nott." Jo grimaced. "I feel so badly for Miss Worsley, as it seems her affections were not reciprocated."

"And yet, he was quite happy to bed her," Lazarus said

with disgust. That was a true reprobate. Was it any wonder she preferred to marry someone else?

"The timing is also perfect, as far as aligning with your fox-hunting party," Jo continued. "The affair with Tremblay occurred from late October into December. Apparently, he and Nott visited Haverstock Hall the first week of December to continue Miss Worsley's instruction. That was when he was dismissed. Nott presumes they were caught, but Tremblay didn't share the details with him."

"But Tremblay told him he'd been paid to be quiet?" Shefford asked.

"Yes, because he gave a portion to Nott to ensure his silence as well. However, it seems it was a *very* small portion, as Tremblay lived a rather lavish lifestyle until recently. Perhaps he is now out of funds. Nott seemed a trifle peeved."

Shefford turned his head to Lazarus. "I say we continue with our plan to seek out Tremblay."

"Agreed." Lazarus couldn't wait to find the man. "Jo, where can we find him?"

"*If* you can find him, but perhaps you'll have better luck at some of his usual haunts around Leicester Square. He lives on Gerrard Street." She gave them the number of his lodgings and also provided Nott's address.

"Jo, you are a marvel." Lazarus leaned over and kissed her cheek.

"You can't go about kissing other women anymore," Shefford said in a mock scolding tone. He looked toward Jo. "He's gone and got himself betrothed." He rolled his eyes and scoffed.

Jo grinned. "Congratulations. I was not present when Gwen returned this afternoon, but I will assume she shared the happy news with Min and Ellis, who were."

"Once I deal with this situation and put it behind me, I

will call on her father," Lazarus said, wishing he didn't have to wait. "I am hoping that will be tomorrow."

Shefford stood again. "I don't see why not. Since tomorrow is when you are supposed to offer for Miss Worsley else she will inform her father and grandfather, we need to conclude this matter."

Jo rose, and Lazarus did the same, meeting her gaze. "I can't thank you enough for your assistance in this. You are helpful in a great many ways. Some man will be lucky to have you one day."

A dark laugh leapt from her wide mouth. "That man doesn't exist. I am as committed to remaining as unwed as Shefford there." She gave him a commiserative nod, and he returned it.

"Solidarity," he said in a low tone. He looked to Lazarus. "Come, our prey awaits."

Lazarus anticipated his capture.

CHAPTER 19

*N*either Tremblay nor Nott had been at their lodgings or anywhere else Lazarus and Shefford had looked last night. They'd finally gone home in defeat hours after midnight.

Lazarus intended to try again this morning, but Tremblay was still not at home. Nor was there anyone Lazarus could ask who could perhaps indicate where he was or when he would return.

Frustrated beyond words, Lazarus made his way to Nott's lodging, hoping for a better result.

The man lived in a small set of rooms above an apothecary. Lazarus climbed the two flights of stairs to the second floor and knocked loudly on the door. "Mr. Nott?"

Lazarus was fairly certain he heard movement inside and was prepared to break down the door if the man didn't answer. Thankfully, he did.

Exhaling with relief, Lazarus tried to set aside his irritation. He would get more out of the man if he could be charming or at least pleasant. He summoned a smile. "Good morning. Pardon my interruption at this early hour."

Glancing over the short, slight man's head, Lazarus saw a valise in the middle of the floor. Was he going somewhere? He met Nott's gaze and noted the apprehension in their blue depths. "I am Lord Somerton."

"Good morning, my lord." He twitched his shoulders nervously. "It is rather early, and I've a coach to catch."

"I see. And where are you going? To visit a relative, perhaps?" He tried to make it seem like he was making idle conversation, but he wanted to know why the man was leaving now amidst all that was happening. Had Jo's visit yesterday provoked him to want to leave London?

"Ah, yes. A relative."

"How splendid. Well, I shan't take too much of your time then, but I do require a few moments." Lazarus easily pushed his way inside past the man. The lodgings were neat, if shabby, with a spartan collection of furniture.

Lazarus turned as Nott closed his door. He stood to the side of it, his brow deeply creased and his mouth turned down.

"Since you are in a rush, let me get straight to the point," Lazarus said almost cheerfully. "I understand you are a witness to a love affair between your employer, Mr. Tremblay, and one of his students, Miss Melissa Worsley." Lazarus paused as the man paled slightly. "Yes, just so," he continued with a faint smile. "I believe you are aware that Miss Worsley is expecting a child. Unfortunately, she has decided to embroil me in this tawdry situation and claim, falsely, that I am the child's father. As you can surmise, I am not interested in being trapped into marrying Miss Worsley."

"No, I don't imagine you are," Nott said, his gaze wary. "What is it you want from me?"

"I am trying to prevent my name being dragged into this scandal, and I do hope you can help me by accompanying me to call on Mr. Worsley and perhaps Lord Haverstock to explain the affair you witnessed." Lazarus thought that was the best, and perhaps only, course of action at this point. Miss Worsley and her mother would tell those gentlemen today that Lazarus had fathered the child, and if Nott could share his knowledge to the contrary, Lazarus was certain Haverstock and Worsley wouldn't force the marriage.

But Nott went gray. He flicked a glance at his valise, then clasped his hands tightly before him. "I really do need to leave. I shall miss my coach. I'm afraid I can't help you."

Lazarus's answering smile was practically malevolent this time. "And I am afraid you must." He recalled what Jo had said about the man being vexed about the amount of money he'd been paid to remain silent as compared to his employer. Now, he was suddenly leaving town. "Did Mrs. Worsley pay you to leave?"

Nott's eyes rounded. "How did you know?"

"I wasn't certain, but I can deduce that you seem keen to leave. Since I know you were visited yesterday about this matter, I presumed the two events could be related. Did you go to them after my friend spoke with you?"

The smaller man's shoulders sank. "Yes." He straightened, as if he'd found his backbone. "Since they'd already paid Tremblay to be quiet and not me, I decided I would ask for money too. You can't expect me to continue working for that libertine. I'd already decided I needed to find other employment. I'm going to try my luck in Bath."

"How good of you to finally grow a conscience." Lazarus couldn't help thinking of how this man ignored Tremblay's treatment of his students. "How long have you witnessed his grotesque behavior and said nothing?"

Nott's jaw worked, though he didn't have much of a chin to move about.

"I don't know what the Worsleys paid for your silence, but I will pay you more if you will speak. Do yourself a favor and don't inflate the price. I will be asking Mrs. Worsley what she paid you." He looked down his nose at Nott. "Furthermore, I'm sure a letter of reference from a viscount will go a long way to ensure your future security in Bath."

He nodded furiously. "Indeed, it would, my lord. I would be most grateful. She paid me twenty pounds, but with your letter, I would be happy to accept ten from you."

"How magnanimous." Lazarus withdrew the notes from his pocket. "You may have the money now, and you'll receive the letter after you deliver your testimony to Haverstock and Worsley. Shall we go?"

"Now?" Nott fidgeted with the buttons on his coat.

"Is there a better time? Besides, as you said, you need to catch your coach."

"I'll have to take a later one," he replied sullenly.

"But you shall be the richer for it." Lazarus started for the door. "Come, Mr. Nott."

As they left the man's mean lodgings, Lazarus felt a soothing calm. This would all be over very soon. Then he could call on Mr. Price and set his future in motion.

$\approx$

*A*ll morning, Gwen felt as though she were walking across a thinly iced pond waiting for it to break. Or in this case, waiting for something to happen. Either Lazarus would call and their betrothal could be made official, or Markwith would arrive eager to negotiate a marriage that wasn't going to happen.

She'd tried to speak with her father last night, to tell him she couldn't wed Markwith, but he was still not home when Gwen had gone to bed. Her efforts to talk to her mother instead had also been foiled, as she'd retired early with a headache. Her maid had confided that the stress of the Eberforce rumor was taking a toll.

Gwen felt terribly about that. If not for her secretly meeting Lazarus at Tamsin's, Eberforce would not have spread the gossip.

Before Gwen thought it would be reasonable to disturb her father, which was any time before noon, she was summoned to his study. She dearly hoped she wouldn't arrive to find Markwith already there.

Worrying her hands as she walked downstairs, she rehearsed what she would say to Markwith if he was here. He was a very nice gentleman, and she hated to disappoint or hurt him. She reminded herself she'd never done anything to indicate she would marry him. Up to now, she'd enjoyed dancing with him and taking a promenade. That did not equate to an entire courtship that would result in marriage.

Particularly since she didn't love him.

Her love for Lazarus, however, was so strong and keen that she felt like skipping, which would probably be disastrous. Or singing, which would definitely be painful for those around her.

Instead, she walked sedately to her father's study and peered around the partially open door. "You wanted to see me, Papa?" A quick scan of the interior revealed him to be alone. Relief swept through her.

"Come in, Gwen," he said from where he sat at his desk. He stood as she entered. "Markwith has just sent a note. He intends to call this afternoon." Papa smiled. "He was quite enthused about the marriage."

Gwen sagged. "I had hoped to speak with you last night, but you didn't return home until after I retired. If I'd known you were about this morning, I would have sought you out." In hindsight, she should have told his valet that she wanted to see her father first thing today.

He frowned. "Is aught amiss?"

"I know you want me to marry Mr. Markwith, and he is very pleasant." She dropped her hands to her sides and straightened her spine, lifting her shoulders as if she could become larger. She could be a bear or a stag, something of impressive stature. "However, I am in love with someone else. Indeed, this gentleman has already asked if I will marry him, and I said yes."

"What the devil is this about?" Papa rarely became angry, but he looked to be that now. His face had darkened, and his eyes narrowed. "You said nothing of another gentleman yesterday when we informed you that you would wed Markwith."

"His proposal happened since then," Gwen replied. Seeing her father open his mouth, she was certain he would ask when. "I encountered him at Henlow House yesterday, by chance."

Her father was nearly scowling. "And who is this gentleman?"

"Lord Somerton."

As Papa's eyes tried to bulge from his face, Gwen heard her mother speak from behind her.

"Somerton? The man you are alleged to be having an affair with?" Mama's voice sounded raspy.

"Look what you've done to your poor mother." Papa raced to Mama's side and helped her into a chair. Indeed, Gwen's mother did look pale.

"I'm sorry, Mama," Gwen said, rushing to her and taking her hand, which was rather cool.

"This will be a terrible scandal," her mother said. "I spent so much time at the ball the other night telling people that you had not been meeting Somerton at Lord Droxford's, that it was merely coincidence."

Gwen's father's gaze landed on her as his lips pursed

heavily. "And we're to believe you just happened upon him at Henlow House? Have you no shame?"

Wincing beneath the heat of her father's words, Gwen chewed the inside of her cheek. This was worse than she'd expected.

"I have no shame for choosing Somerton. I love him, and he loves me."

Her mother gaped at her. "How can you be so naive? Men like Somerton don't make good husbands."

Gwen released her hand. "You seemed enthusiastic about his interest when he first began paying me attention."

"As a suitor, yes," her mother said, appearing pained. "But not to marry. Markwith is a far better choice. You must reconsider, my dear. He is everything we hoped for."

"Except I don't love him," Gwen replied.

"Not yet, but you may in time," Papa said gruffly. "You would be foolish to choose Somerton over him—if he really plans to marry you. The man hasn't even bothered to pay me a call." Papa sniffed with disdain. "We only care about your happiness."

How it stung that they assumed Lazarus to be disingenuous, but they only knew of his reputation, not the man he truly was. "I know you both think I'm hopeless. You didn't even want to give me a Season, but I finally wore you down. Then it was nearly a disaster because I am awkward and clumsy. But do you know who turned my Season around? Lord Somerton. He paid me public attention, which prompted other gentlemen to consider me, and he met with me at his cousin's house to advise me on how best to attract a husband. Without his help, I would not have even attracted Markwith's notice. Because of him, I was queen of the Phoenix Club ball. Weren't you proud of me that night, Mama?"

"You were meeting with him?" her mother whispered. Was that all she'd heard?

"Yes, but not to have an affair. We did fall in love, but that was not why we started our association. Indeed, we realized our feelings after we'd already agreed to stop meeting. Somerton was adamant I didn't need him anymore. He worried his further attention and help could be detrimental to my reputation if we persisted." She couldn't reveal the truth of their meetings—that was Lazarus's secret, not hers.

"At least he knew that much," her father muttered. "I can't support this marriage, Gwen. He is not a suitable husband."

Gwen's mother looked to her beseechingly. "You must know that he will make you unhappy. He may say he loves you, but I doubt he will be faithful. He will break your heart, my dearest girl."

"No, he won't. I don't know how to explain to you that he loves me and could not bear me wedding someone else."

"Some men want what they can't have," her father said darkly. "Trust us, Gwen. You must choose Markwith."

Again, she stood as tall as she could and tried to become an intimidating creature. "I can't do that. I've already chosen Somerton. I am of age, and he is the man I will wed. I am deeply sorry you do not approve and hope you will change your mind." Gwen knew in that moment that she wasn't going to let anyone come between her and Lazarus—not her parents and certainly not Miss Worsley's lies. "Furthermore, you will need to tell Markwith you were mistaken about where my feelings lie. I never promised him anything, so the apology must come from you."

Her father's face had returned to his regular color, but now it reddened again. He took a deep breath, and Gwen decided she should go before things deteriorated further.

"Where are you going?" he snapped as she reached the door.

"I'm leaving before someone says something they wish they hadn't. I implore you both to consider me and my feelings. I have found a wonderful man whom I love and who loves me in return. I will be a viscountess, but more importantly, I will be cherished and adored. Isn't that what you want most for me?"

They both stared at her, their mouths clamped shut. Gwen turned and left before she started to cry. She had no time for tears or self-pity. Besides, there was no reason to pity herself, not when she was on the verge of true happiness with the man she loved.

Sniffing, she hurried to fetch her things so she could call on Miss Worsley. It was time for the young woman to abandon her deceitful scheme to snare Lazarus and let true love win out.

CHAPTER 20

*L*azarus stood with Mr. Nott in the Worsleys' drawing room awaiting the arrival of Mrs. Worsley.

He hadn't accepted the butler's response that she was not receiving. Rather, Lazarus had stalked inside, thrown his title at the butler, and said it was a matter of great import.

The butler had shown him to the drawing room with alacrity.

Nott stood off to the side looking even more nervous than he had when Lazarus had burst in on him earlier. "Is this where you met with Mrs. Worsley yesterday?" Lazarus asked.

"No," Nott replied. "I am not a viscount. I was not permitted past the entrance hall. It took me far more persuasion to obtain an audience."

Lazarus arched a brow. "Persuasion or threats?" He supposed it was the latter, else why would Mrs. Worsley have agreed to see him at all?

Nott looked down at the floor instead of responding.

Mrs. Worsley swept into the drawing room a moment

later. Her gaze landed on Nott first. "What are you doing here again?" Then she saw Lazarus standing more toward the center of the room. "Did you come together?"

"We did," Lazarus said benignly. "We had an informative chat earlier, and I invited him to accompany me. I do realize you paid him not to speak to me, but I paid him more."

She sucked a breath, her cheeks flushing bright pink. "I can't think why you would bring him here. Haven't you come to propose to Melissa?"

"Absolutely not." How Lazarus delighted in saying that. "I'm amused that you would think so given what Mr. Nott knows. Or did you think I'd brought him along for some other reason? Perhaps we're friends." He laughed and noted that Nott had to stifle a smirk.

Lazarus sobered as he gave in to his anger at this woman's machinations and continued belligerence. "I am not here to propose marriage to your daughter, because I am not the father of her child. That man is a dancing master called Tremblay, a fact of which you are fully aware."

She glared at him, but said nothing.

"Where is he?" Lazarus asked softly. "I and others have sought him out, but he is nowhere to be found."

"I'm sure I don't know. You've concocted this entire story. You say you paid this man. Did you pay him to lie and say this dancing master is the father of Melissa's child?"

"I am weary of your schemes," Lazarus said loudly, his patience razor thin. "You surely know that Mr. Nott here is— or was—Tremblay's musician assistant. You are also, I hope, completely aware that Tremblay carried on an affair with your daughter while he was her dancing master." He advanced on her. "I know you dismissed him and paid him to keep silent about what transpired between him and your daughter. What I don't know is why you decided to pin the blame of your daughter's circumstances on me."

She opened her mouth, but Lazarus went on, "And don't think to deny anything. Please recall that I have Mr. Nott as my witness, and he is prepared to tell your husband and your father, Lord Haverstock, the truth."

The color drained from her face. "You would see my daughter ruined," she whispered brokenly.

"I am not inconsiderate of your daughter's troubles, Mrs. Worsley, but involving me was not the way to solve them." Lazarus truly felt for the girl, especially with a calculating mother such as Mrs. Worsley. "I expect to not ever hear from you or her again. I do wish you all the best of luck."

Lazarus inclined his head toward Nott and walked around Mrs. Worsley to the door. He did not look back as he made his way to the staircase.

"That was most impressive," Nott said as they descended. "I didn't even have to say anything."

"Your presence alone was enough," Lazarus said. "I owe you a letter." Which he could not write without considerable effort. *Dammit.*

They moved from the staircase hall to the entrance hall, and Lazarus stopped short. Standing in the center was Gwen. Her lips curved in a happy smile upon seeing him.

"What are you doing here?" he asked, moving toward her. He was so glad to see her and couldn't wait to tell her that their path forward was entirely clear.

Well, he hoped it was clear. He wondered if she had news about her proposed marriage to Markwith.

"I came to speak with Miss Worsley," Gwen replied. "I have just informed my parents that I will be marrying you, and it became apparent that I needed to remove the other obstacle in our way—Miss Worsley's outrageous claim. I was hoping that if I tell her that you and I are in love, she will give up on her ploy."

To Lazarus's left, Nott sniffed. "That's so lovely," he murmured.

Lazarus smiled just as Mrs. Worsley yelled from behind him. "You will not be the ruin of my daughter!"

"Lazarus!" Gwen shrieked as she shoved him roughly.

The report of a pistol filled the hall, and Lazarus looked in horror as Gwen's face registered shock. She grasped her right upper arm as she crumpled.

Lazarus somehow kept from falling himself—she'd pushed him very hard—and leapt toward her, catching her before she collapsed in a heap. "Gwen!"

Another shriek sounded, and Lazarus looked to see that Nott had taken the pistol from Mrs. Worsley and pointed it at her.

"There aren't any more bullets," she spat.

"I don't care," Nott said, his voice shaking. "This makes me feel better."

There had been a footman near the door, but he'd hurried to help with Gwen. Lazarus looked at him. "Go and fetch a physician!"

"I'm fine," Gwen said as Lazarus swept her into his arms. "It barely hurts." Except she winced.

Lazarus glanced about for a place to take Gwen. "I need a room with a chaise or a long settee."

"Just in here," Miss Worsley said, leading them to a room to the left of the entrance hall. She must have arrived at some point.

"I don't need to lie down," Gwen said. "It's only my arm."

Lazarus carried Gwen to a settee and set her down carefully. She cradled her right arm with her left. Her sleeve was bright red with blood. Kneeling beside the settee, he loosened his cravat and stripped it away then gently wrapped it around her arm.

"We need to hold this against the wound," he said softly,

clasping her arm and feeling the warmth of her blood against his palm as it seeped through the cravat.

"Fetch water and bandages," Miss Worsley said to someone. "Mother, come in here."

A moment later, Mrs. Worsley staggered into the sitting room, her face ashen. Nott followed, still pointing the empty pistol at her.

"Sit," Miss Worsley snapped at her mother.

The woman did as she was told, which Lazarus found surprising. "How could you bloody shoot my betrothed?" Lazarus roared.

"I was trying to shoot *you*," Mrs. Worsley mumbled.

"Mama!" Miss Worsley's shoulders began to shake as soft sobs fell from her lips. "How could you do that?"

"I didn't have a choice."

"Of course you did," Gwen said, flinching as she settled herself against the back of the settee.

"I'm so sorry this happened," Lazarus said, pressing a kiss to Gwen's temple. "What were you thinking pushing me out of the way?"

"I was thinking I still wanted to marry you, not bury you. If you hadn't moved, her bullet would have hit you square in the back."

"You don't know that."

"Neither do you," Gwen said darkly. Her features softened, and he thought she might cry. "I couldn't lose you."

"Nor can I lose you." Lazarus brushed his lips over hers. He turned his attention back to Mrs. Worsley. "Why would you shoot at me?"

"Because you refused to marry Melissa. She *must* wed."

"Then wed her to Tremblay," Lazarus bit out.

"He wouldn't marry me," Melissa said quietly. "He didn't love me the way I loved him. When my mother dismissed him at Haverstock Hall, I told her he would come back for me. But he didn't. Because she paid him not to."

Mrs. Worsley's jaw was tightly clenched, the veins of her neck stark and visible.

"She also paid him not to say anything," Nott added.

"Why did you involve me?" Lazarus asked.

Melissa met his gaze with tears in her eyes. "When I told my mother about the babe, it was March. I was already several months gone. I was stupid not to realize what was happening. Mama calculated the dates and, though it was a few weeks earlier than when the babe was conceived, decided someone at the fox-hunting party could be the father. She chose you because she'd seen you return very inebriated late one night. She said it would be easy to convince a man like you that the babe was yours."

Lazarus narrowed his eyes at Mrs. Worsley. "How did you see me? Shefford and I returned near dawn."

"She was stealing from her lover's room," Miss Worsley said bitterly, casting her mother an awful look. "But *I* am the immoral one."

"What you did was despicable," Gwen said, glaring at Mrs. Worsley.

"And where is Mr. Tremblay?" Lazarus asked. "Did you by chance shoot at him too?"

"No." Mrs. Worsley tossed a sneer toward Nott. "After I paid him yesterday, I went to see Tremblay. I gave him more money to leave London immediately."

"Who will I marry now, Mama?" Miss Worsley laughed, and Lazarus wondered if she was finally at her wit's end.

"No one," Mrs. Worsley snapped. "You'll go the country and whelp the brat. Then you'll return next Season. At least your condition is not widely known." She looked toward Lazarus and Gwen. "Is it?"

"I haven't said anything," Lazarus replied. "I wouldn't want to cause Miss Worsley further harm. Although, it will be difficult to keep the fact that you shot Miss Price from circulating."

"Not if no one here says anything." Mrs. Worsley narrowed her eyes in a thoroughly Machiavellian fashion.

"I think you should send for Bow Street," Nott said to Lazarus.

"You mustn't do that!" Mrs. Worsley cried.

"No, you can't," Gwen agreed. She reached over and touched Lazarus's arm with her uninjured appendage, whispering, "Think of Miss Worsley. She will already suffer great consequences for her actions. I would hate for her to suffer for her mother's actions too. I will say I was wounded by a falling book. Or something." She gave him a faint smile.

"You are kinder than I," he murmured, kissing her brow. "But I can't disagree that Miss Worsley will already endure enough." He turned his head toward Mrs. Worsley. "We will leave Bow Street out of this for your daughter's sake. Not yours," he added sharply.

"Are you certain you wish to do that?" Nott asked. "The woman is a menace."

"My betrothed and I don't wish to cause Miss Worsley additional heartache." He fixed his narrowed gaze on Mrs. Worsley once more. "However, if you come anywhere near my wife in the future, you will regret doing so. I advise you to disappear into the country with your daughter for a good, long time."

Mrs. Worsley nodded, but did not look pleased about it.

"Thank you, my lord," Miss Worsley said. "I greatly appreciate your kindness."

Gwen looked up at Miss Worsley. "I am sorry you got tangled up with a true rogue. There are rules for that. I'm going to give you a copy for future reference."

Miss Worsley appeared confused.

"She'll explain later," Lazarus said.

The physician arrived shortly and set a dozen stitches into Gwen's torn upper arm. He prescribed laudanum or strong alcohol for the pain and bade her to keep her arm elevated for the next day.

When he was gone, Gwen addressed Miss Worsley. "I will tell people that I called on you after meeting you at the ball the other night so we could become better acquainted. While here, you were kind enough to show me your library—do you have a library?" At Miss Worsley's nod, Gwen went on. "When I tried to pull a book from a high shelf, I dislodged a few, and they fell onto my arm. No one will see that I have a wound that doesn't match that description."

"You would go to that trouble for me?" Miss Worsley asked somewhat incredulously. "After what I tried to do to your betrothed?"

"I understand you were desperate and that you were trying to please your mother. I know what it's like to want to make our parents proud. While it is a meaningful endeavor, in the end, I think it's more important to have pride in yourself and the choices you make."

"I have little pride in my actions the past several months," Miss Worsley said softly, but with a sharp bitterness.

"You can start anew," Gwen said. "Your past behavior needn't dictate your future." She glanced toward Lazarus, and his chest constricted. How had he been so lucky to find a woman like her, let alone receive her love?

"Let us go, my love," Lazarus said. "I'll carry you to the coach."

"That isn't necessary."

"It absolutely is." He picked her up gently and carried her outside. Nott followed them, and Lazarus offered him a ride.

"Thank you, but I'll grab a hack," Nott said with a smile.

"I do owe you that letter," Lazarus said. "And probably more money."

"Not at all. I was very glad to help." Nott looked at Gwen nestled in Lazarus's arms. "I do hope you will be well, miss. And may I apologize for Mr. Tremblay's behavior and my lack of interference?"

"Mr. Tremblay's behavior is not yours to apologize for," Gwen said warmly. "But I will accept the other one. Thank you."

Lazarus carried her to the coach and gently set her inside on the seat. She grimaced faintly, but she'd had a shot of rum while the physician was preparing to sew her up, which Miss Worsley had provided along with a small glass for herself.

"What am I going to tell my parents?" Gwen asked as the coach started forward.

"You probably shouldn't tell them you were shot. They will be horrified."

"Nicked by a bullet," Gwen corrected. "I can't, in good faith, call this a true gunshot wound." She met his gaze with worry, however, and the smile fell from his face. "My parents *are* horrified—that we're getting married. They're certain you will break my heart, though I assured them you would not."

"I would never," he vowed. "Our hearts are now one, and if yours breaks, so too shall mine."

She lifted her gaze to his. "Now, you sound like a romantic poet."

"You certainly make me want to spout words of love and beauty." He kissed her temple. "If you'd rather wait to get married so your parents can become accustomed, I don't mind."

"No!" The vehemence of her response shocked him.

"Careful, or you'll upset the physician's needlework," Lazarus said.

"We are getting married as soon as possible. When can that be exactly?"

"I can purchase the license tomorrow. I don't want to leave your side today."

"I would argue that you must get it immediately, but I can't say I mind you wanting to stay with me. Shall we set the ceremony for Wednesday?"

While that would be best since he didn't need to be in the Lords—which was where he should be going shortly but would not—he knew his mother would be devastated if she couldn't be here for the wedding. She was going to be shocked enough that he was getting married. She would not want to miss it.

"My mother will want to be here," Lazarus said. "If I send word to her immediately, she could be here perhaps Wednesday afternoon. She is still in Kent with my middle sister."

"The one who had the baby recently," Gwen said with a nod. "Yes, we must wait for your mother. Should we say Friday just to be safe?"

"Thursday should be fine." Though that was the day he was giving his speech. They could get married in the morning, as they would be required to do. Perhaps it would bring him luck.

She sucked in a breath, and he worried she was in terrible pain. However, she said, "You're delivering your speech that day. We should wait until Friday."

He kissed her. "No. Thursday is perfect."

"Have you memorized the entire speech?" she asked.

"I think so, but I confess it hasn't been a priority the past few days."

"Then we will make it so, starting today," she declared firmly.

"You think your parents are going to let me linger in your company that long?"

"They will if they want to attend our wedding ceremony." Her eyes narrowed slightly.

He put his hand to his chest. "My darling almost wife, you can be quite savage."

She used her free hand to cup his head. "When it comes to you, I will do whatever is necessary in whatever manner is required."

He gave her a sly smile. "How I love this commanding side of you."

Her eyes glittered with promise. "I know." She glanced out the window. "We have arrived, unfortunately. Let us go deliver the second-most shocking news of the day."

Lazarus laughed. "I love you, my sweet Gwen."

"I hope you never stop."

He kissed her fast but deep, then locking his eyes on hers, fiercely vowed, "I will never."

~

*L*azarus stepped out of the carriage and held his arms up. "I'm ready."

Gwen shook her head. "You are not carrying me into the house. That will send my mother into a complete upset. You may escort me."

He frowned. Deeply. "I don't care what your mother thinks or does."

"Honestly, I don't need you to carry me," Gwen said. "As delightful as that is. Please just let me walk? If I feel faint at all, I will tell you at once."

Exhaling, he lowered his arms. "Fine. But I dissent."

Gwen couldn't keep from smiling. "Noted." She gave him

the hand of her uninjured left arm and allowed him to basically lift her from the coach.

He put his arm around her waist and supported her as they moved toward the door. "All right?"

"Quite." There was a steady pain in her arm, but it wasn't terrible. The rum had likely helped. She didn't particularly want to take the laudanum the physician had given her, so she would see what liquor her father could provide.

Lake opened the door and immediately gasped, his bushy gray brows drawing together. "My heavens, Miss Price! What has happened?"

"Just a minor injury," she said with a smile.

"She does need to rest," Lazarus said.

Gwen removed her hat and handed it to Lake. "Please inform my parents that I will be resting in my chamber. If they would like to visit, they may do so."

"Has Gwen returned?" Her mother's voice carried into the entrance hall just before she moved into it. Her gasp was louder than Lake's, and her hand flew to her mouth as her eyes goggled. "What happened?" She glanced toward Lazarus.

"I'm fine, Mama," Gwen said, having little patience after their earlier conversation. "Lazarus is going to help me up to my chamber, where he will sit with me for as long as I require. Tomorrow morning, he will obtain our license to wed."

"Congratulations, miss," Lake said, his gaze warm.

"Thank you, Lake," Gwen said, happy to have *someone's* support. "Lazarus, let us go up."

He helped her to the staircase at the back of the entrance hall and they ascended slowly. Gwen's mother followed behind. "Lake, fetch Mr. Price, please. Gwen, what happened?"

In the coach, they'd decided to tell her parents the truth.

Gwen didn't want to lie to them. "It's a rather sordid tale, but all has ended well. I am safe and whole, and Lazarus and I will be wed on Thursday."

"Thursday?" her mother sputtered.

When they reached the landing, Gwen asked Lazarus for a brief respite, adding, "Just one more story."

"The hell with it," he muttered as he swept her into his arms and carried her up the next set of stairs.

Gwen held her right arm over her middle and directed him to her chamber. Once inside, he set her on the edge of the bed. "Thank you." She met his gaze, giddy with love and the love she saw reflected in them.

Lazarus began unlacing her walking boots as her mother stared at him.

"Gwen's maid can do that," her mother said, appearing aghast.

"Her maid is not present at the moment," Lazarus said pleasantly. "As her almost husband, I don't mind performing the task." He sent a wicked look toward Gwen, and she dearly wished her mother wasn't there.

"What is this I hear of an injury and a wedding?" Gwen's father's voice boomed as he strode into the bedchamber.

"I will explain," Gwen said as Lazarus lifted her legs onto the bed and positioned pillows behind her so she could sit up against the headboard. She then launched into a detailed narrative of the Worsleys' attempt to force Lazarus into marriage. When she arrived at the part about Tremblay being the father of the baby, Gwen's mother had to sit down in a chair near the hearth.

"Wasn't that your dancing master?" Gwen's father asked.

"Briefly," Gwen said. "However, I didn't care for his demeanor, and I told Mama I didn't wish to see him again."

"I should have listened to you after the first lesson," Mama said, her face nearly gray.

Gwen looked at Lazarus standing beside the bed, his hand resting next to her uninjured arm on the coverlet. "You can sit, if you like," she said to him softly, inclining her head toward a chair that he could pull close to the bed.

"When they leave," he whispered with a wink.

"You still haven't explained your injury," her father noted with a stern frown.

"Will you allow me to share this part?" Lazarus asked Gwen. "I think your heroism will shine more with my telling."

Gwen grinned. "By all means."

Lazarus detailed his visit to Tremblay's musician assistant, which was new to Gwen. She had wondered why the man was there, but there hadn't been time to ask about that. Then Lazarus explained how he'd informed Mrs. Worsley that he would not be marrying her daughter. She'd been upset, but Lazarus had never imagined she might become violent. Then he told of how he encountered Gwen and what happened after with Mrs. Worsley shooting at them.

Gwen worried her father's head was going to burst. She'd never seen his face so red. And was he shaking?

"What were you thinking, putting yourself in danger like that?" he asked angrily.

"I did ask her the same thing," Lazarus said.

"Good," her father grunted.

"Papa, I am sure you would have done the same for Mama. We don't think when we see the person we love most in harm's way. We just act." She lifted her shoulders in a light shrug, then winced as pain shot up her right arm.

"Oh, my poor dear, you must rest," her mother said urgently.

"We need to send for a physician." Her father started toward the door.

"That isn't necessary," Lazarus said. "She has already been seen, stitched, and dosed with rum."

"Stitches?" her mother asked faintly.

"I am fine, Mama. Truly. It barely hurts."

Lazarus looked down at Gwen. "You need to rest." Then he lifted his head to address her parents. "We decided not to notify Bow Street. No one wants a scandal, and Miss Worsley has already suffered a great deal."

"She tried to force you into marriage," Gwen's father said. "I would not be so charitable."

Gwen looked to her father. "Papa, we would just like to put this behind us. We just want to focus on our upcoming nuptials."

Lazarus looked squarely at her father. "We do hope you will be happy for us."

Her father glowered at Lazarus. "I expect you to make her happy, and not just in the short term before you lose interest."

Gwen felt Lazarus tense and saw his pulse ticking rapidly in his neck. "Papa, that isn't going to happen."

"On my life, it is not," Lazarus vowed. "I love Gwen with everything that I am. I could never have imagined I would find someone as wonderful as her, but I will spend my days working to deserve her love."

Gwen's mother smiled, then she sniffed. Her father's frown lessened.

"Mama, will you please make the arrangements for the wedding ceremony on Thursday morning? We won't be able to have a breakfast as Lazarus has an important speech in the Lords that day. We can have a dinner or other celebration another time." Gwen knew that would be important to her.

Rising, her mother nodded. "I'll take care of everything, including a new gown."

"Mama, I don't need a new gown," Gwen said, trying not to roll her eyes.

"Of course you do. It's your wedding." Her mother came around the other side of the bed and leaned over it to kiss Gwen's forehead. She looked over at Lazarus with gratitude. "Thank you for taking care of our daughter."

"It is now my primary purpose in life."

"We couldn't ask for anything more," her mother said. She glanced toward Gwen's father, and he gave an imperceptible nod.

They left a moment later, and Gwen briefly closed her eyes. "Thank goodness," she whispered. Looking up at Lazarus, she added, "I worried there would be a scene."

"I'm glad there was not—for your sake." He tucked a strand of hair behind her ear. "Before I go, I should tell you that I do need to write a letter of recommendation for Nott. He is relocating to Bath and will be seeking a position there. It was part of how I persuaded him to accompany me to see Mrs. Worsley. However, after his assistance today, I am quite happy to provide it."

"But you are concerned about the writing of it," Gwen said, taking his hand. "I will help you, though I can't write it either, because of my arm. At least not today. You must write it yourself."

"There you go, ordering me about again." He grinned. "Please don't ever stop."

CHAPTER 21

They made very convincing gentlemen, if Gwen said so herself. That she'd gone from bride to gentleman in disguise in a few hours amused her greatly. But she would have gone to any lengths to see Lazarus's speech. And dressing as a man was required, as women were not allowed in the gallery in the House of Lords.

It came as no surprise to her that her friends—Tamsin, Min, Ellis, and Jo—had insisted on joining her in this folly. And now they would wait until whenever it was that Lazarus would deliver his speech. Since Parliament could work well into the night, Gwen hoped it wouldn't be too late.

"We should at least have put a flower in your lapel," Min said as they situated themselves behind the bar with a group of members from the House of Commons. "I can't believe this is how you are spending your wedding day."

"I can think of no better way," Gwen said earnestly. Truly, this was perfect, in her mind.

"I wish you'd all seen how pretty Gwen looked," Tamsin said. As Lazarus's cousin, she was the only one of Gwen's friends who had been invited. Gwen's mother had been insistent that only family be allowed to attend. Gwen was just glad that Lazarus's mother had arrived in time. His oldest sister, who lived near London, had also been in attendance.

"I understand why we weren't invited, but I'm still a little sad about it." Min sniffed.

"My mother is planning a dinner party for next week, and you will all be invited."

"Including me?" Jo asked with a wry smile. "I will not be offended in the least if I do not receive an invitation."

"You are most definitely on the list of invitees," Gwen assured her. "I do hope you will be able to come. I know you are at the Siren's Call most nights."

"Yes, but my mother will likely insist I go—if I tell her about it. She thinks I spend too much time at the Siren's Call." Jo shrugged.

Ellis leaned around Min to look at Jo. "If you did not, you may not have been so exceptionally equipped to aid Gwen and Somerton with that horrible Worsley situation."

In the coach on the way to Westminster, Gwen had explained the entire Worsley affair, much to her friends' outrage and horror. There was no way she would keep the truth from her friends.

"I still can't believe she shot you," Tamsin said with a faint grimace. "Or that you got married three days later."

"Or that they let Mrs. Worsley get away with it," Jo put in.

"It was the right thing to do for Miss Worsley. She's been through enough and still has a baby to deliver," Gwen said.

"How is your arm?" Min asked.

"It's not bad, actually." It had hurt quite a bit yesterday, which had made Gwen glad she'd chosen today for the wedding. Today she was feeling a far sight better, however. The wound was bound with a fresh bandage beneath her shirt.

The session started, and they fell silent. There was to be a debate regarding former soldiers, and Lazarus stood to deliver his speech.

A movement to the right drew Gwen's attention. A few more gentlemen had entered. One of them was her father. She pivoted so he wouldn't be able to see her, then whispered to Tamsin that she needed to move to Gwen's other side to block her father from seeing her.

Eyes wide, Tamsin adjusted her position. Then she lifted her hand and appeared to giggle silently behind it. Gwen couldn't help grinning—this was a terrible risk, but one she was gladly taking.

After addressing the members of Parliament, Lazarus offered a dedication. "I dedicate the speech I am about to make to my lovely new wife, Gwendolen. Yes, as of this morning, I am no longer the reckless rake." There were murmurs and laughter.

"I am proof that love can transform a man. In meeting Gwen, I have found not only a brilliant spouse, but a true partner in everything. She has given me hope where I had little, for you see, I have struggled to read my entire life."

Gwen sucked in a breath, but quickly clapped her hand over her mouth. What was he doing?

"Some have discounted me as unserious or unintelligent, and I have been rather absent from this fine chamber. However, today I rededicate myself to my duty and share with you the challenge I have long faced."

He took a breath and glanced down briefly before continuing. "I have always had trouble reading. I can read, just very slowly and it is a chore. My father did all he could to help me as a child. I made slow but steady progress. After his death, I did not continue to improve in this arena. He was the only person who understood my deficiency. However, he never made me feel deficient."

Gwen realized tears were streaking down her cheeks. She

hastened to wipe them away lest someone notice the odd gentleman crying.

"When I recently became better acquainted with my darling wife, I decided to share my difficulties with her, for you see, she is quite brilliant. She can read multiple books in a day." He smiled, and Gwen felt as though her heart might burst.

"Unsurprisingly, she came up with a methodology to help me improve my reading and also to ensure I would be able to deliver my speech today. I have memorized it, but if I lost my place and needed to refer to my written copy, it would have been a disaster."

Over the past few days, they'd written his speech out in small passages on different pieces of parchment so that he could easily find his way. He'd practiced countless times, and Gwen had never been prouder.

There were more murmurs and a bit of laughter, and Lazarus smiled once more. "What is most remarkable about my wife, however, was the risk she took in tutoring me. She'd agreed to meet with me at my cousin, Lady Droxford's, house."

Gwen heard Tamsin gasp softly beside her and reached over to touch her arm. She would have held her hand, but couldn't very well do that in their current disguises.

"During those meetings, she helped me become better at reading and ensured I would not make a fool of myself today. We were not having an affair as that idiot I shall not name has alleged. He was merely seeking vengeance against Lady Somerton after she accidentally spilled orgeat on him at Almack's. It was a hideous waistcoat, and honestly, can you think of a better use for that drink?"

This was met with a loud burst of laughter. Moving her head back slightly to peer behind Tamsin, Gwen looked toward her father. He was smiling, and the man beside him was guffawing.

Straightening, she refocused on her magnificent husband. How he'd found the courage to say all this was astounding. She could hardly wait to see him later tonight.

"But as it happened, I fell in love with Gwen as she so generously gave me her kindness, her cleverness, and her trust. Without her, I would not be the man I am today. And now, I suppose I shall deliver my actual speech, though I guarantee you this bit was far more interesting." He flashed his signature roguish grin, and Gwen fell in love with him all over again.

Tamsin quickly put her arm around Gwen's waist and gave her a gentle squeeze. "Thank you for helping my cousin. I had no idea he struggled or that you were meeting for such a noble and wonderful purpose."

"It was a secret," Gwen whispered. "Indeed, I am in shock that he would share it like this."

"But perhaps it will help someone else," Tamsin noted.

"I hope it does." Again, Gwen felt a swell of pride. And love. Both of which only grew as Lazarus delivered his speech nearly perfectly. She watched as he carefully moved the paper in his hands as he spoke so that he always had the part he was saying within sight. He only had to check the parchment once, and he barely faltered.

When he was finished, there was a resounding round of applause. And then the debate began. Unsurprisingly, his advocacy was not as popular here as in the Commons.

Gwen and her friends listened for a while, but then decided to depart. Outside, they all laughed and congratulated Gwen, marveling at what Lazarus had revealed.

"How wonderful that he was able to take down Eberforce too," Ellis said with a laugh.

Jo smiled. "That was my favorite part."

Gwen looked around at her dearest friends. "Thank you all for your support. I could not imagine how I would have navigated the past few weeks without you."

"We will always be here for one another, and that includes Persey and Pandora. Though they are not here in person, they are in spirit," Min said. "And I did visit Persey a couple of days ago to inform her of all that was happening. She was agog."

"I hope I'll get to see her soon," Gwen said. And Pandora would certainly write—Gwen had written to her about the wedding. She'd also painstakingly recalled the events of the past several days, which she realized would read like a scandalous novel penned by some anonymous lady.

"Shall we remove ourselves from these clothes?" Tamsin asked. "I do think my breeches are rather tight." She giggled, and they made their way to the coach.

Gwen had never been more grateful. Her heart was full.

～

*I*t was after midnight when Lazarus practically raced up the stairs to his bedchamber. He was so eager to see his wife that he'd thrown off his hat and gloves without a care. Presumably, the efficient footman would retrieve them from wherever they'd landed in the entrance hall.

The debate had lasted hours, and then there'd been other business. Lazarus had resolved to skip tomorrow's session in favor of bestowing all the attention his wife deserved and didn't receive today. He felt horrible for arriving so late on their wedding night.

He threw open the door to his chamber and closed it firmly, then began disrobing immediately. He scanned the chamber, but didn't see Gwen. It was awfully late. Had she fallen asleep? Would she be disgruntled if he woke her? He'd no idea what sort of sleeper she was.

Wearing just his breeches and shirt, he padded toward the bed on his bare feet. Then he stopped cold at the sight that awaited him.

Gwen lay amidst the rumpled bedclothes wearing nothing but a...cravat? Had she donned that because of how she'd been dressed the other day when they'd first shared a bed together?

"I'm so sorry I'm late," Lazarus said, his body tight with desire.

Her lips curved in a seductive smile that made his cock jump. "I expected that."

"And why the cravat?" he asked, taking his shirt off.

Eyes widening slightly as she fixed on his chest for a moment, she stroked the end of her cravat. "I was wearing this earlier today when I visited the House of Lords. I thought you might like to see how I looked in it."

He goggled at her. "You were there today?"

"I was. Along with Tamsin, Min, Ellis, and Jo."

"All dressed like men. Because you had to be, of course." He shook his head. "I'd no idea. I did see your father, however."

"I wasn't too far to the left of him—from your perspective." She continued to stroke the silk of the cravat, and Lazarus was becoming most distracted. His cock somehow grew harder.

"You're going to have to leave that cravat alone if you expect me to carry on a conversation." He drew a deep breath, but the haze of lust remained. "It's good I didn't recognize you. I would have been more distracted than I am right now."

Her hand stilled, and she sat up. "I can't believe what you

said today." Her eyes shone with admiration. "I'm so very proud of you."

"You can't know how much that means to me," he said quietly. "When I lost my father, I never thought I'd have someone who would support me as you have. To know that you are proud of me is the most wonderful gift."

Her gaze met and held his. "I *can* know. All I wanted with this silly Season was to make my parents proud. Yes, I wanted a marriage, but in large part because that was what they wanted for me. I wanted their approval and praise, but I realize what I wanted more than anything was a love of my own. And you gave me that. Now tell me why you said what you did in the Lords today about your reading problems. You didn't have to share any of that."

"I know, but I wanted to. Mostly, because I want the world to know how brilliant you are and how much I adore you. I don't want anyone to doubt that I would ever dishonor or hurt you."

"There is little chance of that now, but I would never doubt it. You sounded so wonderful today. Your delivery was outstanding."

He grinned. "Our scheme with the short passages was the key to my success. And I have you to thank for that. How did I get so lucky to find you? And for you to choose me?"

"I have asked myself the same questions multiple times this past week. Let us lay them to rest. We are both lucky, and we chose each other because we were simply meant to be."

Lazarus's heart soared. "I can see you have seduction in mind, and I have no quarrel with that."

"It is our wedding night," she said.

"How is your arm? Wedding night or not, I am not going to cause you pain or discomfort."

She gave him a saucy smile. "You won't because I am

going to be on top. I believe you said I could ride you, is that correct?"

"Yes," he rasped, quickly unbuttoning the fall of his breeches. He climbed onto the bed and kissed her, gently cupping her face.

Pivoting, she pushed him lightly backward, not that he needed direction or encouragement. "I recall I said I wanted to explore this magnificent chest last time we were together like this."

"You did," Lazarus managed despite the need building to a crescendo within him. How had he lasted four days without her? He wasn't sure he was going to make it through the next four minutes.

He closed his eyes and focused on her hands moving over him, each caress driving him deeper into desire. Then her mouth followed, spreading kisses over his flesh and flicking her tongue to taste him.

When she curled her hand around his cock, he opened his eyes and watched her through slitted lids. As she stroked him, her dark hair fell against his thigh and the ends of her cravat tickled his flesh. He twitched, arching his hips off the bed. In answer, she put her lips to the hood of his cock.

Lazarus groaned, closing his eyes once more, but only briefly for he wanted to watch her suck him. She opened her mouth and drew him inside tentatively, her tongue sliding along his length. Then she released him and met his gaze.

"Am I doing this right?"

"There isn't really a wrong way." His voice rose as she moved her hand down his shaft and cupped the balls beneath. "Ah, that is quite perfect."

"I'm glad to hear that. I do try to be a good student." She returned her mouth to him, this time sucking him in with more confidence, her tongue swirling around him as she gently played with his sac.

Lazarus dug his fingers into the bedclothes, then fisted them as she began to move more quickly. If he didn't stop her, he was going to come down her throat.

He clasped her head with one hand. "Gwen, you must stop before I shock you."

She slowly released him from her mouth, her lips shining as she looked up at him. "How?"

"I will come in your mouth."

"Is that not done?" she asked, blinking.

"It *is*, but you should consent to my doing that."

"I absolutely consent," she said without hesitation. "And what happens with your seed? Will I swallow it?"

"If you like." Her curiosity was both adorable and arousing. All this talk of coming in her mouth was making him even more desperate for her.

"I would like." She made to put her mouth back on him, but he tugged gently on her hair.

"If you don't mind, I would prefer to come in your pussy tonight. Time for you to ride."

Rising up, she straddled his hips. Her breasts jutted out, high and proud, the nipples taut. Lazarus reached up with both hands and stroked her, rubbing his thumbs over her nipples.

She grasped the end of her cravat. "I suppose I don't need this anymore."

"Leave it," he said quickly. "I like how it looks, the ends hanging between your breasts. When you move, the silk may caress your flesh. You may find you like that."

"I do like the sound of it." She wriggled her hips over his. "Show me what to do."

Lazarus skimmed one hand down to her sex and rubbed her clitoris. He slid a finger between her folds and found her hot and wet. "Put my cock inside you. You'll need to lift up slightly."

Her hips rose, and she grasped his sex, guiding it to her sheath. He used both hands to part her folds as she took him inside herself.

Gripping her hips as she worked herself down over him, Lazarus moaned with pleasure. When her thighs met his and he was fully embedded within her, he met her gaze. "Take your time to become accustomed, but then you will set the pace."

She rocked forward slightly, pressing her clitoris against his pelvis. "Oh, that's lovely."

"When you move faster, the friction there will be exquisite."

He guided her movements—up and down—holding her hips as she quickly learned. She ground down hard, and ecstasy shot through Lazarus. He cried out her name as he dug his fingers into her. "Ride me, Gwen. Hard."

She complied, increasing her speed and grinding on him so her clitoris was receiving the attention it deserved. Lazarus managed to keep his eyes open and watched her breasts jostle, the white silk swaying against her nipples as she pitched slightly forward. It was the most erotic sight he'd ever beheld.

Then she began to ride him with such a sharp precision that he could no longer focus on anything but the rapture building inside him. Together, they bucked and panted, their bodies straining for release.

She began making high-pitched, nonsensical sounds, and her movements became more frenzied. Lazarus slid one hand between them and rubbed her clitoris with hard, fast strokes. The muscles of her sex clenched around him, and he felt her thighs tense.

She cried out his name over and over as her body shuddered around him with her climax. Lazarus pumped up into her a handful of times before he too was swept away.

When their bodies slowed, he carefully guided her away from him, easing her onto the bed while cautious with her injured arm. She was breathing rapidly, her breasts rising and falling heavily. Now, she tore the cravat away and flung it to the floor.

Smiling, she looked over at him. "How did I do?"

"You were spectacular. Top marks." He kissed her shoulder, then bounded off the bed to fetch a cloth to tidy her.

As he approached her from the other side of the bed, he cleaned his seed from her, then deposited the cloth in the basin. Then he tidied himself and rejoined her in their bed.

Their bed. No longer just his. Everything he had he would share with her. Gladly. Eagerly. For all their days.

He helped her into the bedclothes. She lay on her back, and he pressed himself to her side. "I'm not going to Westminster tomorrow."

"Is that all right?"

"I have rarely spent much time there," he said drily. "No one will miss me."

"They will after today. I daresay you made quite an impression on everyone with that speech. You certainly impressed me. And my father, I think. He laughed at your jest regarding Almack's orgeat."

Lazarus smiled. "Did he? That's good to hear. I know he has his reservations about me, but I will prove to him every day that I deserve to be your husband, that I will make you the happiest woman in the world."

"Already accomplished," she said with a sigh. "I am curious to know what Eberforce thought of your speech. I presume someone will have told him of it. You have ruined his plans to ruin me."

"If he does anything untoward regarding you, I will put an immediate stop to it. Indeed, at the first opportunity, I plan to inform him that if he causes you any distress or maligns you in any way, I will ensure he's never able to purchase a fashionable waistcoat in London again. He'll have to learn to make them himself."

Gwen laughed. "You can't have that much power."

He arched a brow at her. "I'm willing to find out."

She leaned over to kiss him, her eyes glowing. "Thank you for being my champion, from that night at Almack's to today at Westminster. There can be no woman luckier than me."

"We've already established our luck as fact," he said soberly. "I thank you for also being my champion, for reminding me of my worth. I am only sorry my father isn't here to meet you. I do think he would love you nearly as much as I do."

"He lives on in you, my love," she said with a brilliant smile that encapsulated every delightful aspect of who she was. "And he will live on in our children, should we be blessed with them."

"I should hope so. You will be an excellent mother." He kissed her again, and his body began to stir once more.

"And you will be a magnificent father." She kissed him back, her tongue sliding along his as she caressed his chest.

"We should go to sleep," he said.

"What if I prefer to take another ride?" she asked.

"It's rather soon, and you are new to the sport. Perhaps I will wake you with another method of lovemaking that will not put pressure on your arm."

Her brow puckered as she looked at him with rampant curiosity. "And how is that?"

"You'll lie on your uninjured arm."

She rolled to her left arm, presenting her back to him. "Like this?"

Blast, now she was going to tempt him sorely. "Yes. And I will bend your top leg like this." He moved her leg into position, opening her sex. He dragged his fingertips along the back of her thigh and stroked them across her folds. She was wet again, and now he would be lost.

"I was going to wake you this way, but now it seems this is how I will say good night," he said softly as he worked his fingers into her eager sheath.

"I can think of no better way to welcome sleep." She moved her hips with his thrusts.

Lazarus kissed her neck and whispered, "Are you ready for me, my love?"

"Always." He entered her from behind and rocked into her, thrusting deep as he clasped her thigh.

"I love you," she moaned, as they raced for ecstasy once more.

EPILOGUE

Ten days later
Marriage Celebration Dinner

Gwen gathered with her friends in the library at her parents' house following dinner. The other women were in the drawing room while the men were having their port. Gwen's friends had insisted they needed a few minutes to share a private conversation—and a gift.

The best part of the dinner was the surprise attendance of both Persephone and Pandora. It was Persephone's first social engagement since having her baby, and likely the only one she would make for the rest of the Season. She hadn't wanted to miss the celebration.

But Pandora coming from Bath was the greatest gift. Gwen was thrilled to have everyone together, including the newest member of their set, Jo. She and Pandora had already become fast friends.

"It's time for your gift, Gwen," Pandora said with a broad

smile. She handed her a wrapped parcel, but Gwen already knew what it was.

Tearing open the paper, she was thrilled to see her very own embroidered copy of the rogue rules. The design was decorated with books. "Of course you stitched books in the corners," she said, trying not to cry.

"Of course," Pandora said. "Now, how many of those did you break with Somerton?" she asked with a wink.

Scanning them though she knew them by heart, Gwen said, "All but the last." There had been no reason to ruin Lazarus, for there was never any fear that he would ruin her.

"Naughty!" Pandora winked at her as she laughed, and everyone joined in.

"Will you be staying in London, Pandora?" Ellis asked.

Pandora nodded. "For a while. I'd come when Jonathan was first born, but I should have stayed longer, so I'll remain with Persey and Wellesy for a few weeks at least. But do not ask me to attend anything. I am *not* entering Society."

Gwen could understand why. Still, she hoped that someday Pandora might be able to find a man she could love, who would treasure and honor her as she deserved.

Persephone looked to Min. "How is Sheff handling the loss of yet another dear friend to the shackles of matrimony?"

"Terribly," Min said with a snort. "One would think Somerton had *died*." She paled suddenly and looked away from everyone.

"What's wrong?" Persephone and Tamsin asked practically in unison.

Ellis patted Min's arm and looked at everyone. "It's best if we don't discuss it."

"Did someone die?" Gwen asked, thinking the word "died" had prompted Min's reaction.

"Yes," Min said quietly. "But no one you know."

"You should tell them," Ellis said. "Even Pandora."

Gwen shot a look at Pandora whose jaw tightened.

"Who died, Min?" Pandora asked.

Min met her gaze. "Bane's wife died in childbirth recently."

"How awful," Persephone said, her features stricken as she reached for her sister's hand.

Pandora gripped her and swallowed. "That is truly sad. I am sorry for him. What of the babe?"

"She also died," Ellis said. "We just found out yesterday and wondered if we should say anything. This is a happy occasion, and anyway, it's Bane."

"He still deserves our pity," Tamsin said.

Everyone seemed to send tentative looks toward Pandora. She nodded once. "Yes, he does." Taking a deep breath, she summoned a serene smile. "But let us do that another time. Tonight is about Gwen and Somerton and the start of their happy life together. We should return to the drawing room so we can toast their marriage."

They all agreed and rose. Gwen looked at her embroidery once more, then gave Pandora a fierce hug. Her arm was still a little sore now and again, but the stitches had been removed and the physician had declared it was healing nicely.

"Thank you, Pan," Gwen said softly. "I love it. And you."

"I am so happy for you," Pandora said. They parted smiling, and Gwen hoped the news of Bane's wife and babe wouldn't trouble her friend.

They returned to the drawing room just as the men came up from dinner. Toasts were made, and by the time Gwen and Lazarus were on their way home, she was feeling a bit tipsy.

"Did you hear about Bane's wife?" she asked as she snuggled against her husband.

"I did," he said in a low voice. He pressed a kiss to her temple. "It was rather sobering news. I feel quite badly for him."

"I do too. Rogue or not, no one deserves that."

"Agreed. I wonder if he will return to London. Only Sheff has seen him since he moved to the north when he wed, and that was last summer."

"I suppose time will tell," Gwen said. "Does this make you nervous for me to have our child?"

"I'd be lying if I said no, but I would be nervous anyway. It's a great imposition to carry and bear a child. It's unfair that you have to shoulder the entire burden."

Gwen laughed. "I am sure we can find ways for you to share it with me. But we've time to work that out. Or not. At the rate we keep coupling, I may be carrying next month."

Lazarus grinned. "I hope that isn't a complaint."

"Not at all. In fact, if the trip to our house were just a little longer, I might like to give coach sex a try."

Groaning, Lazarus kissed her deeply. "I shall plan an excursion to Richmond for Wednesday. We will have coach sex and picnic sex and tree sex."

"Tree sex?"

Lazarus kissed her throat. "Vertical."

Gwen giggled. "I can hardly wait."

Ready for the next installment in the Rogue Rules?

Pressured by his parents to take a wife, Clive Halifax, Earl of Shefford selects the most inappropriate bride he can find: the outspoken daughter of a gaming hell owner.

Don't miss Jo and Sheff's story in AS THE EARL LIKES coming in October!

In the meantime, check out the first book in my new historical mystery series, Raven & Wren. Don't miss A WHISPER OF DEATH coming July 30!

Would you like to know when my next book is available and to hear about sales and deals? **Sign up for my VIP newsletter** which is the only place you can get bonus books and material such as the short prequel to the Phoenix Club series, INVITATION, and the exciting prequel to Legendary Rogues, THE LEGEND OF A ROGUE.

Join me on social media!

Facebook: https://facebook.com/DarcyBurkeFans
Instagram at darcyburkeauthor
Pinterest at darcyburkewrite

And follow me on Bookbub to receive updates on pre-orders, new releases, and deals!

Need more Regency romance? Check out my other historical series:

The Phoenix Club
Society's most exclusive invitation...

Welcome to the Phoenix Club, where London's most audacious, disreputable, and intriguing ladies and gentlemen find scandal, redemption, and second chances.

Matchmaking Chronicles
The course of true love never runs smooth. Sometimes a little matchmaking is required. When couples meet at a

house party, provocative flirtation, secret rendezvous, and falling in love abound!

The Untouchables

Swoon over twelve of Society's most eligible and elusive bachelor peers and the bluestockings, wallflowers, and outcasts who bring them to their knees!

The Untouchables: The Spitfire Society

Meet the smart, independent women who've decided they don't need Society's rules, their families' expectations, or, most importantly, a husband. But just because they don't need a man doesn't mean they might not *want* one...

The Untouchables: The Pretenders

Set in the captivating world of The Untouchables, follow the saga of a trio of siblings who excel at being something they're not. Can a dauntless Bow Street Runner, a devastated viscount, and a disillusioned Society miss unravel their secrets?

Marrywell Brides

Come to Marrywell, England where the annual May Day Matchmaking Festival has been bringing hopeful romantics together for hundreds of years. The dukes and rogues of the Regency will meet their matches with spirited and captivating ladies who may very well steal their hearts.

Wicked Dukes Club

Six books written by me and my BFF, NYT Bestselling Author Erica Ridley. Meet the unforgettable men of London's most notorious tavern, The Wicked Duke. Seductively handsome, with charm and wit to spare, one night with these rakes and rogues will never be enough...

Love is All Around

Heartwarming Regency-set retellings of classic Christmas stories (written after the Regency!) featuring a cozy village, three siblings, and the best gift of all: love.

Secrets and Scandals

Six epic stories set in London's glittering ballrooms and England's lush countryside.

Legendary Rogues

Five intrepid heroines and adventurous heroes embark on exciting quests across the Georgian Highlands and Regency England and Wales!

If you like contemporary romance, I hope you'll check out my **Ribbon Ridge** series available from Avon Impulse, and the continuation of Ribbon Ridge in **So Hot**.

I hope you'll consider leaving a review at your favorite online vendor or networking site!

I appreciate my readers so much. Thank you, thank you, *thank you*.

ALSO BY DARCY BURKE

Historical Romance

Rogue Rules

If the Duke Dares

Because the Baron Broods

When the Viscount Seduces

As the Earl Likes

The Phoenix Club

Improper

Impassioned

Intolerable

Indecent

Impossible

Irresistible

Impeccable

Insatiable

Marrywell Brides

Beguiling the Duke

Romancing the Heiress

Matching the Marquess

The Matchmaking Chronicles

Yule Be My Duke

The Rigid Duke

The Bachelor Earl (also prequel to *The Untouchables*)

The Runaway Viscount

The Make-Believe Widow

The Untouchables

The Bachelor Earl (prequel)

The Forbidden Duke

The Duke of Daring

The Duke of Deception

The Duke of Desire

The Duke of Defiance

The Duke of Danger

The Duke of Ice

The Duke of Ruin

The Duke of Lies

The Duke of Seduction

The Duke of Kisses

The Duke of Distraction

The Untouchables: The Spitfire Society

Never Have I Ever with a Duke

A Duke is Never Enough

A Duke Will Never Do

The Untouchables: The Pretenders

A Secret Surrender

A Scandalous Bargain

A Rogue to Ruin

Love is All Around

(A Regency Holiday Trilogy)

The Red Hot Earl

The Gift of the Marquess

Joy to the Duke

Wicked Dukes Club

One Night for Seduction by Erica Ridley

One Night of Surrender by Darcy Burke

One Night of Passion by Erica Ridley

One Night of Scandal by Darcy Burke

One Night to Remember by Erica Ridley

One Night of Temptation by Darcy Burke

Secrets and Scandals

Her Wicked Ways

His Wicked Heart

To Seduce a Scoundrel

To Love a Thief (a novella)

Never Love a Scoundrel

Scoundrel Ever After

Legendary Rogues

Lady of Desire

Romancing the Earl

Lord of Fortune

Captivating the Scoundrel

Historical Mystery

Raven & Wren

A Whisper of Death

A Whisper at Midnight

A Whisper and a Curse

Contemporary Romance

Ribbon Ridge

Where the Heart Is (a prequel novella)

Only in My Dreams

Yours to Hold

When Love Happens

The Idea of You

When We Kiss

You're Still the One

Ribbon Ridge: So Hot

So Good

So Right

So Wrong

ABOUT THE AUTHOR

Darcy Burke is the USA Today Bestselling Author of sexy, emotional historical and contemporary romance. Darcy wrote her first book at age 11, a happily ever after about a swan addicted to magic and the female swan who loved him, with exceedingly poor illustrations. Join her Reader Club newsletter for the latest updates from Darcy.

A native Oregonian, Darcy lives on the edge of wine country with her guitar-strumming husband, incredibly talented artist daughter, and imaginative, Japanese-speaking son who will almost certainly out-write her one day (that may be tomorrow). They're a crazy cat family with two Bengal cats, a small, fame-seeking cat named after a fruit, an older rescue Maine Coon with attitude to spare, an adorable former stray who wandered onto their deck and into their hearts, and two bonded boys who used to belong to (separate) neighbors but chose them instead. You can find Darcy in her comfy writing chair balancing her laptop and a cat or three, attempting yoga, folding laundry (which she loves), or wildlife spotting and playing games with her family. She loves traveling to the UK and visiting her beloved cousins in Denmark. Visit Darcy online at www.darcyburke.com and follow her on social media.

facebook.com/DarcyBurkeFans

instagram.com/darcyburkeauthor

pinterest.com/darcyburkewrites

goodreads.com/darcyburke

bookbub.com/authors/darcy-burke

amazon.com/author/darcyburke

threads.net/@darcyburkeauthor

tiktok.com/@darcyburkeauthor

Milton Keynes UK
Ingram Content Group UK Ltd.
UKHW030722300824
447605UK00004B/109